CREATURE DISCOMFORTS

THE BEELER LARGE PRINT MYSTERY SERIES

Edited by Audrey A. Lesko

CREATURE DISCOMFORTS

A Dog Lover's Mystery

SUSAN CONANT

BEELER LARGE PRINT

Hampton Falls, New Hampshire, 2001

Library of Congress Cataloging-in-Publication Data

Conant, Susan, 1946-
   Creature discomforts : a dog lover's mystery / Susan Conant
      p.   cm.—(The Beeler Large Print mystery series)
   ISBN 1-57490-360-8 (lg. print alk. paper)
   1.   Winter,   Holly   (Fictitious   character)—Fiction.   2.
Cambridge (Mass.)—Fiction. 3. Women journalists—Fiction. 4.
Women dog owners—Fiction. 5. Dogs—Fiction. 6. Large type
books. I. Title. II. Series.

PS3553.O4857 C74 2001
813'.54—dc21   2001035742

Published in Large Print by arrangement with
Doubleday, a division of Random House, Inc.

BEELER LARGE PRINT
is published by
Thomas T. Beeler, Publisher
Post Office Box 659
Hampton Falls, New Hampshire 03844

Typeset in 16 point Times New Roman type.
Printed on acid-free paper, sewn and bound by
Sheridan Books in Chelsea, Michigan.

CREATURE DISCOMFORTS

To Carter, Rowdy, and Kobi,
my hiking partners
on the trails of Acadia

Acknowledgments

I HOPE THAT READERS WHO SHARE MY LOVE FOR THE novels of Margery Allingham will take pleasure in recognizing in this story a small tribute to my favorite mystery writer. Dog lovers will certainly find countless unbridled tributes to my own dogs, Frostfield Firestar's Kobuk, C.G.C., and Frostfield Perfect Crime, C.D., C.G.C., Th.D., and to all dogs everywhere.

For help with some of the background of this story, I am grateful to Jill Hunter; and to the members of Malamute-L, a discussion group for fanciers of the Alaskan malamute, and PSG, the Poodle Support Group. Thanks, too, to Deborah Dwyer, Roseann Mandell, and Geoff Stern; to Jean Berman, Dorothy Donohue, Roo Grubis, Margherita Walker, Anya Wittenborg, and Corinne Zipps; to my wonderful agent, Deborah Schneider; and to my editor, the incomparable Kate Miciak.

Steve Rubin, please note that the bichon frise in this story is named Molly. You see? I did put your dog in a book.

One

I CAME TO MY SENSES BETWEEN A ROCK AND A HARD place. The rock was a boulder hurled millennia ago in thankless rage by a reluctantly northbound glacier. Still, it was a rock of ages: cleft for me. My bruised body fit so neatly into its riven side, a deep, narrow fissure, that the rock might almost have been cleft to measure. Too sick to move, I remained hidden in the rock. Only my head protruded. I rested face up in what proved to be a puddle of rainwater and blood in a shallow depression in the hard place, a ridge prettily embellished with lacy lichen in a deceptively soft shade of pastel green. Around the boulder and into its cleft grew stunted blueberry bushes that bore, here and there, clusters of tiny wild berries and dried-up bits of what had once been fruit, single berries mummified, perhaps even petrified.

In retrospect, it feels peculiar to owe my life to a boulder and its surrounding cushion of lowbush blueberries, but the giant rock is undoubtedly what broke my fall, and without the masses of wild shrubbery to absorb the impact, the body-on-boulder slam would almost certainly have killed me. As it was, I lay unconscious for what I now estimate to be an hour. During that lost time, I half-roused for seconds or even minutes. In moments of forgotten semiconsciousness, I must have slipped my body feet-first into that opening in the rock, acting as my own kindly undertaker. In dog training, we happily recognize anticipation as a sign of learning. A dog who comes before he is called has

1

figured out what to expect next. In my case, however, the Great Handler did not call me to my final reward.

I'm tempted to romanticize my return to consciousness. It's difficult to control the corny urge to drop allegorical hints about spiritual renaissance: Naked came I, slithering out of a dark passageway into water and blood, double-cured of sin, enlightened, born again. My actual revivification was disgustingly different from the kind of rebirth that would've put me permanently in the ribbons in the My-Soul's-Better-Than-Yours class. The first thing I did was to roll painfully over, gag, and then pollute the water and blood in the would-be-symbolic baptismal font with what looked, even from my perspective, like copious ropes of saliva cascading from the jowly mouth of some drooly giant-breed dog. In my own ears, I sounded like an allergic dog in the throes of what's known as "reverse sneezing." The phrase even crossed my mind. Oddly enough, it was comforting to diagnose myself with a canine malady.

The nausea and choking began to subside. What took their place was a global sensation compounded of pain, cold, and terror. A sensible person would have assumed that the acute fear was an adaptive response to my real plight. The pain began to differentiate. The burning of torn skin was worse on my knees and my right hand than it was elsewhere. My scratched face stung. Stabs and throbbing radiated from my right elbow down to my fingers and up to my shoulder. An object dug mercilessly into my abdomen. A foreign object? One of my own ribs? My head hurt less than the bad elbow but, without my consent, had moved someplace it didn't belong—to the middle of my stomach and ten feet away, both at the same time. But pain wasn't going to kill me. *Died of exposure,* I thought. *Exposure* meant hypothermia, a life-threatening drop in the body's core temperature.

Instead of rolling over, sitting up—offering a paw, perhaps?—and seeking heat, I took satisfaction in the word itself: *hypothermia.* How delightfully poly-syllabic! Counting the syllables seemed like a grand idea. Hypo—made two. By the time I reached the end, I'd not only lost the subtotal, but forgotten the word I was playing with. *Polysyllabic?* For a giddy second, the sound of the final syllable struck me as a brilliant comment on my situation: Ick! The childish assessment triggered a moment of clarity. Shifting my head ever so slightly away from the puddle, I propped my chin on the lichen and made an effort to take stock of myself. My face, I realized, must be the same whitish green as the miniature forest around me.

That reflection, if you'll pardon the forthcoming pun, brought with it the hideous realization that if I were to look in a mirror, I would have no idea what image to expect in the glass. In panic, I tried to move my right hand. Pain roared up my arm. I did, however, manage to roll onto my back and, with my left hand, clumsily unzip the top six or eight inches of my anorak. My left hand answered a fundamental question. Breasts. The fear ebbed as I savored the joy of dawning self-knowledge. Sex: female. Skin color: green. Handedness: right. Vocabulary: polysyllabic. Body temperature: hypothermic.

Having discovered the rudiments of *who,* or at least *what* I was, I made the mental leap to wondering *where* I was. Instead of remembering where I'd been that morning or how I'd hurt myself, I had an hallucinatory recollection of a Gauguin painting that hung, I was certain, in Boston's Museum of Fine Arts. The picture

3

showed Tahitians across the life span. It was titled *D'où venons-nous? Que sommes-nous? Où allons-nous?* The name of the language lingered on the tip of my tongue, but I translated easily: *Where Do We Come From? What Are We? Where Are We Going?* Gauguin's images inspired me to decide, mostly on the basis of incipient hypothermia, that I was not in Tahiti. As it turned out, I was correct. Good girl! Sharp. Excellent. A triple-digit IQ lay only a few mental steps ahead.

Finding it a bit difficult to survey my surroundings while sprawled flat, I struggled to get to my feet. Dizziness stopped me. The nausea returned. And retreated. The whirling abated. Shuddering with cold, I was now sitting on the lichen-covered ledge with my legs stretched in front of me. The fog was so thick that my new vantage point provided little information. I wore jeans with recent-looking rips in the knees. The skin visible through the holes was raw. The heavy hiking boots I wore were undamaged. What came as a surprise was my backpack, which I hadn't known was there. It was a lightweight pack suitable for day hiking, bright red, with an unpadded hip belt that had slipped upward and twisted to cut deeply and painfully into my abdomen. The second I released the clasp, the pain lessened. Once the ground around me stopped spinning, I realized that I was on the side of a steep hill or mountain. The ledge, my hard place, sloped upward. I had obviously fallen, and then bounced and rolled downhill and across the ledge until I collided with the boulder. Uphill, bordering the ledge, grew dark green moss interspersed with a few infant evergreens, huckleberry bushes, and what I thought might be azaleas. Below were a few oak saplings and a beautifully gnarled pine that looked like a giant version of the artfully pruned trees in those Japanese dish gardens. What were they called? Everything else, on all sides, hid in the fog. I'd been dimly aware of sounds that were now easy to identify as distant foghorns and, far below me, tires speeding along pavement. The ocean. A blacktop road.

Instead of feeling relief at my proximity to civilization, I again fell victim to dread. *Something* was urgent and frightening. I remembered everything about this dangerous, terrible something—every nuance of fear, every trace of desperate worry that the responsibility to act was mine alone. Entirely missing was all memory of what this terrible something was.

The memory startled me as violently as if it had been a snake suddenly slithering through the fog bank. I held perfectly still in an effort to keep my equilibrium as I teetered between the shaky here-and-now and the unbalanced moments of half-arousal when I'd overheard the scraps of conversation. The sounds had come from somewhere to my right. Somewhere above? How far away? I couldn't guess. Like a picky eater, the fog swallowed some words and phrases and spat out others.

"Tragic." The voice was a man's. "Tragic accident. No one could've survived." The fog ate whatever came next. "Keep your name out of it. You have my absolute assurance."

His soft-spoken companion's reply was lost to me, but I heard the first speaker's attentive murmurs of agreement. "Yes . . . huh . . . Yes." In apparent response to a suggestion, the man exclaimed, "Out of the question! The media would seize on it." The fog exercised its appetite. A word reached me: "Death." Then, with a note of finality, the man said, "Anonymity is, after all, anonymity."

As the memory faded, the voice rang itself to silence in my ears.

Tragic accident. Whose? Whose death?

The ledge was reassuringly devoid of harps. The recollected conversation didn't meet my expectations of an angel choir. The fog had an earthy odor, like old compost, with a tinge of balsam and wild thyme, maybe, or some other herb. Still, perched as I was high in a cloud in some nameless region, I had to consider the possibility that the death under consideration was my own.

Two

SPEAKING OF HAVING DIED AND GONE TO HEAVEN . . .

Musical metallic jingles and the crash of bodies through underbrush heralded the twofold apparition that zoomed out of the mist. Was I seeing double? Thickly furred in a lupine shade of dark gray, the beasts radiated the wild and primitive aura of protocreatures cast forward in time from some shining netherworld ruled by a Creator who'd mated wolves to teddy bears. Speeding down the ledge, however, the animals moved like great cats. Before I could either rise or curl in fetal protection against their onslaught, they fell on me, knocked me flat to the rock, and began to scour my raw face with huge pink tongues.

"Off!" I demanded. "Off! Off!"

In what struck me more as accidental cooperation than as anything remotely like obedience, the dogs leaped to their big-boned snowshoe paws and wagged plumelike white tails before hurling themselves onto their backs, wiggling all over, and foolishly waving all eight powerful white legs in the air. Responding to the friendly invitation, I rubbed the two furry white tummies and scratched the two muscular chests while simultaneously seizing the chance to size up what were clearly going to be my saviors. The heat of the dogs' underbellies was already warming my hands. I was not going to die. With no irreverence, I said softly, "Thank God."

As if performing a well-rehearsed act, both dogs quit squirming. They folded their legs, tucked in their massive forepaws, and fixed deep-brown, almond-shaped eyes on me. On close inspection, the dogs were far from identical. The larger dog, revealed as an intact male, must, I thought, outweigh his female companion by at least ten pounds. He stood about twenty-five inches at the withers. She was perhaps twenty-three. His muzzle was slightly blockier than hers, his triangular ears a hint smaller. His eyes were a deep bittersweet chocolate, a little darker than hers, and he had a notably soft expression, mainly, I thought, because his face was white, whereas hers was heavily masked. Dark markings made goggles around her eyes and blended into a bar that ran down her muzzle and up to a sort of widow's peak cap on her broad skull. Reveling in the tummy rub, she nonetheless studied me with the intensity of a fundamentally serious intelligence. The male, in contrast, sank into bliss with a carefree smile on his face.

But I have neglected to mention the newcomers' most striking characteristics. First, the dogs were utterly and overwhelmingly beautiful. Second, both were dressed in red. She wore a sturdy-looking pack with heavy, bulging saddlebags that had shifted forward and twisted to one side. He was in a state of considerable dishabille: Three black straps with quick-release buckles fastened a red saddle-shaped pad snugly to his back; one strap ran across his big chest, the others around his middle. Down the length of the pad and on each shoulder were strips of black Velcro that must have secured saddlebags like the female's. He, however, had dumped or lost his pack somewhere. The jaunty red vest gave him the debonair look of a canine dandy.

Mindful of the hum of distant traffic, I said in fierce, quiet tones, "If you were *my* dogs, you'd never be allowed to run loose!"

I had to admit to myself, however, that the dogs showed obvious signs of responsible ownership. Although they'd been tearing around on their own, they were dragging red leashes that matched the packs. The leads were snapped to rolled-leather collars with brass fittings, from which dangled the tags I'd heard jangling. Fastened to the male's collar was a bright circle of yellow with block capital letters announcing I AM A THERAPY DOG. Although I couldn't imagine what the declaration meant, the message felt aimed directly at me. Therapy was exactly what I needed. The dogs, in a furry sort of way, clearly intended to provide it. In addition to the therapy-dog tag, the male wore a Saint Francis of Assisi medal. Both dogs were licensed in Cambridge, Massachusetts, and had been immunized against rabies at a veterinary clinic there. They had tags from the National Dog Registry. Identical owner ID tags proclaimed the dogs the property of one Holly Winter of 256 Concord Avenue in Cambridge, Massachusetts, 02138. Her phone number was listed. The dogs' names were not. Whoever she was, she took good care of her animals. The dogs' clean, gorgeous stand-off coats

8

testified to an excellent diet and careful grooming. When the dogs had wiggled their feet in the air, I'd noticed that the nails were short and that the hair between the black pads had been trimmed to neaten the appearance of the feet. Even so, I felt a flash of outrage. This Winter person with the silly, Christmassy name should damned well have held tightly to those leashes! No matter what, you never let go of a leash! Never! My anger brought insight. Not for a second had I felt any fear of these big, powerful dogs. On the contrary, from the moment they'd barged out of the cloud that surrounded us, I'd felt increasingly strong and self-confident. Good! In what I now see as one of the monumental understatements of the millennium, I congratulated myself on being a person who liked dogs.

By now, I was on my feet. To my amazement, the female had stationed herself in a solid stand at my left side and hadn't budged as I'd rested my weight on her and hauled myself up. I'd had to keep lowering my head to let the blood reach whatever disconnected bits of my brain had survived my crash. Each time my head descended, the handsome male planted wet kisses on my face.

Heartened, I finally took the practical step of searching my day pack and the female's red dogpack. My pack yielded a staggering number of brand-new, medium-size pale brown plastic bags with handle ties, an old and sadly cracked Nikon camera, a ring of keys, and the kind of survival blanket that looks like a giant sheet of aluminum foil. After swathing myself in it, I ripped the female's pack from its Velcro fasteners and began to empty its contents onto the ledge. The dogs took a tremendous interest in the unpacking, mainly, as I rapidly saw, because some of the supplies were ready-to-eat snacks: a blueberry muffin tightly encased in plastic wrap, cheese and crackers wrapped in aluminum foil, and a Granny Smith apple. Driven by some unexamined impulse, I quickly stashed the food in my own pack and zipped it shut. In a burst of common sense, I realized that there was something terribly wrong with me. The precise word eluded me. What came to mind was *head injury*. I couldn't remember whether a person who'd sustained one was allowed to eat. The dogs had no such worries about themselves. As I stashed the goodies, they posed rather formally, wagged their tails over their backs, lifted their heads, and favored me with twin expression of irresistible charm. On its own, my left hand reached into the pocket of my anorak and emerged bearing small cubes of cheese dusted with lint.

Some of the remaining items in the dogpack made sense: two big bottles of spring water, a fabric water bowl for dogs, four heavy-duty nylon dog booties, two leashes, a flashlight, a pocket knife, a first-aid kit in a plastic box, hand towels apparently used as padding to prevent hard objects from poking into the dog, a collection of very small bungee cords, a hiking guide to Acadia National Park folded open to a page about Dorr Mountain, a map of Mount Desert Island, and a cobalt blue fleece pullover covered with what appeared to be dog hair. After unwrapping myself from the survival blanket and removing the waterproof anorak, I donned the pullover, then put the anorak back on, and again wrapped myself in foil. Acadia National Park! Mount Desert Island! (Let me note in passing that in mentally pronouncing *Desert*, I correctly stressed the second syllable, making the word sound like *dessert*, as in chocolate mousse, as opposed to the Sahara. French: *Ile des Monts Deserts,* Isle of the Barren Mountains.) The coast of northern Maine! No wonder the weather was cool and foggy! But the flashlight, the knife, the first-aid kit, and the water? What fool had put survival gear in a *dog's* pack? The essentials belonged with the person, not with the dog!

The dogpack also contained something that utterly mystified me, namely, fourteen pounds of plain, uncooked generic-brand rice in plastic bags that had never been opened: two five-pound bags, two two-pound bags. All four packages of rice were separately sealed in extra-strong food-storage bags. I could understand why someone had wanted to guard against having the original packaging give way and fill the saddlebags with loose rice. But why set out with this ludicrous quantity of rice? Clearly, the two dogs had an Asian owner with a morbid fear of starvation. I decided that the owner, Holly Winter, had anglicized her name or taken her husband's last name.

Comforted by the certainty that I, at least, was not about to die of hunger, dehydration, or hypothermia, I drank some of the spring water and used the handy little fabric bowl to water the dogs. With the towels, the water, and the first-aid kit, I bathed my wounds and patched myself together. By now, New England being what it is, the temperature was abruptly shifting from too cold to too hot. As the fog evaporated, land appeared in the valley below. Sunlight beat on the side of a hill or mountain opposite this one. If I could see, I could be seen. The red of my day pack and the matching red of the dogs' gear might have been selected to grab attention. Minute by minute, the ledge became increasingly exposed. Had I wanted to attract human help, I'd have had to do nothing but wait. Far from

11

wanting to summon human rescuers, I felt an ardent desire to shun people in favor of Holly Winter's self-possessed dogs. If necessary, I'd steal them. I felt sure that I needed them more than she did.

After an abortive effort to fasten my day pack to the male dog's vest, I decided to abandon the heavy, bulky bags of rice. Without them, the female's saddlebags had room for my own pack and its contents. It seemed unfair to ask her to haul everything, but I reminded myself that she was now carrying less weight than when her pack had held the water we'd drunk and those fourteen foolish pounds of rice. Still, I promised myself that if she showed any discomfort, I'd transfer her burden to the male's powerful shoulders. *Leave nothing but your footprints, I* thought, with no memory of where I'd learned the maxim. I swore to myself that I'd return here to retrieve the plastic bags of rice.

Until now, I had, perhaps unwisely, trusted my new companions to stick around. Afraid that they'd desert me once I began to move, I took their leashes. Far from objecting, the dogs shook themselves all over and bounced around with a gleeful eagerness to get going. Yes, but where? The open page of the guidebook had originally been headed *Dorr Mountain: A Long, Difficult Hike over a Quiet Mountain.* Someone had scratched out the words *Long, Difficult* and scrawled in their place *Pleasant.* I tried to read the paragraphs about the long, difficult or, alternatively, pleasant hike, but by the time I got to the end, the beginning was swimming in my head. The page opposite the description showed a map. Two landmarks on it were blessedly familiar: Cadillac Mountain and the town of Bar Harbor. Dorr Mountain appeared to the right of Cadillac. Many trails led to its summit. At the bottom of its east face was a tiny body of water called The Tarn. Visible directly below me now was a small pond, an elongated oval of water shaped just like the one on the map. Therefore, I was on Dorr's east face. The traffic I'd heard earlier was now visible. Cars, vans, motor homes, and an occasional pickup passed along a strip of blacktop on the far side of The Tarn. On the map, the road was labeled Route 3. My malfunctioning brain managed to define *tarn:* a glacial pond. Even in my demented state, I found it peculiar and offensive that anyone would have routed a paved road and busy traffic along the shores of an interesting geographical feature. Still, The Tarn would serve as a goal. The map showed two parking areas nearby. With luck, the keys I'd found in my backpack would fit one of the vehicles in one of the lots.

Despite my desire to avoid people, especially this Winter person, who'd certainly reclaim her dogs, I set out to make my way down what I now felt confident was Dorr Mountain, which, I should add, from my present perspective rather than the one I made do with then, rises to the less than Alpine height of 1,270 feet above sea level. Cadillac, the highest peak on Mount Desert Island, soars to 1,532 feet. By the standards of the Rockies, it's an island of hills, of course, but these are granite hills, and many rise not merely from sea level, but directly from the breakers of the Atlantic. In other words, I have to make the disappointing confession that although I'm crazy about those books of the "How I Stupidly Went to Some Godawful Place and Almost Died" genre, Acadia National Park is the opposite of godawful. Also, I now realize that I hadn't come all that close to dying.

Still, bushwhacking across and down the face of the little mountain was out of the question; the descent was impossibly steep, and the remains of ancient rock slides lay everywhere. The guidebook map showed trails running up and down Dorr. I found one only by blundering after the dogs, who headed uphill, stopping occasionally to sniff undergrowth or mark territory. The female lifted her leg almost as high and often as the male did. To my annoyance, when we reached a stretch of damp earth, both dogs began to scarf down mud with apparent enjoyment. Lingering as the dogs feasted on their disgusting snack, I could hear hikers on what was evidently one of the trails up Dorr's east face. The brightening sky was hatching a crop of tourists. Refreshed and energized from glutting themselves, the dogs took the lead. If I intended to stay with them, I could do nothing but cling to their taut leashes and follow.

In almost no time, we came to a trail paved with beaten earth and smooth rock. With no hesitation, the dogs turned right and, only a minute or two later, hauled me past a fork in the trail and a cedar post that bore wooden trail markers. Feeling frightened and confused, I knew I should read the trail signs and consult the guidebook, but I lacked the strength to stop the dogs. The trail rapidly became more a piece of monumental outdoor sculpture than a woodland path, a massive staircase that melded into the land as if Nature herself had constructed it, with each wide stone step neatly and solidly set between its higher and lower neighbors. Trees, both evergreen and deciduous, loomed overhead, and wild vegetation edged the stones as decoratively as a tasteful gardener's carefully selected groundcover. The effect was at once cozy and otherworldly, as if gentle giants had lumbered out of the pages of a fantasy novel to carve an enchanted route through this sloping mass of shattered boulders.

Now and then, the trail ran uphill, and I worried that my guides were leading me in the wrong direction, but we eventually reached an intersection, where the dogs decided all on their own to take a short break that they devoted to marking another cedar post. Fastened to it were wooden arrows. One confirmed my guess that this was the Dorr Mountain East Face Trail. According to two arrows marking the right-hand turn, it led to the Kurt Diederich Trail and, at a distance of only four-tenths of a mile, The Tarn.

The dogs selected that trail. Happy with the route, they charged at a dangerous pace down flight after flight of stone steps, which proved damp and treacherous. Ignoring my near-falls, quiet gasps, and frantic entreaties, the beasts bounced and dashed downward. At moments, I may have flown through the air. To the surprise of a pair of tourists, a man and a woman, these maddeningly agile dogs dashed down the final flights of steps and exploded into a picturesque clearing where giant, flat stones formed a naturalistic mosaic. A little stream passed beneath the stone trail to empty into a pond: The Tarn. Close behind the dogs, I frantically fought to stay upright while maintaining my grip on the leads. The first thing I noticed about the woman tourist was that she was not Asian and therefore not the dreaded Holly Winter hellbent on stealing her dogs back. In fact, she was a Caucasian woman in her mid thirties who had prepared for what was apparently going to be a hike by protecting her feet with open-toed, high-heeled sandals. She wore yellow shorts and a T-shirt that read *Cool as a Moose, Bar Harbor, Maine.* She carried a small straw purse decorated with artificial flowers. Her friend wore the same T-shirt over the men's version of her yellow shorts. His sandals had flat soles. He carried nothing but a video camera. I was back in civilization.

It was the man who greeted me jovially by asking, "Who's taking who for a walk here, huh?"

I didn't mind the rib-poking. On the contrary, I felt grateful to the unsuitably dressed couple for giving me the chance to catch my balance and my breath. The dogs had abruptly abandoned their hell-for-leather forward dash to devote themselves to performing a song-and-dance routine for the tourists. The a cappella music consisted of prolonged peals of a repeated syllable: *Woo-woo-woo! Woowoo-woo-woo-woo!* The male spun twice around in a circle. His polished, show-off manner suggested that he was executing a well-practiced trick. Perhaps hampered by her pack, the female settled for wagging her whole body to the rhythm of her tail. Then, as if on cue, the dogs planted themselves in neat sits in front of the hypnotized couple and, in unison, raised their right paws. I couldn't tell whether they were offering to shake hands or were simply waving. By now, the man had the video camera going.

"Look, Harold!" the woman exclaimed. "That one's wearing a backpack! Isn't that cute?" To me, however, she said, "It looks awfully heavy."

"Making the dog do all the work, huh?" agreed Harold, eyeing the absence of a pack on my own back.

I merely said yes.

"Looks like you took a tumble," he said. "You all right?"

"A little scratched," I replied. "I'll be all right."

"Some old guy got killed here today," the man reported. "Fell on the rocks."

Smiling with undisguised excitement, the woman added, "Right near here!" If she'd been passing along

16

the news that the Second Coming had just occurred at the summit of Doff, she couldn't have sounded happier. "On something called the Ladder Trail," she went on. "Would you happen to know where that is?"

"I don't know my way around here." By *here,* I meant the world.

The woman scornfully pointed to a legend carved into the stone of the staircase I'd just descended. Kurt Diederich's Climb, I read. A short time earlier, I'd seen the name on a trail sign. Shortly before that, I'd read it on the map in the guidebook. Even so, the words looked brand new.

"The Nature Center's right down that way." The man pointed to one of several well-worn trails. "And the spring. Not worth visiting." He glanced at his partner. "Well, I guess we'll be on our way." Equipped only with the video camera and the contents of the woman's purse, the pair took a few steps toward the start of Kurt Diederich's Climb. The man looked back. "Nice huskies," he said.

All on their own, the words seemed to activate a tape recorder stored in my throat. "Thank you," I said automatically. "Actually, they're Alaskan malamutes. Bigger than Siberian huskies. All malamutes have brown eyes."

"Well, beautiful dogs, whatever they are," the man said in parting.

The correction had leaped from my lips without the aid of my mangled brain. I looked at the dogs, who had transferred their attention from the tourists to me. "Alaskan malamutes," I said. "Of course. Alaskan malamutes." The syllables fit the shape of my vocal cords. I'd uttered them thousands of times. Strangers had admired my huskies. "Thank you," I'd replied.

"Actually, they're Alaskan malamutes."

I was not, after all, stealing these oddly friendly and staggeringly beautiful dogs. On the contrary, they were miraculously my own.

I felt ferociously proud. *My* dogs.

Three

IF THE DOGS WERE MINE, SO WERE THE DOGPACKS, which, I now realized, matched the bright red of my own backpack. Pretty corny, that. A bit too much like the dressed-as-twins tourist couple I'd just met. In panic—was I, like the high-heeled hiker, the female half of a human twin set?—I examined the third finger of my left hand. It was bare. Good! If I had a husband, at least we did not have a traditional marriage. Or maybe we didn't have a traditional *American* marriage. All that rice in the dogpack? The Asian owner. Myself! Holly Winter, of Cambridge, Massachusetts, a right-handed Asian woman with a polysyllabic vocabulary and utterly magnificent dogs. He, Mr. Winter, was American. Or English? But we'd been joined in holy matrimony in the Far Eastern rite of my native culture. Back home at 256 Concord Avenue, our address, a ceremonial symbol of our union lay reverently preserved in the bejeweled cask handed down from generation to generation in what I somehow suspected was my devoutly religious family.

The Asian marriage fantasy only temporarily distracted me from thinking about the nameless man who'd fallen to his death. The ghoulish tourists had been heading up. I'd just come down. Therefore, I must have been nearby when the man died, right? This sense of jeopardy? And responsibility? Since the miraculous arrival of the dogs, my fear had begun to lift a bit, yet there remained a biting feeling of danger. For the first time, I desperately wanted to get away from here. My anxiety now had a practical element. Although I was feeling physically and mentally better by the moment, the prospect of being questioned by park rangers about the fatal accident scared me silly. I'd be unable to answer simple questions about where I'd been and what I'd done today. The dogs might be taken from me! We had to leave right now.

The male tourist had pointed to a trail that led to a spring that wasn't worth seeing and to something called the Nature Center. I'd seen the name on the map. The place had a parking lot. And park rangers? I had no idea, of course, where I'd parked my car. I felt sure that I had one. After all, I had a ring of keys, and the dogs and I had arrived here in something. I somehow imagined my car as a vehicle befitting my splendid dogs: a luxurious four-by-four with leather upholstery and a great sound system. A Land Rover. A Mercedes. No, a Bentley! That was it! A Bentley! Dogs like these traveled in magnificence. I'd know my Bentley anywhere. It would, of course, have Massachusetts plates.

More to the point, the dogs would know their Bentley anywhere. Better yet, they'd remember where it was. Looking to the dogs for direction, I let their leads go loose. In uninformative fashion, they sniffed the ground, anointed a couple of trees, and then looked at me. For direction! I felt ashamed of myself for letting them down. Having no idea what else to do, I took a few random steps and said brightly, "Let's go! Come on, guys! Let's go!" After pitying the poor creatures who

19

evidently relied on me to take the lead, I found it disconcerting to have them suddenly strike out down a trail with swaggering self-confidence. To my relief, the path they chose was not the one to the Nature Center. Rather, it was a flat continuation of Kurt Diederich's Climb that went past The Tarn and soon led to a small parking area next to a substantial blacktopped road. Route 3? Certainly.

The small lot was evidently not where I'd parked my Bentley. Tired-looking parents and a large number of screaming children were piling into an admirable red van with mountain bikes on a carrier at the back and a sea kayak on top. It had a Michigan plate. A new cream-colored VW bug was from Massachusetts. It would barely have held one of these dogs, never mind both of them and a driver, too. Besides, it wasn't a Bentley. Neither was anything else in sight. To my chagrin, the dogs unhesitatingly made for the oldest and most battered-looking car in the lot. The blue, dirt-covered Ford Bronco had, damn it, a Mass. plate and a lock on the driver's side door that fit one of the keys on my ring. The floor mats in front were decorated with large, stylized paw prints. Echoing the motif, dog hair was interwoven with fabric through the car. The windows bore translucent designs of what I guess should be called "saliva art" or perhaps "tongue painting." The rear passenger seat was folded down. Tucked between it and the driver's seat was a woman's leather shoulder bag. It contained a wallet, a cosmetics bag, a purse-size photo album, tissues, pens, a steno pad, and other pocketbook junk. In the back were an old blanket, a couple of stainless steel dog bowls, and two big bottles of Maine spring water.

Ripping the female's saddlebags from the Velcro strips that held it to her vest, I dumped it in the car, and then got both dogs in. After adding water to the steel bowls, I lowered myself into the driver's seat, started the engine, and put on the air conditioning. Tepid air drifted from the vents. Damn. Worse, an accidental glance in the rearview mirror revealed that rice or no rice, I was unmistakably Caucasian. My first impression was of a human golden retriever.

But the car offered at least a little good news. According to the gas gauge, the tank was full. Opening the big map that had been in the dogpack, I located the Nature Center, which was just off Route 3 near the intersection with the Park Loop Road. In one direction on Route 3, at no great distance, was the town of Bar Harbor. Did I have a motel room there? The Blackwoods Camp Ground lay in the opposite direction. Were we camping out? Could we rent a hotel room? The wallet held, among other things, a bank card with a MasterCard number and seventy-six dollars in cash. The deciduous trees here in the valley between Dorr Mountain and what the map identified as Huguenot Head held yellowish green leaves tinged with red. My ailing brain sputtered out the warning that autumn was still tourist season in Bar Harbor, which even off-season was an expensive resort.

In desperation, I rummaged through the glove compartment. It yielded another map of Mount Desert Island, a guide to the carriage roads of Acadia National Park, and two sheets of the sort of heavy cream writing paper I associate with wedding invitations. On one sheet, however, was a note handwritten in charmingly baroque script. The other sheet, in the same script, was headed *Directions to the Beamon Guest Cottage.*

21

The note read:

Dearest Holly and Pups,

What a treat for me that your work calls you to M.D.I! I will be positively thrilled to see you and to have you and your beautiful dogs fill the lonely emptiness of the Beamon Guest Cottage, which, although perfectly private, is quite near the Big House. Consequently, I look forward with great eagerness to inflicting (!) my hospitality on you for as long as you care to stay.

All best wishes,
Gabrielle Beamon

The directions instructed me to take Route 3 from Ellsworth, cross the causeway onto Mount Desert Island, go left on 3, and follow it through Bar Harbor, past the Jackson Laboratories, the Sieur de Monts Spring entrance to the park, and quite a few other landmarks. After a considerable distance, I was to watch for a small arrow on the left pointing toward the Beamon Reservation. There, I was to turn. A hand-drawn map at the bottom of the page depicted various rights and lefts that would eventually take me to a threeway split in the dirt road. Directly ahead of me would be the parking lot for the Beamon Reservation. To the right would be a private road that, on the map, ended at an X labeled "Quint and Effie's." An X beyond the one for Quint and Effie's was marked "Axelrod." I, however, was to go left on another private road. The Beamon Guest Cottage would be the first house on my right: yellow with green shutters. The door would be open, the key on the kitchen table. The dogs and I were to make ourselves at home. I assumed that we already had. The car that wasn't my Bentley contained no luggage.

Soon after pulling out of the lot and turning right onto Route 3, I passed The Tarn and then came upon a Park Service truck and sedan parked on the sandy shoulder, together with civilian vehicles that probably belonged to hikers still on the trails. The guidebook map of the area had somehow failed to photocopy itself onto my memory. Still, I had the sense to realize that the man who'd fallen to his death must have done so in this area, on the face of Dorr, beyond The Tarn.

Still fighting the irrational fear that a ranger would stop me to ask unanswerable questions about what I remembered, I drove by at the speed limit. Continuing, I scanned the roadside in search of the sign for the Beamon Reservation. On my first pass, I overshot the turn because, as I discovered after reversing direction, the arrow pointing toward the reservation was the approximate size of a toothpick. The hand-drawn map, however, proved accurate. Turning off Route 3, I followed twists and turns over dirt roads until smack ahead of me was the entrance to a small, unpaved parking lot with a gigantic sign mounted on a rustic wooden frame. The sign read:

WELCOME TO THE BEAMON RESERVATION!

Hours: Open daily from dawn to 5:00 P.M.
No vehicles beyond the parking lot.
No overnight parking.
No strollers.
No bicycles.
No pets allowed.

23

No camping.
No campfires.
No picnicking.
No alcoholic beverages.
No smoking of cigars, cigarettes, or pipes.
No littering.
Hunting prohibited. No firearms of any kind!
No ball playing.
No fishing or clamming.
No gathering of mussels.
No swimming.
No berry picking.
No boat launching.
No radios, tape players, or CD players.
Do not feed or approach the seals or other wildlife.
Stay on marked trails. Respect private property!
Groups desirous of visiting the Reservation must make arrangements in advance.

Parents are responsible for assuring that children abide by the regulations of the Reservation.

At the bottom of the sign was yet another injunction. Considering the list of prohibitions, it hit me as a jarring afterthought:

ENJOY YOUR VISIT!

Four

THE RULES OF THE BEAMON RESERVATION STOPPED just short of banning human beings from setting foot on the property. Consequently, it gave me an illicit thrill to veer left onto a narrow road plastered with Private Property, Keep Out, No Trespassing, This Means You signs. I, of course, had been invited; therefore, I was among the elite to whom the Private Property, Keep Out, No Trespassing, This Means You malarkey did not apply. As I'd wound through the lanes toward the Beamon Reservation, the dogs had begun stirring. The female, who'd been dozing at the rear of the Bronco, got to her feet and gave herself a preparatory shake-all-over. The male, who'd had to be prevented from leaping into the front and then, presumably, into my lap, was now happily taking in the less-than-spectacular scenery. It consisted of low balsam firs, dull maples, ordinary birches, and other secondary and tertiary growth. Now the two big dogs were up on all paws, and both plumy tails were wagging.

Before long, a yellow clapboard cottage with green shutters appeared on our right. The tidy little house looked unfamiliar to me, but then, so did everything else. As I pulled into a grassy, lightly rutted parking area next to the cottage, waves of anxiety sent hot blood to my face. What was so frightening? The guest cottage had been freshly painted in an especially inviting shade that blended buttercup with rich cream. Far from dangling in sinister disrepair, the deep green shutters created the happy illusion that the cabin's front

25

windows were two bright eyes radiating a thick-lashed welcome. White geraniums and mottled ivy grew lushly in window boxes, and the shiny green front door practically smiled.

Hansel and Gretel.

But where else could I go?

By now, the handsome male had squeezed his big head past my left shoulder to stick his face out the half-open driver's-side window. When I twisted around and made a brave, if futile, effort to force him to the rear of the car by shoving on his massive white chest, the female took an opportunistic dive into the front passenger seat. With exquisite delicacy, she stretched her powerful neck and aimed those intelligent almond-shaped eyes past my face toward the opening in the window, as if calculating the odds of soaring over me and into the outdoors. In desperation, I cranked up the window and fished for both leashes, which were still fastened to the dogs' collars. Gripping the leashes as tightly as my sore hands allowed, I eased open the door. Seconds later, I found myself braced in the bent-knee, flexed-arm semicrouch appropriate to a Godzilla-like professional wrestler with the bulk and muscle to control these beasts.

It never occurred to me to let the dogs loose. My own vigilance failed to register on me. I did, however, find a peculiar reassurance in my body's mindless preparation to have both dogs simultaneously hit the ends of their leads in a massive double wham that could otherwise knock me to the ground. The wrestler stance was unnecessary, not because the dogs spontaneously decided to behave themselves, and certainly not because I exerted any influence on their behavior. Rather, it was the appearance of a brand-new white Volvo station wagon that diverted the beasts from what was evidently going to be a headlong gallop for the cottage door. The car approached from the direction opposite the one I'd just driven.

The driver slowed and stopped alarmingly close to the dogs and me. When she lowered her window, it took my eyes a second to distinguish between the woman herself and the curly-haired white powderpuff of a dog in her lap. As testimony to the erratic and bizarre effects of head injury, let me point out that I not only instantly identified the dog as a bichon frise, but remembered her name: Molly. With absolute certainty, I also knew that the woman had chosen the car to match the white of her dog and that if Volvo had offered a model with a fluffy coat, she'd have been driving it now. The woman herself had straight hair in flattering transition from blond to white. The short, soft cut framed her face. She'd clearly never bothered to protect her fair skin from the sun; her face was tan, and her slightly plump arms were mottled with sun spots. She wore a plain white T-shirt and no jewelry except tiny pearl stud earrings. With that incredible bone structure, she needed no flattery, no defenses against age, no fancy wardrobe, no gold or silver. She had gorgeous blue eyes.

"You've *heard* about poor Norman Axelrod," she informed me in an incredible voice: low-pitched, warm, husky, sensuous, and utterly unselfconscious. Although no one was around to overhear, she switched to a tone that made me feel singled out as the chosen recipient of an opinion that she wouldn't have shared with just anyone. "I keep thinking that he must have had some sort of premonition and that's why he always hated the outdoors. He must've had a vision of falling on a wet day. No wonder he hated hiking! He was right! The

27

park was the last place he should ever have gone." She sighed affectionately. "Norman was a terrible curmudgeon, but he was *our* curmudgeon, wasn't he?"

Whose, exactly? Hers and mine? I'd evidently known Norman. But how?

Caressing the little white dog, who sat alertly in her lap, she went on. "I just talked to your father."

Was this my mother? I couldn't ask. I'd sound like some foolish animal character in a children's book: *Little Holly the Hedgehog asked, "Are you my mommy?"* Besides, I was too busy trying to control the dogs to respond. Having been diverted by the arrival of the Volvo, the beasts were now straining to get into it. Or maybe they just wanted to jump on the door, poke their heads through the window, and lick the woman's face. From nowhere, however, a phrase replete with warning popped into my consciousness: *hors d'oeuvre breeds.* Small dogs. As seen through malamute eyes. Worse, as crunched by malamute jaws. Oh, my aching arms!

"I was hoping my hero would get here tonight," the woman continued, "but he can't." Her hero? My father? "He'll be here tomorrow. I wanted him to have a chance to get together with Malcolm Fairley, but maybe it's just as well. I've gone ahead and invited Opal and Wally." Her eyes had a mischievous gleam. "That bumper sticker might make things just a tiny bit awkward. Quint and Effie are going to be very peeved with me, but it's my party, not theirs, and as developers go, Opal and Wally are better than most. And Opal and I have been friends since forever. I simply will not cut her off." She paused. "Holly, are you all right? Your face is scratched to pieces."

"I slipped on some wet rocks," I said dismissively. "I'll be okay."

Restarting the Volvo, then shifting gears both automotively and conversationally, she said, "I have to run and get the lobsters! I'll see you at seven. Do bring the dogs. Everyone else will." With a smile and a wave, she and the bichon frise drove off. I felt a little bereft. According to the directions with Gabrielle Beamon's letter, her house was at the end of this road. Therefore, the woman running out to get lobsters just about had to be Gabrielle Beamon. She was clearly not my mother. The letter and directions were from a hostess to a guest, not from a mother to a daughter. And how many wives refer to their husbands as "my hero"?

As the dogs impatiently dragged me to the side door of the cottage, names danced in my head: Opal and Wally, Quint and Effie, Norman Axelrod, Malcolm Fairley. My father, whose name I didn't even know. Ridiculous though it may sound, my only memory of my father was that he was unforgettable. Suddenly, for the first time since I'd regained consciousness, I was close to tears. Whatever his name was, he'd be here tomorrow. And for reasons I couldn't understand, the prospect did nothing to alleviate my anxiety.

The interior of the cottage was normal and cozy. The back door opened into a tiny, old-fashioned kitchen with a small gas stove, a noisy refrigerator with rounded shoulders, an old white sink, and shelves stacked with cast iron pans, muffin tins, aluminum cooking pots, heavy mixing bowls, and a great many serving dishes, plates, cups, saucers, and drinking glasses. Almost everything except the microwave, the coffeemaker, a set of big pottery coffee mugs, and a few utensils dated from forty or fifty years earlier. On top of the refrigerator, a twenty-pound bag of premium dog food and a wastebasket escaped plunder. Boxes of cereal and crackers, a loaf of bread, and other edible odds and ends had been tucked between dishes and glasses on high shelves.

The tiny kitchen opened to the living room. Since the one-story cottage was uninsulated, the interior walls and the high ceiling showed bare wooden planks and beams. The grain of the wood and the age-darkened knotholes made the kinds of eye-of-the-beholder pictures you see in clouds. The living room had one obviously new feature: a sliding glass door that led to a deck. At the far end of the room was an old fieldstone fireplace with a raised hearth. Bookshelves filled the walls on either side of the fireplace. Grouped invitingly around a glass-topped coffee table in front of the hearth was a set of white wicker furniture with fat cushions covered in a cheerful print of pastel flowers. At the opposite end of the room, by the kitchen, was an almost antique dining-room table with six mismatched chairs that somehow belonged together. Against a wall near the table, a small desk held a tall pile of notebooks and manila folders, and a combination telephone and answering machine with the message light blinking.

The digital display showed one message. I didn't want to hear it. In fact, the innocuous flashing of the tiny red light made my heart pound. In a desperate effort to relieve the stupid, senseless tension, I pressed the Play button. *"Holly? Bonnie here."* Nothing dire so far. Bonnie, whoever she was, sounded altogether friendly and pleasant. What was I expecting? Not, in any event, what I heard next. *"Just wondered about any progress you might've made on the arsenic front,"* Bonnie added blithely. *"Give me an update when you have a chance! Hope you're getting in some hiking. I can use that, too. Bye!"*

Dumbfounded, I replayed the message four times. *Arsenic?* Progress I might've made on the arsenic front? I struggled to connect the poison to my fear. A phrase came to mind: *Arsenic and Old Ladies.* I knew there was something wrong with it. I couldn't think what.

Five

THE AMORAL BONNIE ENGAGES HOLLY WINTER, professional assassin, to rid her of an inconvenient husband. Or a hated rival. Little care I! Like a catalog clothes shopper mentally trying on an outfit, I slipped into the role of contract killer. It was a bad fit. For one thing, wasn't arsenic a strange choice of weapon for a hired *gun?*

If I were a killer, my most likely victim seemed to be the late Norman Axelrod, who'd apparently been the man who'd fallen to his death. I had, admittedly, been nearby. I did not, however, feel like the sort of indecisive or doubly cautious person who'd have dosed Norman with arsenic and *then* shoved him onto some rocks; it seemed to me that I'd have made up my mind one way or the other. Besides, if I'd had a contract to do him in, wouldn't I be reveling in the afterpleasure of a job well done? Or greedily collecting my pay?

Most of all, what I'd learned about myself so far suggested that I was a decent human being. Caligula probably felt the same way about himself. Still, the worst character trait I'd discovered in myself so far was a harmless, if pathological, attachment to uncooked rice. I was kind to animals. Clean, too!

At the moment, for example, I was under a hot

31

shower shampooing my hair. Naked, I'd found far less physical damage than I'd expected. My knees were scraped, and the area around my right elbow was badly bruised and abraded, but most of the blood that had pooled with rainwater had been from superficial scratches on my face. The muscles that ached now would scream tomorrow morning. From my scalp rose a large, tender lump that seemed to account for something important. The medical term eluded me. What I caught was a fleeting memory about the need to awaken a victim every two hours to check the pupils of her eyes. For what? When I got out of the shower, I wiped the steam off the mirror over the sink and stared at myself. To my persisting annoyance, I was definitely not Asian. Although my eyes were distinctly Caucasian, there was nothing else wrong with them, at least that I could see, except for fine lines at the corners. The pupils weren't of different sizes and appeared neither enlarged nor contracted. Great! I wasn't a drug addict. I tried to guess my age. I remembered looking at my driver's license, but if I'd read the birth date, I'd now forgotten it. The face was over thirty and under forty. As to its aesthetics, my main response was considerable relief that I looked less like a golden retriever, even a wet golden, than my earlier glance in the rearview mirror had led me to suppose.

As to my devotion to animals, observation of my own behavior suggested that my reflexes knew a lot more about my dogs than my brain remembered. For example, after I'd listened to the unknown Bonnie's arsenical phone message, the dogs had performed an energetic song-and-dance routine that hadn't fooled me one bit. In response to the performance, which consisted of prancing around while emitting unearthly yet identifiably Arctic yowls and yips, I had not mistakenly decided that the three of us were a vaudeville team. Rather, my legs had taken me to the kitchen, where I'd automatically checked the clock over the stove to make sure that it was after five and thus canine dinnertime. More importantly, I hadn't just naively doled out dog food. Without pondering the matter at all, I'd led the incredibly gorgeous male—what the hell *was* his name? I knew it better than my own!—to one of two large VariKennels in the bedroom. Having incarcerated him, I'd then filled two dog bowls, replaced the food bag on the top of the refrigerator, put the beautiful female's dinner on the floor, and dashed back to the male's crate, where he quit screaming and thrashing the second I fed him. In other words, empty though my head was, my body wisely expressed a practical knowledge of the malamute vocabulary. It is a lexicon that does not extend to the word *share*.

What the hell *were* their names? How could I have forgotten?! What ingratitude! There I'd been, exposed on a mountainside like a doomed female infant, when these ungodly beautiful dogs had materialized from the mist. Here I was now! Still astounded at heaven's bounty in blessing me with this massive, furry evidence of hope and strength in an otherwise bewildering and menacing universe! And what had *I* done in return? Failed to recognize my saviors as my own dogs! Effaced their names from my witless so-called intellect!

Having staged my own internal revival meeting and confessed myself a sinner before the altar of Almighty Dog, I resolved to atone. I longed with religious fervor to know the dogs' names. What drove me was, among other things, the conviction that the ability to call the dogs by their own names would somehow release me from the fear that still gripped me.

Before ransacking the cottage for rabies certificates, dog snapshots, or other artifacts of my lost past that might bear the magic names, I made myself slow down, breathe calmly, and carefully check both dogs for subtle injuries. Neither was limping or bleeding. Still, the female, with her Lone Ranger mask and her air of acute self-possession, struck me as too proud to whine about pain; and the male, with his soft, glowing expression and his debonair charm, seemed capable of ignoring a bodily injury if it competed with his zest for the joys of the here-and-now. I began with the female. She readily sprawled tummy-up on the floor as I ran my fingertips over her, extended and flexed her legs, and peered closely at the pads of her feet. Despite a rivalrous gleam in his dark eyes, the handsome boy suppressed what I suspected was an incipient rumble of complaint about having to watch his chum get all the attention.

"Okay, Big Boy," I finally told him. "Your lady friend seems fine. Let's take a look at you." Eager to join the game, he dropped to the floor and rolled over, tucked in his chin and forepaws, and let me repeat the examination on him. As I did so, his companion remained on her back, and the two sets of warm, almond-shaped eyes stayed fixed on my face. Finding nothing alarming, I finished by giving the two massive chests and tummies a simultaneous and vigorous rub.

"I swear to God," I promised, "that somewhere in this house is something with your names written on it. In the predicament we're in right now, the crucial thing is to have a plan, right? So, here's the beginning of it. First, I am going to get myself cleaned up. And then I am going to find out who you two are. And then we'll take it from there."

So, after I'd showered, toweled myself off, and dried

my hair with what felt like someone else's hair dryer, I examined Holly Winter's clothes, which consisted almost exclusively of jeans, T-shirts, and sweatshirts. The jeans and a couple of fleece tops were free of adornment, but almost every T-shirt was embellished with a team of sled dogs, the head of an Alaskan malamute, the logo of the Cambridge Dog Training Club, a boast about what Big Dogs did or didn't do, or some other blatantly canine motif. Furthermore, although a queen-size bed, a dresser, and the big dog crates occupied almost the entire floor space of the cottage's one small bedroom, I'd managed to cram the space available for storage with dog gear. In an open alcove that served as a closet were a set of portable PVC obedience hurdles and a large duffel bag jammed with leashes, dumbbells, scent articles, white work gloves, and other paraphernalia that I didn't bother to explore. In one corner of the room, fleece animals, thick ropes, and hard chew toys formed a neat mound. Only the two top dresser drawers held human clothing. The bottom drawer contained wire slicker brushes, undercoat rakes, and other grooming supplies. All were neatly sealed in heavy plastic bags.

It came as a relief to find that I did have a few respectable possessions of my own and at least a few interests other than dogs, albeit not many. The coffee table by the fireplace held a pair of binoculars and a field guide to birds with my name written on the flyleaf. Stacked next to the binoculars were books about Acadia National Park: *Trails of History, Mr. Rockefeller's Roads,* several photographic essays about Mount Desert Island. Two or three big maps of the island and several different guides to the park's hiking trails also bore my name. On the desk by the answering machine I found a thick pile of bulging manila folders, some steno pads, and three large notebooks. I leafed through the pads and notebooks, and skimmed a few of the loose sheets of yellow legal paper in the folders. The handwriting was almost illegible; I found it hard to tell where words began and ended, and the characters might as well have come from the Cyrillic alphabet as from the ABCs. The thickest of the file folders was, however, ominously labeled *Arsenic.* In addition to yellow sheets covered with Cyrillic gobbledygook, the folder bulged with copies of articles. I skimmed a few titles: "Toxicology of Arsenic," "Herbal Horror Stories," "World Health Group Tackles Arsenic Poisoning." In case the World Health Group was devoting itself to Mount Desert Island, I scanned a couple of paragraphs. In certain areas of India, I learned, arsenic-contaminated wells provided the only source of drinking water. The chronic poisoning caused cancer, leprosy-like skin lesions, and, ultimately, death. How monstrous! But why had I collected this material? What had it meant to me?

I was losing sight of the plan. Step one had been to get cleaned up. Task completed. Step two had been to discover the real names of the Lone Ranger and Big Boy. On the dining table was a medium-size green notebook neatly labeled *Hiking.* Next to the notebook, as if I'd been writing in it that morning, was a pen. Underneath the notebook was a book entitled *A Guide to Backpacking with Your Dog,* by Charlene LaBelle. What seemed to be the final page of a typewritten letter served as bookmark. I read:

a chance to see for yourself how bossy Gabbi can be! But she is really very sweet and such a contrast to Malcolm. No matter how headstrong or

36

overbearing and difficult Malcolm was, he was charming, too, and we still miss him.
    Hugs to Rowdy and Kimi.

                                              Fondly,
                                              Ann

P.S. Did you know that a Trophy Edition *is a Bentley?*

In the margin, for reasons I couldn't guess, I'd scrawled in big letters GOD *spelled backward!!!* Ann was evidently a friend of mine who also knew Gabrielle Beamon and the man named Malcolm whom Gabrielle had mentioned. She'd wanted Malcolm to have a chance to get together with my father. I liked the idea of family friends. In our brief encounter, Gabrielle hadn't struck me as particularly bossy, but she had been perfectly sweet. My own forgotten opinion of Malcolm might also differ from this Ann's. I might not view him as in the least bit headstrong and difficult. He might not charm me. And maybe my other car really was a Bentley! But the great news the letter conveyed was, of course, the names of my dogs.

"Rowdy!" I called. Both dogs came flying. "Kimi!" I exclaimed. Both sets of eyes gleamed. Both wagging tails picked up the tempo. "Rowdy! Kimi!" I repeated. Both dogs sat. Which was which? Rowdy was probably the male, Kimi the female. My hiking notebook confirmed the guess. For reasons I didn't understand, I'd kept a log of hikes. I'd study it later. Now, I found what I sought almost immediately. My penmanship here was better than the foreign-alphabet speed-writing on the papers in the folders. I'd obviously cared about this hiking diary; I'd wanted to make sure I'd be able to decipher it. One of the last entries was dated September 9. It opened with a complaint: "Clear, *hot* day with the sky an unrelieved blue! Carriage road up Day Mountain, then trail down." My notes went on to specify the weight each dog had carried. Rowdy had packed fifteen pounds, Kimi twelve. "Fifteen was nothing for him," I had noted, "and Kimi could easily have taken more, but gravel on the damned carriage roads is brutal on the dogs' feet." So, fifteen was nothing for *him?* For Rowdy! And Kimi could have carried more. *She* could have. Big Boy: *my* Rowdy. The Lone Ranger: *my* Kimi.

Holly, Rowdy, Kimi. Mount Desert Island, Maine. By now, I knew what day it was, too. Fastened to the refrigerator with a lobster-shaped magnet was Gabrielle Beamon's invitation to the event for which she was picking up lobsters. The invitation had been photocopied onto cheery yellow paper. "Come to a clambake!" it read. "In honor of Malcolm Fairley and in celebration of the Pinetree Foundation for Conservation Philanthropy! Wednesday, September 13!" The invitation went on about the time, 7:00 P.M., and the place, the Main House, and the phone number for obeying the request to R.S.V.P. In the same lovely script I'd already seen in her letter to me, Gabrielle Beamon had added a note at the bottom. "Holly, do come! Bring your beautiful dogs! Gabbi." So, as my correspondent, Ann, had written, Gabrielle—Gabbi for short—was bossy and sweet. If Malcolm was headstrong and difficult, why give a party in his honor? Because of his charm?

The kitchen clock read 6:30. I congratulated myself. Besides knowing who I was and where I was, in a minimal way, I knew the date and the time. I'd pass a mental status exam! An undemanding one. But a short time ago, I'd have flunked hopelessly. "Where Do We Come From? What Are We? Where Are We Going?" Ah yes! Gauguin's painting. Three questions. I now had two answers. We come from Cambridge, Massachusetts. We are an injured, vulnerable, frightened woman and her two ungodly powerful dogs. We are a trinity destabilized, for the moment, by its weak human element. As to the third question, the dogs have faith either in themselves or, God help them, in me. They do not worry about where we are going. Kimi has retrieved a fleece ball from the heap of toys in the bedroom. She lies with her belly on the cool floor, her toy globe immobile between her forepaws. The world is hers to chew and sniff. Rowdy has been rummaging in a pile of newspapers, magazines, and junk mail in a wooden basket by the fireplace. He parades around with a treasure in his mouth. It is an envelope. Intuition tells me that a certain magic word will persuade him to relinquish his plunder to me. Intuition stops just there. The magic word is in eclipse. I manage, however, to see that the envelope is addressed to Current Resident. Therefore, it is my envelope. It is mine to give to my dog. "Good boy, Rowdy," I say, simply for the joy of speaking his name. "Good girl, Kimi." For the same reason, of course.

Where are we going? *I* am not going to a hospital, because *we* would not be admitted. The idea skips across my mind that I might consult a veterinarian. I decide I must be temporarily insane. Consequently, we are not going home. Massachusetts is a long way from Bar Harbor, Maine. The trip is too long to be undertaken by a mad person unwilling to put her dogs at risk. Besides, I am convinced that there is something here I must do. Must tell someone? Must, at a minimum, *remember.*

I concoct a theory: As I was about to die, my whole life passed before my eyes and out of my memory. As my life returns, my lost mission and I will reunite. In the meantime, we must hunt for it: my hunting dogs and I.

Six

SOON AFTER ROWDY, KIMI AND I HAD BEEN introduced to the other canine and human guests at Gabrielle Beamon's clambake, I started to worry about what I mistook for a bizarre new neurological symptom caused by my recent fall. The particulars: Having been introduced to Pacer, Demi, Isaac, and twenty or so human beings, I exhibited an instantaneous case of perfect recall for everything about every dog and immediately forgot the names of all the people. I now recognize the phenomenon as spiritual rather than medical. Heaven knows that there was nothing new about it! But at the time, instead of feeling appropriately relieved to discover that the core of my being was intact, I fell prey to mental hypochondria: Ridiculous though it now seems, a lifelong sign of God's grace seemed to represent the unhappy effect of a brain injury. Also, I was frightened. And preoccupied with arsenic.

All this is to excuse my inability to give an entirely reliable and coherent account of the evening. If you've ever looked in a looking glass at yourself looking in a looking glass and so forth forever and ever, you won't require my apology. Instead of reflections of reflections of reflections, of course, I have recollections of recollections of recollections. Memory: It's all done with mirrors.

Remarkably enough, I remember why I decided to

40

accept Gabrielle's invitation. The reason was fear. Was I in real danger? If so, my best course must be to carry on as usual, to the extent that I could guess what usual was. If I holed up in the guest cottage, I was certain to make no progress. Only by venturing out did I have a chance of discovering what it was that frightened me. Furthermore, the persistent fear evidently disinterred my buried knowledge of predators and prey. If I screamed, ran, flailed around, and revealed my injuries, I'd mark myself as an easy victim. Flight invited attack. The alternative to flight was fight. But fight what? Or whom? What was the conflict? And which side was I on? I might not know whose human side I was on, but the dogs, miraculously, *my* dogs, were as strong as I was weak. I was on their side, and they would stay at mine. I dismissed the worrisome thought that despite the presence of the dogs, something terrible *had* happened to me today. My fall, I told myself, had been an accident. I could have been running from something. I could just have tripped.

I made myself as presentable as I could. The scratches on my face and the bruises on my right hand were impossible to disguise, but a pair of almost-new jeans, a long-sleeved blouse, and a purple fleece pullover covered the remainder of the damage. As the dogs and I walked along the well-worn road, I decided that the best camouflage for my mental bruising would be pleasant, neutral silence. "We'll keep our eyes and ears open," I told Kimi and Rowdy, "and our mouths shut." The resolution should have sounded familiar. It embodied the advice I was always giving myself and other people about how to avoid trouble in the sometimes gossipy and always hypersensitive atmosphere of a dog show. My memory of the context

41

had, however, vanished. I'd also forgotten that having sworn not to utter a word, I always ended up chattering at least as much as everyone else at a show.

According to the map Gabrielle Beamon had sketched on the sheet of directions, the dirt road that ran past the guest cottage soon ended at her house, which sat on a small peninsula that jutted into what she had marked as Frenchman Bay. As the map had promised, we quickly reached Gabrielle's house, a sprawling three-story version of the yellow clapboard guest cottage. Like the cottage, it had green shutters and trim. The road ended at a wide parking area at the back of the house. Five or six SUVs were parked there. The doors of a two-car garage were closed. Gabrielle's white Volvo had been pulled onto the rough lawn near the back door of the house. What I noticed now was that each of the Volvo's headlights had its own tiny windshield wiper. Headlight wiper? That's understated luxury for you: a minor feature no one needs and most people can't even name. There was nothing flashy about the house, either. It probably had its original kitchen, old baths, and a mere ten or fifteen other rooms. Location, location! Prime. On Mount Desert Island. Smack on Frenchman Bay. On how many totally private acres? With how many zillion feet of deep-water frontage? Abutting conservation land, too: the Beamon Reservation.

"This lady," I said under my breath to the dogs, "is a class act." It was a stupid thing to say. I mean, Rowdy and Kimi were the ultimate class act. The misfit was . . .

"Holly! Oh, wonderful! You *have* brought the dogs." Gabrielle sailed out the back door. She wore old jeans and boating shoes. The source of the nautical effect was a loose off-white muslin blouse trimmed with a few unobtrusive ruffles. At first glance, I mistook the ruffles

42

for something they were not, namely, lace. *Old* lace. As in arsenic and . . . That was it! Not old ladies. But the ruffles were just ruffles. Gabrielle's little white dog, Molly the bichon, was still where she'd been the last time I'd seen her, apparently joined to Gabrielle at the middle in the manner of a Siamese twin. Rowdy and Kimi behaved themselves a lot better than they had at our last encounter, only because I'd taken the precaution of stuffing my pockets with cubes of cheddar cheese I'd found, already diced, in a plastic bowl in the cottage refrigerator. I'd felt a stab of guilt. Was I chronically guilty of *bribing* my dogs? But I was weak and desperate, and the cheese worked wonders.

"Wally is taking care of the lobsters for me," Gabrielle went on. She threw one arm toward the side of the house. With the other, she supported Molly, who showed a happy interest in every word Gabrielle spoke. "I can't bear to murder them, especially slowly. It's one thing to plunge their heads in boiling water—you know they can't survive long—but this is different. Grisly. Although, when you think about it, they're just big insects. But I still don't like doing it. And there are clams and corn and potatoes, and that's going to be it, except for a salad and dessert. You can let the dogs go. The other dogs are running around. We're all down at the water."

As I accompanied Gabrielle across the lawn, toward the ocean, she overwhelmed me with human names. A few minutes later, when we joined the other guests, Gabrielle performed cheerful introductions and reintroductions. As I've explained, the human names didn't stick. Consequently, I'll call by name only the people I got to know later in the evening or saw subsequently: Opal and Wally; Quint and Effie;

43

Gabrielle, of course; and Malcolm Fairley, who hadn't yet shown up. At least a dozen other adults, plus a gaggle of children, were sitting, standing, or, in the case of the children, cavorting around on the wet rock-and-pebble beach created by the fall of the tide. But I have leaped ahead of myself. I must take care, I find, not to inflict my disorientation on others.

Gabrielle's house, I should first mention, faced the ocean. A wide, generous porch ran across the front; it was a definite porch, a roofed veranda. Steps ran down to a front lawn punctuated with a few tall pines, their lower limbs removed to open up the view, which was ungodly spectacular: blue-green ocean, lobster buoys, barren islets that would vanish when the tide rose, and in the distance, tree-covered islands, the line of the mainland, and white-sailed boats. As the lawn crept toward the ocean, it gave way to great stretches of smooth rock. The coast of Mount Desert Island has those tremendous cliffs you see in pictures of Acadia National Park: Otter Cliffs, lots of others. This was a gentle stretch of shoreline. It was easy to find natural staircases that started as dry rock and became damp and barnacle-covered near the seaweed, tide pools, and stones of the beach. Here, directly in front of Gabrielle's house, the rocks ran out into the water to form a point that probably had a name. Beamon Point? To the left, low cliffs rose to pine forest. To the right of the rocky point, the shore abruptly cut inward to form a large cove.

A prominent sign demarcated the boundary between Gabrielle's property and the grounds of the Beamon Reservation. The land directly in front of the house was private property; the Beamon Reservation began only a short distance to the right. In style, the rustic sign was identical to the one by the reservation parking lot, but this one limited itself to the words *Beamon Reservation.* Beyond the sign, on what was clearly conservation land, Gabrielle's guests were engaged in a blatant, if merry, demonstration of how to break the regulations so conspicuously posted elsewhere. As Gabrielle and the dogs and I picked our way down to the shore, I could see that, for a start, the food was being cooked in genuine clambake fashion. Adjusting layers of seaweed and poking at hot stones with a stick was a man with a small, round head, a large, round middle, and puny limbs. His nearly hairless head and circular face were evenly tan, and he wore a yellow sweatshirt. Picture a little apricot atop a big golden apple.

We'll get back to Wally Swan, as the lobster murderer proved to be. I'd evidently met him and his wife, Opal, before. I didn't remember them. Back to the rules of the Beamon Reservation. *No campfires and no picnicking allowed. No alcoholic beverages.* Soon after we reached the guests clustered near the clambake, Gabrielle offered me a drink from a giant cooler that held soft drinks, small bottles of Poland Springs water, cans of beer, and two recorked bottles of white wine.

"Or if you like," Gabrielle added, "someone will run up to the house and get you a real drink. It's no trouble. Gin?"

In the manner of people at parties, Wally, Opal, and most of the other adults had drinks of one kind or another. I felt a little embarrassed about refusing something *real,* as Gabrielle phrased it. "Maybe later," I lied politely. "At the moment, I'm just thirsty." Memory! It's bizarre. It is possible, I assure you, for the mind to hide the name of your ailment while retaining the warning that if you suffer from whatever-it-is, you

45

mustn't drink.

"All that hiking," Gabrielle remarked. "Speaking of thirst, where has my wine gone to? Didn't I leave it . . . ?"

"Sorry about that," said a woman seated in a low folding beach chair. "One of the dogs knocked it over."

"Opal," Gabrielle said, "you remember Holly." With a coy smile she added, "My hero's daughter. He'll be here tomorrow."

Although Opal looked about fifty-five, her gray-streaked brown hair was pulled into a ponytail smack on top of her head and cascaded halfway down her back. Except for the juvenile hairdo, her appearance was unremarkable. Her skin was neither light nor dark, her features were moderately small and moderately attractive, her eyes were a medium hazel, and her makeup was unobtrusively flattering. She wore a heavy navy blue sweater and tan corduroy slacks. I wondered whether her character, too, had a jarringly childish element. The question struck me as comfortingly intelligent. Then I realized I'd forgotten the ponytailed woman's name. I did, however, have the sense not to ask how my father, whoever he was, had become Gabrielle's hero; the tale was obviously one I should know. I tried to smile comprehendingly. I probably simpered.

But to return to rule breaking—*no pets allowed*—Gabrielle's drink could have been knocked over by any of the three dogs, Pacer, Demi, and Isaac, who were enjoying the illegal freedom of the Beamon Reservation. I can't remember Demi's owners, but Pacer was Wally and Opal's. Isaac, an apricot mini poodle, was now in Gabrielle's care; he had apparently belonged to the late Norman Axelrod. Pacer was a golden retriever, Demi a black Lab. Pacer "bunny-hopped," as it's called; he ran like a kangaroo. His whole hind end rocked and rolled like a boat on a rough sea. Classic signs! Some deep social reflex kept me from asking Opal whether she realized that her dog probably had hip dysplasia. Had I been myself, I'd surely have blurted out the question.

No swimming. All three dogs were drenched. *No berry picking! Stay on marked trails!* Twin red-haired boys of five or six appeared from the woods bearing saucepans they'd used, or maybe just intended to use, in gathering berries. *No ball playing!* A red-haired couple joined the twins in a game of catch. Since the only wildlife in sight consisted of gulls, there were no seals for anyone to feed or approach, and there were no bicycles or strollers being pushed and no boats being launched. No one was toting a gun. In other words, not every regulation was being broken. Even so! A clambake *alone,* never mind everything else? On conservation land! I kept my mouth shut about that, too.

By now, I was sitting quietly on a reasonably dry rock near most of the other people, which is to say, close to the clambake. Rowdy and Kimi, having spent who knew how much time tearing around on their own on Dorr Mountain, were models of canine good citizenship, especially when I patted my cheese-packed pockets. Big, flashy, friendly creatures that they were, they attracted considerable attention. Since it was apparent to me, the recent victim of a head trauma, that my dogs were content to roll onto their backs and accept the adulation of strangers, it should have been equally apparent to people whose brains hadn't just been run through a food processor. But it wasn't. No, no! My poor leashed dogs became the object of group sympathy: *Don't they ever get to be free? Just look at those precious faces! Oh, they're just dying to play with the other dogs!* And so forth, all of which palaver the dogs regarded as verbal liver treats and gobbled up. Alaskan malamutes don't merely *have* big brown eyes, but *use* them. If I'd been in my normal state of consciousness, I'd have explained that malamutes operate on the principle that if it *could* be dinner, it *is* dinner. Fish corpses and decomposing crabs deposited by the receding tide: dinner. Your lobster, my lobster, everyone else's lobster, all the clams, corn, and potatoes? The hot stones? The seaweed? Maybe even the coals and embers? Dinner. I'd have given examples of objects devoured in their entirety by Alaskan malamutes: leather jackets, zippers and all, songbirds caught on the wing.

Malcolm Fairley's arrival spared me the need to explain. He didn't deliberately rescue me; he just happened to turn up at the crucial moment. Still, I felt grateful. Even if I hadn't, I'd have liked him the second I saw him, in part because everything about him, from his Yankee jaw to his plaid flannel shirt to his wholesome, weathered face, looked solid and familiar. Although I did not, of course, remember the man, it was instantly apparent to me that I knew men like him. Trusted them, too. Consequently, I felt doubly grateful to Malcolm Fairley. Without so much as uttering a word, he'd not only saved me from an awkward little situation, but had softened my edgy feeling of groping in an alien world. Although he was late for a celebration in his honor, no one seemed to feel annoyed or slighted. If he'd been three or four hours late, everyone would probably have been delighted that he'd arrived. Perhaps I can best convey Malcolm Fairley's impact by noting his dramatic effect on the canine guests. As soon as he

48

appeared, Pacer, Demi, and Isaac dashed toward him, tails and bodies wagging in undisguised delight. Even Molly wriggled out of Gabrielle's arms to join the scramble. Rowdy and Kimi jumped to their feet, pointed their noses toward him, and burst into the characteristic malamute greeting, that prolonged, human-sounding *woo-woo-woo*. Human inhibitions being what they are, the rest of us didn't go flying toward Fairley or sing aloud for joy. Those who'd been lounging sat up. Eyes brightened. We radiated a collective, doglike happiness. Malcolm Fairley was one of our own. Now that he'd arrived, our pack was complete. *We miss him*, Ann had written. I could see why. So far, his headstrong, difficult streak was unapparent.

Maybe I've overstated the subtlety of the human greetings. Gabrielle Beamon didn't pound across the rocks toward Fairley and certainly didn't mimic the dogs by hurling herself to the rocks at his feet, and she didn't carol a chorus of *woo-woo-woos*. Still, it's fair to say that as Gabrielle hurried toward him, the ruffles of her shirt caught the salty air like the sails of a boat catching a fresh breeze. When she reached him, he transferred his right hand from Demi's smooth black head to Gabrielle's shoulder and kissed her on the cheek. I was startled. Malcolm Fairley had struck me as the kind of male Yankee whose typical object of public affection is a Labrador retriever.

Gabrielle didn't seem to share my surprise. After returning his kiss, she stated the obvious: "You're here!" That extraordinary voice of hers, at once mellow and husky, made the banality sound warm, genuine, and wildly seductive.

"Anita offers her apologies," Fairley said, "and Steve's. They should be here in time for dessert."

Nature had designed Gabrielle for talking about romance. "So! We get to meet the boyfriend," she said with satisfaction. "Serious?"

Fairley just smiled and nodded. I'd already heard enough, though. His voice had hit my gut like a mallet pounding a gong. Although it was far less distinctive than Gabrielle's, I'd recognized it instantly. It was the voice I'd heard during those fleeting, dreamlike moments of half-awakening. The man who'd promised anonymity to his quiet companion? The man who'd talked of death? Malcolm Fairley. I'd have known that voice anywhere.

Seven

"I'M CURIOUS ABOUT THE PINE TREE FOUNDATION." I ripped a leg from my lobster's body.

Effie O'Brian's response was a bit snippy. "I would've assumed Norman Axelrod'd talked you to death on the subject."

Her husband, Quint, called her on the slip. "Effie, find another expression, if you don't mind."

Quint O'Brian, I'd managed to discover, was Gabrielle Beamon's nephew. Although he and Effie looked barely old enough to be out of high school, they'd graduated from Oberlin three years earlier, married soon after that, traveled in Europe, and then settled in as the caretakers of the Beamon Reservation. Because of Effie's chattiness, I hadn't had to ask many questions, and those I'd asked had been vague enough to hide my ignorance. Quint and Effie's house, she told me, was on the private road to the right of the

50

reservation parking lot, opposite the road to the guest cottage and main house; I remembered seeing it on Gabrielle's map. Effie used one room as a pottery and weaving studio. Quint, she informed me, was a cabinetmaker. The couple shared a homespun look. Effie's long, dark hair was French-braided. She wore layers of flowing cotton garments. On her feet were Birkenstock sandals over thick woolen socks. Quint had cherubic blond curls and was dressed in jeans and a multicolored woolen jacket that looked Guatemalan or Peruvian, but may have been handcrafted by his wife. Without actually looking like the Campbell Kids, the O'Brians radiated a New Age version of red-and-white soupy wholesomeness. Effie was at that very moment pouring steaming vegetable soup from a thermos into a small pottery bowl. She's already told me, with a censorious look in her husband's direction, that as a vegetarian, she didn't eat lobster or clams.

"Quint," she'd explained, "is a pesco-ovo-lacto-vegetarian, meaning that he eats fish. And eggs. And milk."

"Meaning," Quint had expanded, "that to a purist like Effie, I'm not a vegetarian at all."

They'd locked eyes and burst into laughter.

"We have an ongoing purer-than-thou competition going here," Quint told me. "Pardon us. We're obnoxious."

They weren't. Or I didn't find them so. In fact, when Wally Swan finally disinterred the lobsters, steamers, corn, and potatoes, Quint and Effie invited me to eat with them. They also went out of their way to include the Pine Tree Foundation's secretary, a dark-haired, pixielike young woman named Tiffany, who clearly knew the other guests but had still been cast to the

51

social periphery. Luckily for me, Tiffany took an instant liking to my dogs, who used a variety of mournful expressions, smiles, vocalizations, and similar tactics to convince her that they perceived unique and fabulous traits in her character that no one else, human or canine, had ever noticed before. Tiffany's captivation by malamute voodoo freed me to eat dinner. With what I now see as astonishing competence, she took Kimi's leash and assumed the task of preventing Kimi from filching the food on people's paper plates. With a quick hand signal, she promptly got Rowdy, too, to drop to the ground in a sphinx-like pose. "Well-trained dogs," she commented. "Stay!"

Anyway, I was thus able to disjoint my lobster and ask a vague nonquestion about the Pine Tree Foundation for Conservation Philanthropy. For all I know, Effie's snippy response was justified; maybe Norman Axelrod *had* talked me to death, so to speak, on the subject. Still, I ignored Quint's objection to the expression about death and said, "No, not really."

"Well, I'm surprised to hear that," Effie said, "because it was one of his favorite, uh, points of contention, although as you probably noticed even on short acquaintance, he had so many that it's a wonder he didn't, uh, prick himself to death on one of them long ago."

"Effie!" Quint apparently devoted himself to monitoring his wife's figures of speech.

"Well, it's the truth," Effie insisted. "He was like a bull that went through the world seeing red flags everywhere." After taking a bite of a sandwich she'd brought with her—bean sprouts wiggling from slices of a whole-grain loaf—she swallowed, and amended the claim. "Not everywhere. Axelrod operated on the

52

principle that if other people *wanted* something, or liked it, or supported it, or whatever, then no matter what it was, he was violently opposed to it. Except for his thing about celebrities. Especially Stephen King. Not that Norman stalked Stephen King. He just liked people to think they were friends."

"They weren't," Quint added. "It was just that he was a name-dropper. Norman, not Stephen King. Norman would kind of alternate between this adulation of some famous person he was pretending he knew and, on the other hand, this mean-spirited opposition to—"

Effie interrupted. "Quint and I could never see that he had any causes he really cared about, I mean, for their own sake. His whole life was like a reaction *against* anything someone else gave a damn about."

"It wasn't so much that, Effie," Quint said. "He was a crank. He couldn't just accept that a good idea was a good idea. He always had to see some dark scheme surrounding things. If something *seemed* good, he had a kind of compulsion to go ferreting around to find out what was bad about it."

"Mr. Axelrod was always writing letters to the papers," Tiffany informed me. "And they got published, too! Like, he wanted the park to close the road to the top of Cadillac Mountain, which is like maybe the most popular place in the entire park, the top of Cadillac."

"You see?" Effie cut in. "The tourists love it, so Axelrod wanted to close it down."

"Not close down the *summit*," Quint clarified. "Close the road to *traffic*. People could still hike up. Or bike. Ski. That's different. And it's not such a bad idea."

"Oh, admittedly, Quint," his wife said, "overuse is a tremendous problem. Three million visitors a year, and practically all of them pollute the air with their *infernal* combustion engines *driving* to the top of Cadillac and the Thunder Hole and Otter Cliffs without ever getting out of their cars. But the realistic way to address the problem is collective action, public education, raising money for conservation, like the Pine Tree Foundation, and preservation of what's left, the way we do here. It isn't writing crazy letters all on your own about banning cars from Cadillac."

"Nobody ever answered your question," Tiffany said to me. "What the foundation does is to let people invest their money in a way that benefits the environment. The investors put their money in the foundation, and the foundation reinvests in environmental concerns and makes grants to conservation groups. And then it pays the investors back, just like a bank, only with a lot higher interest."

"Malcolm is the founder," Quint said. "And C.E.O. Malcolm Fairley. You probably know that."

"Yes, of course," I said as knowingly as I could. Then I turned my attention to the clams. Steamers are disgusting only if you're used to cherrystones, littlenecks, and other kinds of quahogs. With steamers, you remove the clam from the soft shell and then peel an icky-looking membrane off the neck before dipping the clam first in clam broth, then in butter, then into your mouth. Steamers have big, squishy, creamy bellies and chewy necks. Eating steamers keeps you busy enough to explain any lack of full participation in conversation.

"What's special," said Effie, tossing a superior glance toward her husband and Tiffany, "is that besides having investors and grantees, the Pine Tree Foundation also has donors—benefactors, they're called—which is what makes a lot of the grants possible and makes the foundation such an attractive investment. So, the investors—like the people here, some of them, and lots of others—can put their money in the foundation instead of in stocks or bonds or whatever, and do very, very well, and benefit the environment, all at the same time. It's a perfect example, actually, of what I meant about Norman Axelrod. He saw everyone and everything around him benefitting from the foundation. He even knew the people, like Malcolm—everyone knows Malcolm Fairley—and knew that they were committed to Acadia and to preserving the island and to keeping Maine green and all the rest. Everyone else knows what a good thing the foundation is for everyone! It's obvious! So, naturally, Norman Axelrod wouldn't have anything to do with it and didn't have one good word to say about it."

"Cutting his own throat," Quint remarked.

"Quint! Now look who's using the wrong—"

"Sorry," Quint said. "What I meant was he could see for himself that the investors had done very well. My aunt, for example. Gabbi was one of the initial investors, and she did so well that she keeps reinvesting, and so do plenty of other people. So Norman Axelrod knew what a good investment the foundation was, and he still turned down the opportunity. Just to be oppositional."

I tried to speak in a tone that was half statement and half question. "But he and Gabrielle stayed friends . . . ?"

"Oh, that's Gabbi." Effie said it affectionately. "If you want an extreme case in point—"

Quint interrupted her with a soft, growly, "Effie, not here!"

Tiffany helped me out by whispering, "Quint means Opal and Wally Swan."

I swallowed a clam. "And . . . ?"

Tiffany looked aghast. As if confiding that Wally and Opal were convicted child molester serial chainsaw murderers, she whispered, "They're developers! Swan and Swan. They build houses! And condo complexes, when they can get away with it. The whole idea of the foundation is keeping Maine green. And the whole idea of Swan and Swan is cutting down every tree on Mount Desert Island. Quint hates the Swans just as much as Effie does."

Despite Tiffany's low volume, Quint must have overheard, because, in normal tones, he said, "Mount Desert Island has a fragile ecosystem. We're bombarded by threats from the outside, like air pollution blown in from the Midwest, acid rain, acid fog, acid snow. But we've also got water pollution that originates here. And habitat fragmentation. You can't preserve a habitat bit by bit, one spot here, one spot there. It's an integrated whole. Take the rain forests. What happens there has a direct impact on what happens here. That's why Malcolm is involved with Guatemala, too. The big problem right here, really, is overuse. You can literally see it on the popular trails. You can see and hear the cars, and you can smell the exhaust in the air. And yes, you can encourage the tourists to go to the less frequented places, but it just shifts the problem. It doesn't solve it. And the more development there is, the more houses, the more motels, the more everything, the more overuse there's going to be."

"You can't ban visitors from a national park," I pointed out.

"More's the pity," Effie said.

"Mr. Axelrod used to joke about shooting tourists on sight," Tiffany said brightly. "That was his favorite

56

joke: If it's tourist season, why can't you shoot them?'"

"What makes you think he was joking?" Effie asked.

Eight

"SHORT OF BRINGING POOR NORMAN BACK TO LIFE," said Gabrielle, "it seemed like the most useful thing I could do." She was explaining how Axelrod's mini poodle, Isaac, happened to be in her care. "Especially because Isaac hadn't been feeling well—he's fine now—and I wasn't sure who else had a key to Norman's house. Norman was *not* the most trusting individual. So I went over and let myself in. Poor Isaac! He was so happy to see anyone. He came dancing to the door, and I scooped him up, and I grabbed a few of his toys and his crate and brought him back here, poor boy. He's no trouble. If anything, he's not *enough* trouble! He's a funny little duck. Some of these show dogs are all too used to being stuck in their crates and ignored for days at a time."

After a swim in the Atlantic, the happy-looking Isaac was far from ready to enter the show ring. In what I now see as a positive prognostic sign, however, I took pleasure in recognizing the link between Isaac's enjoyment of his dip in the Atlantic and his breed's origins, which despite the pop term "French poodle," are German. *Pudeln:* to splash in water. The standard poodle, the largest of the three varieties—standard, mini, toy—was originally a water retriever. The miniature poodle, with a height between ten and fifteen inches at the withers, was bred down from the standard poodle and was never meant as a sporting dog. Even so!

Here before my delighted eyes, his mane of apricot curls and his apricot pompoms drenched, his shaved hindquarters bare to the world, the adorable little Isaac unconsciously proclaimed his functional heritage. An unsettling reflection cut short my joy. How, I wondered, can someone possibly recall the derivation of the word *poodle* and the origin of that wonderfully intelligent breed while struggling to remember her own name?

Darkness was now falling, but the temperature remained surprisingly mild, and the air was still. Although most of the food had been eaten, people continued to pick at their lobsters. After sucking the juice out of a leg, Gabrielle went on. "Horace Livermore, Molly's handler, is always after me to send Molly on the circuit, but I can't see it. He's always pointing out that we could finish Molly in no time and get her Canadian championship if I'd turn her over to him the way Norman did. Horace Livermore has what's called a string of dogs. Like a string of prostitutes. Isn't that grand! But I want Molly with me, and *Buck*"—Gabrielle beamed at me—"tells me that I'm perfectly right. What we do is called 'ringside delivery.' There's also something called 'ringside pickup.' Isn't that a wonderfully licentious expression? But Molly and I don't do that. We make advance arrangements to meet Horace at the shows, except that half the time I have trouble finding him. Anyway, before Norman got into one of his snits and fired Horace, Isaac was hardly ever here. He was always with Horace Livermore."

I was about to ask a gossipy question about why Norman Axelrod had fired his handler, Livermore, when Opal commented that it was just as well, in retrospect, that Isaac hadn't had the chance to get too attached to Norman. If something happened to her or to

Wally, Pacer would be grief stricken. And what would Molly do if Gabbi died? She'd be heartbroken!

"But Isaac knows!" Gabrielle insisted. "Or he'll figure it out. Sooner or later, he'll know something is dreadfully wrong. He's so bright! I keep thinking there ought to be a way to help him understand what happened. If I could just explain it to him—"

"Since the rest of us don't know what happened," Wally Swan said in grouchy tone, "I don't know how you expect to explain it to a dog. I, for one, don't have a clue about what Axelrod was doing near the Ladder Trail. As I understand it, he fell on the upper part of it, above the ladders. And Malcolm, I have to say . . . Well, it's already been said. Norman Axelrod was a crank. Let me tell you, when he heard about Opal and I volunteering to help on the Homans Path, he didn't have a good word to say about that project or anything else you were connected with, Malcolm. And that's the truth."

Tiffany, the Pine Tree Foundation secretary, again filled me in. "The Homans Path goes up Dorr from the Nature Center," she said quietly. "It's one of those old trails with stone steps, but the Park Service abandoned it ages ago, for no good reason. They cut down trees at the bottom and top to block it off. So, Malcolm got people together to restore it, and he got permission, and the foundation gave a grant. Malcolm does a lot of the work himself, and he got Opal and Wally to be part of his trail crew, and also a new guy named Zeke, who isn't here tonight. That's what Malcolm's like. He doesn't just want to sit in an office and talk about the environment. He gets right out there and does the work."

"Opal and Wally?" I whispered back. "Swan and Swan?"

"That's Malcolm Fairley! Who else would've asked *developers?* I mean, talk about hands-on learning about the environment! He's actually got them involved, really involved, not just on paper. You aren't going to get developers to change their attitudes by yelling at them or lecturing them. It's a waste of breath. But Malcolm's got them out there clearing brush and moving logs and opening up the trail, so eventually they'll figure things out for themselves. No one else would even have thought about asking them, never mind gotten them to do it. And the Homans Path is really beautiful. The steps aren't even in terrible shape. Once you see it, it's just so obvious that it's worth saving. If you ask me, once it's done, the park ought to rename it after Malcolm Fairley."

When I tuned back in to the general conversation, Malcolm Fairley was saying that yes, Norman Axelrod was the last person you'd expect to find hiking anywhere. "You'd hardly call it hiking," Fairley said ruefully. "I knew he wasn't fit for a real hike, but I had no idea he was in such bad shape. He was only about my age, and he had to stop every five or ten steps to catch his breath. When we started out, it was raining, not hard, but the stone was wet, and he had a rough time with the footing. We hadn't gone more than a quarter of a mile when I started asking him if he didn't want to call it quits. And this was on Kurt Diederich. Anyone who can walk up an ordinary staircase ought to be able to do Diederich. Or that's what I thought."

Fairley was in radiantly robust condition. His notion of a slow, gentle walk might be most other people's idea of an exhausting climb. And two *males?* Contrary to popular stereotypes, self-confident females, especially malamute females, do lift their legs, but it's males who are driven by an unreasoning compulsion to mark everything, especially anything that has been or could be marked by another male. With males, one and one doesn't equal two; it equals competition. Human beings? Well, yes, certain trivial interspecies differences exist. A male dog, for example, isn't going to keep turning around to ask the loser in the you-know-what contest whether he wants to call it quits. He's just going to . . . Well, never mind. Sorry. Talk about bias! For all I knew, Malcolm Fairley's dedication to Guatemala, the rain forests, and the global environment extended to the social environment of his own species. Maybe the two men had strolled cooperatively up the trail. Still, Ann's letter had used the word *overbearing*. And there'd been a third person, hadn't there? A man or a woman whose voice hadn't reached me. An anonymous third person.

"I still don't understand why Norman was there at all," Effie said vehemently, "and why he was there with you, Malcolm. He hated exercise, he hated trees, and he was more than slightly antagonistic to the Pine Tree Foundation."

"There was no personal animosity," Malcolm Fairley replied. "Norman disapproved of the Beamon Reservation, too. He needled Gabbi mercilessly about it, if you remember. But they remained friends."

"Was it his idea to go hiking?" Effie demanded. "Or yours?"

"Mine." Fairley looked a little embarrassed. "What can I say? I'm an incurable proselytizer. I'm convinced that if you can make the environment real and meaningful to people, they'll make good decisions. And the old stepped trails up Dorr make a

61

better argument than I can for conservation."

"They're man-made," Quint objected. "They aren't a natural part of the environment." He paused. "Oh, I get it. So there was a chance that Axelrod might actually like them."

Fairley smiled. "The truth is, I offered him a lure in the form of something to complain about. If you remember, one of his gripes with the park was about signs. He wrote letters about how there weren't enough signs, they were confusing, and—"

Gabrielle gave a peal of glee. "And the trail signs on Emery and Kurt Diederich and that whole area really are confusing if you don't already know your way. Isn't *Diederich* misspelled on one of them? And it's hard to keep straight what's the Emery Trail or the Emery Path or the Dorr Mountain Trail or the East Face Trail. Very clever, Malcolm! Well done." She caught herself. "Well, in retrospect, not precisely."

"They're typical Acadia trail signs," said Quint, graciously covering Gabrielle's enthusiasm for a tactic that had ended in Axelrod's abrupt demise. "There's nothing wrong with them if you use a map. They're traditional old-style signs."

A brief discussion about the merits and failings of the trail markers on Dorr ensued. Everyone eventually agreed that Norman Axelrod would've leaped on the inadequacies of the small wooden markers as a fresh cause for public complaint.

"Something really ought to be done about the markers near the summit," Malcolm Fairley said. "That's where we were headed. On a foggy day, it's easy to lose your bearings up there and get yourself twisted around a hundred and eighty degrees. When I told Norman about that, he wanted me to take pictures. I said he had to see for himself. Damn! For once, he was right."

Night had fallen. Everyone but the mosquitoes had finished eating. Although Gabrielle provided aerosol cans of bug repellent, the creatures were feasting on us. To help drive them off and to give some light, Wally Swan had transformed the site of the clambake into a campfire. As he tossed a piece of driftwood onto the fire, I heard Effie whisper, "Quint, please! Make him stop."

"It's Gabbi's business, not mine," Quint whispered back. "It's her reservation."

"We're the caretakers," Effie argued softly. "It's not right. She's *your* aunt! You speak to her! Honestly, a blazing fire! And aerosol cans!"

Meanwhile, Malcolm Fairley continued his narrative. "There's not a lot more to tell. I wish there were. We finally got to the top of the Diederich Climb and onto Emery, and by then, Norman's breath was labored, and we took a lot of rest stops, but he wouldn't quit. You know that fork where the trail to Dorr goes to the right, and if you go left, well, straight, you're on the Ladder Trail. There *are* trail signs. They're old style, but they're unambiguous. Anyway, Norman said he needed to rest, and he looked around for a rock or log to sit on, but everything was wet. It seemed like he was going to stand there for a while, so I, uh, went off into the woods to answer a call of nature. And when I got back, he wasn't there. I couldn't've been gone more than . . . I don't know. Two minutes? Three minutes? Of course, now I'm hollering for him. The first thing that occurs to me is that he's gone off looking for a dry place to sit down, not that there was one. But I couldn't figure why else he would've left except to look for a place to park himself. Or maybe, like me, he's answered a call of nature. I look around, keep calling for him, go a little way back down Emery, take a few steps down the Ladder Trail, and there's not a trace of him. Sound does funny things in that thick fog, and I keep stopping and calling for him and listening. Then, finally, it occurs to me that he's decided to get a head start on me, beat me to the top, so instead of just going in all directions around that fork, I head up Dorr. By now, I'm worried. I'm moving right along. If he'd gone that way, I'd've caught up with him in a few minutes. But I kept thinking that if he got above tree line, before the summit, he'd get lost and end up God knows where. I'm up there in, say, ten minutes. Twenty maybe. It's not far. And he's not there. I retrace my route, back down to where the trail forks. And then I come to my senses and I think, this guy isn't going up a mountain or down some ladders. He's going to turn around and follow the steps back down to my car."

And where was I all this time? I wondered. Lying comatose on the slope below? Had I seen Norman Axelrod, Malcolm Fairley, or both? Had I been seen? What about my dogs? We'd all been wearing red.

"So at that point," Malcolm Fairley continued, "I beat it back down to the Nature Center, where we'd left the car, and as I'm going down, I'm still hollering for Norman and trying to scan all around, because you know how slippery those steps are when they're wet. And the fog's as thick as ever, thicker, and no one's hiking up that I can ask. And I'm telling myself Norman's inside the Nature Center, or he's pacing around in circles by my car, sorry he ever got out of it."

What about the other person? I wanted to ask. I heard you! I heard you talking with someone!

"You must have been terribly worried by this time," Gabrielle said.

"Well, yes, I was! But I expected to hear some kind of explanation. That some hikers had been going down and Axelrod had decided to go with them. Something. It crossed my mind that maybe he twisted his ankle. Maybe he was hurt. Never occurred to me he was *dead*. I still can't understand it."

"So how did you find out?" Gabrielle asked.

"Soon as I got to the Nature Center, I saw three or four park rangers. And you could tell something was up from the look on their faces. So I asked them. His body had already been found. Hikers, a young couple, husband and wife, were going up the Ladder Trail. Experienced hikers. Didn't care about the fog. They were trying to hike every trail in the park. They found him. He was lying right on the Ladder Trail, on that long flight of steps near the top. He hadn't even made it down to the top ladder. From what I heard, he must've fallen and rolled, smashed his skull."

"Probably a blessing he didn't survive," Opal commented.

"A lot of people don't realize it," Fairley said, as if agreeing with her, "but Dorr's the steepest mountain on the island. Not the highest. The steepest. A guy like Norman had no business on God's earth wandering around there alone. I can't for the life of me figure out what he thought he was doing."

Yes, I had been in the vicinity at the time of Axelrod's fatal fall. But only in the vicinity. If I'd been hiking alone, I might have done the Ladder Trail. But Rowdy and Kimi had been with me. Scraps of memory remained: Dogs were banned from Acadia's ladder trails. Even if they'd stupidly been allowed! There was no way I would've started down *any* ladder trail with two big dogs.

"Most common accident in the park," Fairley said. "Falling on rocks. There's a sign at the Nature Center that says so. Thank God, most of the time the worst that happens is a skinned knee. What happened to Norman was a freak accident." He paused. "Tragic," he murmured. "A tragic accident."

Nine

THE ODDITIES OF MEMORY AND ITS LOSS BEING WHAT they are, I retained solid expectations about the spending habits of New England white Anglo-Saxon Protestants. Consequently, I wasn't surprised to find that the toast to Malcolm Fairley was to be drunk with cheap champagne. What amazed me was that there was champagne at all. And lo and behold, more than a single bottle for the whole crowd! Two bottles, to be precise. But by Yankee WASP standards, especially rich Yankee WASP standards, the supply was generous. I'd have bet on ginger ale, and little of that.

In response to the mosquitoes and the darkness, Wally Swan had erected a half dozen bug-repellent torches in a circle around the fire. The flames efficiently illuminated the stinky black plumes of smoke that emerged from the wicks. Effie O'Brian limited her protest to loud coughs and a stagy display of fanning away the fumes with her hands.

"They do smell rather awful," Gabrielle remarked, "but they look festive, don't they!"

Effie grumbled something.

"What's that? Well, you know, I wouldn't worry too much about it," Gabrielle said. "It's only citronella, isn't it? And, really, in no time, it vanishes into the air. That's one of the nice things about being next to the ocean. It washes everything clean."

It was unnecessary to see Quint and Effie to perceive their reaction to this bit of environmental wisdom. I could practically feel a wave of rage emanate from them and churn through the air. Kimi, who'd been peacefully lazing at Tiffany's feet, suddenly got up, moved purposefully to Effie, and planted herself there, as if expecting to be told what the problem was and what she could do about it. Effie reached out and stroked Kimi's dark head. "What an intuitive dog you are. Good boy."

"Girl," I said reflexively.

Meanwhile, Wally Swan, who served almost as Gabrielle's butler, had opened the champagne and was pouring it into small plastic cups that his wife, Opal, distributed to everyone.

"I was hoping Anita would be here by now," Gabrielle said.

"Steve, too," Malcolm Fairley added.

"Yes, of course, and Steve, too. We are all dying to meet him. But what I meant was that all of us who support and, uh, benefit from the foundation owe our thanks equally to Malcolm and Anita."

"Anita's the foundation's attorney," Tiffany muttered to me. "Malcolm's daughter."

Lifting her small plastic glass, Gabrielle intoned in that extraordinary voice of hers, "To Malcolm Fairley! And the Pine Tree Foundation!"

Voices rose. "Hear, hear!"

Malcolm Fairley benignly accepted the tribute. He

had the good manners not to drink in his own honor. I didn't exactly drink to him, either, not out of disrespect, but out of the conviction that champagne in my bloodstream would end up as bubbles in my brain, which felt quite foamy enough already, thank you. I settled for bringing the plastic cup to my lips and miming a sip.

"And to Anita!" Gabrielle added.

After drinking to his daughter, Malcolm Fairley cleared his throat and proposed a new toast. "To the absent friends who make our work possible!" Norman Axelrod's name flew across my mind. I brushed it away. For one thing, Axelrod wasn't just absent; he was *dead*. For another, he didn't seem to have been anyone's friend except Gabrielle's and possibly mine; from what I'd heard, he'd been more enemy than friend to the Pine Tree Foundation. Also, there'd been only one of him, of course, and Fairley has clearly said *friends*. Plural. Fairley elaborated. "To the generous benefactors of the Pine Tree Foundation for Conservation Philanthropy! Our deepest gratitude!"

"They make matching contributions," explained Tiffany, my self-appointed interpreter. "That's why the rate of return can be so high, because of their contributions."

In innocence, I asked aloud, "Who are they?"

Lowering her voice, Tiffany said reverently, "Philanthropists, really. Very wealthy people who are totally committed to the environment. And to M.D.I." She translated. "Mount Desert Island."

In case you've never smashed your head on rocks while visiting Acadia National Park, let me assure you that you can do so without forgetting the name of the park's principal benefactor, mainly, I guess, because it's a household word: *Rockefeller.* Well, not household, exactly. Mansionhold? Anyway, I've subsequently had the occasion to look up a few statistics on John D. Rockefeller, Jr., Mount Desert Island, and Acadia National Park. So, here goes. It won't hurt; it'll only sting a little. M.D.I. consists of about 74,000 acres, of which 34,000 acres belong to Acadia National Park. The park owns another 6,000 acres on nearby Isle au Haut, Schoodic Point, and other gorgeous spots. John D. Rockefeller, Jr., gave more than 10,000 acres to Acadia, which also received gifts of land from the Morgans, Astors, Fords, Vanderbilts, and Pulitzers.

What's famous about Rockefeller's gift isn't just its size or its value. It's what John D., Jr., did with large portions of the land before signing it over to the park. He built carriage roads. Why? Because the principal heir to the Standard Oil fortune hated, and I mean *detested,* automobiles. He saw motor vehicles as the potential ruin of M.D.I. and, in fact, battled to ban cars from the island. What he liked were horses. Consequently, just as you or I might have done in his position, he spent twenty-seven years building fifty-one miles of no-cars-allowed broken-stone roads designed for horse-drawn carriages. Well, maybe just as *you* might have done. *I*, of course, would've spent the twenty-seven years constructing fifty-one miles of groomed paths open only to hikers accompanied by dogs, or a fifty-one mile sled-dog trail, or fifty-one miles of dog-recreational something else. But I'm not John D., Jr. Among others things, having funded and supervised the construction of fifty-one miles of anything whatever, I'd keep it for myself and my dogs, whereas John D., Jr., donated most of his carriage road system to Acadia National Park. Most. Not quite all.

Here and there on the carriage roads near the town of Seal Harbor, you come to a sign announcing you're about to leave the park and cross onto what is discreetly called "private land." It doesn't take half a brain—about what I had left—to know *whose* heirs' private land it is.

So when Tiffany mentioned philanthropist benefactors deeply committed to M.D.I, I took the obvious baby-step mental leap and was just opening my mouth to utter the mansionhold word when Tiffany raised a finger to her lips. "The benefactors prefer to remain anonymous," said Tiffany, obviously quoting the official policy of the Pine Tree Foundation.

I can take a hint. Instead of loudly sputtering, "Wow! The Rockefellers!" I just said, "Wow!"

"Everyone knows, really," Tiffany said. "It's just like, uh, some game they like to play, you know, pretending they're normal. Well, not *normal* exactly. You know, low profile. A couple of times a year, they meet with Malcolm at his house for formal stuff, votes, that kind of thing. They don't want to be seen at the foundation. But I do the agendas for the meetings, so I have to know, really." Her voice glowed. "And in between, they'll call Malcolm, not that they give their names, not outright, not to *me,* or Malcolm will have to consult them about something, and then he'll go see them at their, uh, house, or sometimes in the park. I always know who's involved, really. I do the agendas for those meetings, too."

Malcolm Fairley startled me by swooping out of the darkness beyond the fire and the torches. The dread that had plagued me since I'd awakened on the mountain had been in partial abeyance. The sound of small waves, the unromantic reek of the ocean floor at low tide, the comforting presence of uninjured people and of my big, strong dogs, all of it had beaten back the terror. My grip on comfort was pitifully fragile. What set my heart racing now was, in part, a healthy startle reflex, a primitive what-the-hell-is-that? response. A figure unexpectedly swooped out of darkness. What seriously scared me, though, was my reaction to Malcolm Fairley's voice. His words and tone were benign. In fact, all he did was tell Tiffany in a light, jocular fashion that he hoped she wasn't giving any secrets away. "Anonymity is anonymity! It's a solemn promise." I had, of course, heard him speak of anonymity before. Addressing me, he added pleasantly, "Names are *not* for publication."

"No names have been named," I said flatly, battling the temptation to ask where he expected me to publish any names that might have been mentioned. I enjoyed a fleeting and somewhat frightening moment in which I saw myself as a roving correspondent for some highbrow newspaper or toney magazine. Loose pages of the *Times* and *The New Yorker* drifted through empty brain space. Each page prominently displayed my byline. Recovering from this little fit of journalistic grandiosity, I realized that Fairley might not have been speaking literally. For all I knew, my publications, like the late Norman Axelrod's, consisted of crank letters printed on the editorial pages of local weeklies.

Fairley went on to suggest otherwise. Playfully wagging a finger at me, he said, "I hope that Tiffany hasn't been giving any secrets away." To Tiffany, he added, "Holly's here because Norman promised her a story. A scoop? Is that still the term, Holly? So we need to watch what we say to her, or it'll all end up in print!" Fairley sounded pleased at the prospect: *You're not going to write about ME, are you? Are you?*

71

Another bit of knowledge. I was evidently a writer, a Rachel Carson type, perhaps, whose subject was the environment, pollution, conservation, ozone, global warming, and all that sort of thing. Ah-hah! The mysterious message on the answering machine about the arsenic front! Norman Axelrod's promise of a story! The pieces interlocked. I, Holly Winter, famed chronicler of environmental issues, had been summoned by Norman Axelrod to prepare a special report on arsenic contamination at Acadia National Park. Scandal! Millions of innocent park visitors each year exposed to the notorious toxin! Thousands of M.D.I. residents! Not to mention everyone who ate a Maine lobster! Well, no wonder I suffered from this dreadful sense of mission! And Norman Axelrod? Although I remembered nothing about him, what I'd heard this evening suggested a man who'd never have voluntarily started down a ladder trail on his own, especially not on a wet, foggy, slippery day. Rather, he'd been a man on the verge of exposing mass arsenic pollution at one of the nation's most cherished national parks. But before we'd gone public with our revelation, poor Norman Axelrod had fallen to his death.

Ten

PEOPLE WHO COMPLAIN ABOUT SOMETHING THE CAT OR dog dragged home have obviously never met human children. All of a sudden, a pigtailed girl of seven or eight dashed into the light of the campfire. Dangling a stinky, repulsive length of what appeared to be bubble wrap encrusted with the rotting corpses of sea creatures, she ran up to Quint and demanded, "What's this?"

Far from being put off, Quint showed the eagerness appropriate to the caretaker of a nature preserve. "This is a curious find, isn't it?" he told the child. He pulled out a flashlight and shone the beam on the loathsome thing.

"Is it an animal?" the child asked.

"How about we take it up to the house," Quint suggested, "where we can look at it in good light?"

Skipping after Quint, the child babbled happily. "*Roberta* said it was just an old piece of junk," she gloated. "But Roberta was *wrong!*"

"Sisters often are," Quint said sympathetically. "But they usually outgrow it. Roberta probably just didn't get a good look at this specimen. It's pretty dark here. Once we . . ." His voice trailed off.

Was the repulsive thing an animal? I had no idea. Worse, I had no desire to find out. As a conservation biologist or a famous science writer, I seemed to be on a par with the scorned Roberta. Scratch that hypothesis. So, why *had* the late Norman Axelrod summoned me here? I could hardly beg Quint and the little girl to play scientific detective by deducing my vocation in the fashion of Sherlock Holmes. Malcolm Fairley apparently knew the answer to my question. Still, I could hardly catch his eye and remark, even in an offhand way, *Say there, Malcolm! You've piqued my curiosity about how I earn my living. Do you suppose you could fill me in?*

Trying to dream up a subtle probe, I idly ran my fingertips down Rowdy's throat, as if a bright idea wedged in his vocal cords might transmit itself to my nervous system and eventually excite my enfeebled cerebrum. I studied him. In daylight, Kimi's dark facial markings had made her the more wolflike of the pair.

Now, by the light of the fire and the torch flames, each was as primeval as the other. Huddled around the remains of the clambake, glutted with the flesh of oversize undersea insects, we human beings looked none too civilized ourselves. With their dark, heavy coats, blocky muzzles, neat little ears, and intelligent eyes, my dogs had the advantage of startling beauty. By comparison, mine was a species of mutant ape ravaged by a skin disease.

Watching me, although not quite reading my thoughts, Malcolm Fairley spoke up with his usual joviality. "It's in the genes! I'm not joking!" Lowering his voice only a hint, he added, *"They're* the same way, of course. Dog nuts all."

In perfect seriousness, I asked, "Would you consider me a dog nut?" Not only Malcolm Fairley, but Effie, Gabrielle, and a couple of other nearby people laughed.

"Very good!" Malcolm complimented me. "Wonderfully dry sense of humor."

"It *is* genetic," said Gabrielle, who looked, I might add, far less apelike than anyone else there. Like my dogs, she had an appealing rightness. Whereas others appeared to suffer the hideously revealing effects of a skin and coat disorder, Gabrielle's perfect bone structure was obviously designed to be seen and admired. Her muslin ruffles were utterly correct for her breed. I realize now that the great gift she shared with my dogs was the invisible, elusive ability to make everyone feel special. "The love of dogs, I mean," she continued, eyeing me. "It's genetic. In this case, like father, like daughter."

"Daughter?" Fairley asked. "In general, the foundation deals with—"

"We're at cross-purposes here." Gabrielle slapped a mosquito. "I was talking about Buck and Holly. Her father and I met at a show. A *dog* show," she explained, presumably for the benefit of the genetically challenged. "Buck rescued me."

"I think that's very romantic," said Tiffany, who had persuaded Kimi to stretch out at the base of a boulder and was now using the big dog as a hairy headrest. "How did he rescue you?"

"Oh, everyone's heard this already," Gabrielle replied. "Malcolm knows the story, and poor Holly has suffered through it I don't know how many times."

"Don't mind me," I said, suppressing any hint of eagerness. The notion of this heroic father of mine was inexpressibly comforting. I was ravenous for details.

For once, Malcolm Fairley looked less than jovial. Still, he made a grunt of agreement. I felt sorry for him. Every time he looked at Gabrielle, he went all Bambi.

"Well," Gabrielle said happily, "I was supposed to meet Horace Livermore at the show, but Horace hadn't been too clear about exactly where. Horace has a tendency to assume everyone knows him and he'll be easy to find. But it isn't necessarily true. Shows are all spread out."

"Horace is . . . ?" Tiffany asked. "Maybe you said before."

"Molly's handler. But she does *not* travel with him the way poor Isaac did. I always thought that was very wrong of Norman. In theory, I have Molly all groomed, although I'm not very good at it yet, and then Horace takes her into the ring. Or one of his assistants does, or he finds me another professional handler. Sometimes he has a conflict, when he's supposed to be in two rings at once. Molly and I are not his most important clients."

Teasing Gabrielle, Tiffany said, "This is not very romantic so far!"

Gabrielle patted her arm. "Well, no, Tiffany, it isn't! Horace is a wonderful handler. Even Norman Axelrod admitted that. Norman's gripes about Horace had nothing to do with how Horace presented Isaac. But Horace is not the romantic type. What I'm leading up to is that I drove through this simply terrible rain to get to the show, which was in Portland, at some enormous convention center. Shows are so chaotic! I got up at four o'clock in the morning, and then I drove all the way there. Then I *did* have the sense to carry Molly. To keep her clean, of course. But she'd been in the car all that time, and she really had to go. And once I got indoors, there were these rows of pens with cedar shavings and so forth, and I thought, well, here are the potties! So I let Molly in one, only it turned out that they were private. And some dragon of a woman came charging at me. And poor Molly still hadn't had a chance to relieve herself. So what could I do? I picked her up and took her outdoors again, and I put her on the ground. She ended up dripping wet, with her feet all muddy."

"You have a great future with Harlequin," Tiffany said. "This is getting more romantic by the second."

"Isn't it!" Gabrielle went on. "Well, it does now. You'll see! So there I was, carrying Molly back inside, and she really was a mess. Meanwhile, I still hadn't seen a sign of Horace Livermore. I asked four or five people, and they were about as helpful as that dragon woman with the private dog potties. So I thought, *What am I doing here? This is not fun!* And I turned around and tried to leave. Only it turned out that when I'd taken Molly out the first time, I'd lost the little piece of paper saying she belonged there."

"The entry," I supplied.

"Yes, the entry. You have to have it when you take a dog out of the building. To prove you're not stealing the dog, you see, Tiffany. And I'd had it the first time, so I must've dropped it when I put Molly on the ground. The people at the exit were perfectly nice. They're just ordinary people, volunteers. They weren't going to have me arrested. But they were *not* going to let me take Molly home, either. They kept explaining some dreadful, complicated procedure. I was perfectly miserable." Gabrielle paused. "And along came Buck Winter." Her voice lingered on the name as if it were astoundingly famous and satisfyingly distinguished. *And along came Winston Churchill.* "Buck," she continued, with a verbal caress, "knows everyone. He just swept us up—he's a *big* man—and in no time, he had Molly on his grooming table—he has the most beautiful golden retriever—and he found Horace, and he *made* Horace handle Molly himself. And Molly went Winners Bitch and Best of Opposite."

This time I translated. "Best of Opposite Sex to Best of Breed."

"Molly won?" Tiffany was a little confused.

"It's complicated," I said in what should have rung in my own ears as practiced tones. "She won points toward her championship. If there was enough competition."

"Two points!" Gabrielle said.

"Congratulations," I said.

"But the real *point,*" Gabrielle punned, "is that from the second Buck Winter gathered us up and swept us away, all of a sudden I was having *fun!* All of a sudden, there was no place else on earth I'd rather have been." She gave a coy smile. "And no one else I'd rather have been with."

"Now *that,*" pronounced Tiffany, "really is romantic. I'll bet he's a hunk. What does he look like?"

Unbidden, the reply spoke itself in my head: *A human moose.*

"He's very tall," Gabrielle said. "He looms over everyone else. It's a big advantage at a show. That's how he found Horace, among other things. Everything about him—Buck, not Horace—is large and *solid*. His voice. His personality. Next to him, other men seem sort of . . . washed out."

"Oh, you've got it bad!" Tiffany exclaimed.

"At my age!" Gabrielle agreed. Adopting a practical tone, she said, "It's a good thing he isn't married. He's a widower. We have that in common. We both had happy marriages. Holly's mother died quite a long time ago. She sounds like a wonderful person." As if conclusively proving the excellence of my late mother's character, Gabrielle added, "She bred golden retrievers."

"Another dog nut!" Malcolm Fairley said cheerfully.

Gabrielle was unhappy with him. "Malcolm, that is a disparaging term, and you are talking about Holly's mother."

"I didn't mean it in a disparaging way," Malcolm said. "My apologies if it sounded dismissive. As I was telling Holly, *they* are the same way, and I have the highest regard for, uh . . . What is the preferred term?"

For a second, I thought he meant the foundation's benefactors and wondered why he was asking the question.

" 'Dog people' will do," Gabrielle answered.

"A hybrid species," I found myself adding.

"Hybrids!" Malcolm repeated a bit too enthusiastically for my taste. "Excellent! Very good! A hybrid species."

If I'd agreed that my remark was excellent or even very good, I wouldn't have minded having so much attention drawn to it. I was on the verge of asking Malcolm Fairley whether he'd ever had a dog, but stopped myself in time. I should know the answer. Flustered, I changed the subject. "What kinds of dogs do *they* have?" I clarified the question. "What breed?"

"Oh, more than one," Fairley answered agreeably. "Retrievers. Terriers. That sort of thing."

"Ignore him," Gabrielle said playfully. "He can't tell one breed from another." Rising to her feet, she said, "Well, I hate to give up on Anita, but if we don't have dessert now, we'll be here all night. It's raspberry pie. Last fresh raspberries of the season. I just have to whip the cream. Shall we stay down here? Or go up to the house? Is anyone getting cold?"

For a September evening on the coast of northern Maine, the temperature was still abnormally high, and there was no breeze at all. Several guests remarked that this weather couldn't last. We might as well enjoy it now.

"It's freakish, isn't it?" Gabrielle said cheerfully. "I suppose we have global warming to thank."

Effie succumbed to what passed as a choking fit. Recovering, she said, "Global warming is hardly something to be thankful for, Gabbi."

"Not in general, no, of course not, Effie. I meant in this instance. Ten years ago, at this time of year, we'd have been freezing out here, and the mosquitoes would've been long gone. Speaking of which, if we're having dessert out here, does anyone need more bug spray?" She held up an aerosol can.

No one accepted Gabrielle's offer. With Opal accompanying her to help with the dessert, she left for the house.

"Aerosol cans!" Effie exclaimed quietly. "Canada banned those damned things a long time ago. I don't know what's wrong with this country. It's as if everyone here is hell-bent on destroying what's left of the ozone layer."

"It depends on what's in the cans," Malcolm Fairley told her. "Not all of them—"

"Aerosol industry propaganda!" Effie declared. "From you, of all people, Malcolm! You won't buy those things any more than I will. Gabrielle knows better, too. I don't know what she was thinking."

"She didn't buy those cans," said someone whose name I've forgotten. "She told me. Norman Axelrod gave them to her."

"What a hostile thing for him to do!" Effie spat. "Typical! He couldn't just *be* irresponsible. Oh, no! He always had to flaunt his lack of concern. Like all his bragging about how when he died, his son was going to sell his land to the highest bidder and that the highest bidder was damned well not going to be Gabbi or the Nature Conservancy or anyone else who might preserve it."

Although I couldn't see people's expressions clearly in the darkness, the light from the fire and the torches revealed a subtle turning of heads toward Wally Swan, the developer, who was adding yet more driftwood to the coals. "Effie, let's drop it," he said peacefully. "That's one issue that doesn't need more wood added to its fire."

"Did Norman ever offer to sell you and Opal his land?" Effie demanded bluntly.

"No, he did not," Wally replied.

"Did he promise you his son was going to?"

"No."

But Effie persisted.

"Where *were* you and Opal this afternoon? Just as a matter of curiosity, I'd like to hear where you were when Norman Axelrod *fell* on the Ladder Trail. Did you happen to be working on the Homans Path? Both of you? It's no great distance from there to the Ladder Trail, is it? It's no great distance at all."

Eleven

"WE NEED TO GET YOU SOMETHING BETTER TO DRIVE than this." Anita Fairley is referring to Steve Delaney's van or, more precisely, to its interior, which has an ineradicable odor of dogs. Steve knows all too well how ineradicable it is. Three boxfuls of baking soda sprinkled over the seats and carpeting, left overnight, and then sucked into the bowels of a wet-dry shop vac had no perceptible effect. He has repeatedly saturated the van from ceiling to floor with spray-on stench-control liquids ranging from commercial products to improbable home-remedy concoctions containing everything from white vinegar to feminine-hygiene powder. For a week after the vinegar treatment, the van smelled like a pickle factory. The unspeakable powder left it smelling like a brothel.

"Something that doesn't smell like dogs," Anita adds unnecessarily. She occupies the passenger seat, which she has tilted back until she is reclining rather than sitting. Anita reclines as beautifully as she does everything else. She is more than photogenic; you can't even take a bad glance at her. Holly, Steve reflects,

81

always kept the seat in a fully upright position, as if perpetually prepared for take-off or landing. Out of the corner of his eye, he sees Anita's manicured right hand brush in evident annoyance at the nylon fabric of what she has informed him are called trekking pants. Their color, she says, is known as cigar. Anita has unknowingly enriched Steve's vocabulary by introducing him to new uses of old words—*tobacco*, too, proves to be a shade of brown—and to phrases like *personal trainer* and *personal dresser* that leave him wondering whether there also exist impersonal trainers and impersonal dressers and, if so, what services they can possibly perform.

"You owe yourself something better," Anita tells him. Holly would've told him not to waste his money on a new van because anything he drove would smell like dogs sooner or later, anyway. Besides, she'd have asked, what was wrong with doggy odor? And who was he, a veterinarian, suddenly to display this ridiculous antipathy to the fragrance of God's Own Sacred Animal?

Steve briefly takes his eyes off the road, the Maine Turnpike, to glance at Anita as she reclines seductively where Holly always sat. And talked. Often about her dogs. Or her work. Anita can't talk about her dogs because she has none. Her only pet is a small green lizard, Ignacio. As to Anita's work, Steve, as befits a veterinarian, had had to ferret out her occupation. Anita doesn't talk about her work because . . . Well, because she's sensitive about the negative public image of her profession, he guesses. She is a lawyer or, as she says, an attorney, a specialist in environmental law, conservation easements, all that sort of thing. Steve has no idea what that sort of thing is and never asks. The opportunity seldom arises. In a manner that Steve finds refreshing, Anita usually talks about him.

"A new van'd be a waste of money," he tells her now. "Sooner or later, it'd smell just like this one. It comes with the profession. A harmless occupational hazard."

She laughs uproariously. An almost inaudible voice at the back of his head asks whether she does not, in fact, laugh a bit too uproariously in response to what was not, after all, side-splitting hilarity. He ignores the voice. Unlike Holly, Anita possesses the great virtue of never trying to be funny. *She wouldn't know how,* the voice murmurs.

"Steve, I wasn't suggesting that you get rid of it," Anita says soothingly. "What I was thinking was that you could get yourself something new and fun, and just use this when you had your dogs with you."

The unwelcome voice at the back of his head instantly pipes up. New and fun? As opposed to when the dogs are with you? My boy, if this woman loves you at all, it's not for who you really are. The voice sounds irritatingly like Holly's. Who the hell is she to talk about loving him for who he really is? Or isn't?

"The new one wouldn't have to be big," Anita points out. "You could get a two-seater. Whatever you wanted. Leather seats?"

He feels defensive. His dogs are far too well behaved to think about chewing up leather seats, never mind doing it. Lady, his pointer, has never fully recovered from her initial timidity. Her fearfulness, he believes, is in part constitutional. Still, she trusts him, and with most strangers, she no longer shakes like Jell-O. Prozac is probably unnecessary. She has made progress without it, and he prefers a behavioral intervention. India, his shepherd, has too high an opinion of herself to stoop to

83

misbehavior and too high an opinion of him to disobey. India has, however, developed the embarrassing habit of calmly stationing herself between Anita and Lady, as if to protect the vulnerable pointer from human menace. Fortunately, Anita does not recognize the insult for what it is. What will not fail to register, if Anita happens to see it, is the expression that appears now and then on India's expressive face as she quietly studies Anita. Even Anita would know what that silently lifted lip meant. No one could misinterpret that Elvis Presley sneer.

"Wouldn't that be fun!" Anita exclaims. "You work so hard. You deserve a lot in return. Payback!"

Steve is not a complete fool. The two-seater with its leather seats? Anita would borrow it. Often. Very often. All the time. The voice suddenly sounds like his mother's. It asks what he expects from a woman he picked up in a bar. He almost laughs. After a twelve-hour workday, he'd fed and walked his dogs, showered, dressed, and then indulged himself in the extravagance of a drink and dinner in the bar of his favorite restaurant, Rialto, which is in the Charles Hotel in Harvard Square and about as far from his veterinary practice as you can get without leaving Cambridge. The food is wonderful. Everyone else wears black. No one talks about canine hysterectomies. If the word *castration* is uttered, it is in the Freudian rather than the veterinary sense. Alone at a small table, he was finishing a delectable dinner that he was too depressed to taste when through the doors of Rialto, which is to say, into the bar, stepped a tall, thin young woman with the irresistible combination of brown eyes and naturally light blond hair. Groomed and graceful, she radiated the elegance he has previously seen only in Afghan hounds in the show ring. Neither then nor now does he hint aloud at the possibility of comparing her, no matter how flatteringly, to a dog.

She took a seat at the small table next to his. Her beauty seemed almost unreal. Indeed, his first thought was that he might be the victim of some freakish and previously undocumented reaction to a supposedly innocuous drug. The drug was not Prozac. Soon after the end of a long love affair with a woman who was plainly never going to marry him, probably for good reason, he had considered putting himself on the famous vitamin P. He could easily have prescribed it for Lady and taken it himself. It was as faddish in veterinary as in human medicine. And reputedly as effective. As he'd done with Lady, he'd balked. Compromising, he'd self-prescribed the standard dosage of over-the-counter Saint John's wort and voiced his bitterness to no one but his dogs. In Cambridge, therapists of all persuasions were as thick as fleas on a junkyard dog. Probably as biting, too, he'd decided. Alternative therapies? Acupuncture, for example, would presumably allow him to remain silent. As it was, he felt as though needles were vibrating in all his most sensitive spots. The treatment, he decided, would be redundant.

In response to his mother's imagined remark, Steve reflects that, technically speaking, it was Anita who picked him up. The technical consideration is that it was she who spoke first. Specifically, she asked his advice about what to order from the reduced menu available in the bar. He said that everything was good. Well, okay, the actual exchange was subject to double interpretation.

"So," she said, "what's good?"

"Everything," he replied. "It depends on what you want."

Introductions followed. A waiter in a long apron took her order for the soupe de poissons and the mini Tuscan-style steak, his for brandy. Discovering Steve's profession, she poured out the details of Ignacio's recalcitrant skin ailment, a fungal infection she attributed to the high humidity in her condo. Later, after carefully examining the lizard and its habitat, he tactfully explained that although humidity was probably one factor, the more significant cause of Ignacio's problem was poor hygiene. This is to say that after leaving Rialto, he'd ended up in Anita's condo, one of a great many in a large complex overlooking the Charles River. If she had enticed him with the prospect of the view or perhaps offered to show him her etchings, he might have refused her invitation. Touched by Ignacio's plight, however, he'd accepted.

Ignacio's condition required a week's hospitalization. Professing herself wracked by guilt because of her failure to clean the animal's cage, Anita made daily visits to the veterinary clinic, where Ignacio basked under therapeutic lights behind clean glass walls. Ignacio's condition ameliorated, and with it, Steve Delaney's. Their afflictions were not entirely comparable. It is, after all, one thing to compare Anita Fairley to an elegant show dog, and quite another to compare Holly Winter to a reptilian fungal infection. Still, six weeks after the evening at Rialto, Ignacio is cured. Anita has installed lights for him. A professional pet-care agency makes biweekly visits to her condo to clean the lizard's cage. And Steve Delaney no longer feels the need for Saint John's wort. He again thinks of Prozac only as a treatment option for dogs. He savors Anita's differences from Holly, differences that extend beyond Anita to her refreshingly normal family. Anita's father, in particular, is pleasant, sociable, and immediately likable. Malcolm Fairley heads the Pine Tree Foundation for Conservation Philanthropy. Malcolm is ordinary. It would never occur to him, for example, to own a wolf-dog cross, never mind a pack of half-wild, half-tame misfits. The bumper sticker on Malcolm Fairley's four-by-four bears a wonderfully innocuous message: MAINE: THE WAY LIFE SHOULD BE. The tattered bumper sticker on Buck Winter's van also carries a message about God's Country: KEEP MAINE GREEN. SHOOT A DEVELOPER!

Not that Holly's father is in any way Holly's fault. Still, Steve feels an irrational gratitude to Anita for having a father who is neither a private irritant nor a public embarrassment. As Steve heads north on the turnpike, he looks forward to seeing Malcolm Fairley. Steve reminds himself that if he keeps his ears open at dog shows and flees at the first hint of a mooselike bellow, he will never see Buck Winter again.

Twelve

NOT THAT I WANT TO COMPARE ANITA FAIRLEY TO THE raspberry pies. The simultaneous arrival was a meaningless coincidence. The pies were made of fresh raspberries and topped with whipped cream. Fresh raspberries, as everyone knows, are wildly expensive because they're so fragile. They don't keep. One minute, they're delectable. The next, they're covered with mold. Sometimes it's white fuzz. Sometimes it's green slime. Then you have to throw them out. Whipped cream, when you think about it, pretends to be

87

something it isn't. It's an ordinary liquid puffed up to artificial heights by having a lot of air beaten into it. At bottom, a raspberry pie is just crust. One other thing. Even if the raspberries are beautifully fresh and taste wonderful, they still leave seeds stuck between your teeth. But as I hope to emphasize, there's no comparison. I *like* raspberry pie.

I don't want to compare Anita to a dog, either. And not just because I like dogs. Love dogs. Whatever. The point is that even a resounding crack on the head hadn't eradicated my facility for what I assure you is not mental telepathy or clairvoyance or any other psychic power. Take, for example, my apparently uncanny ability to predict when a dog is going to vomit. Not to brag, but I really can do it. Not years, months, weeks, days, or even hours before the event. But minutes before. Seconds, sometimes. Still, seeing the future is, after all, seeing the future, even if the future in question is only seconds away. I mean, one minute the dog is standing in the middle of a rug that can't go through the washing machine. And the dog obviously intends to keep standing there. Specifically, he has no intention of ambling onto some conveniently washable surface like linoleum, tile, or even wood, and he certainly doesn't plan to run considerately to the bathroom in the fashion of a person suddenly hit with nausea. And the dog, being a dog, doesn't groan, grab his stomach, and say something readily interpretable like, "Hey there! I'm about to deposit a gooey mass of intestinal juices and half-digested food on your rug!" If there's a real dog person around, he doesn't have to. What the dog does, you see, is to lift the corners of his mouth. If you're a dog person, that's what you see, anyway. And in plenty of time to rush up, grab his collar, and hustle him off the rug and onto the nearest washable surface. If you're not yet a dog person, of course, you're so tickled by the dog's darling expression that you exclaim, "Oh, look! He's smiling! Isn't that cute!" But after you've cleaned up after a few of those smile episodes, you make the connection. You develop the apparently inexplicable ability to read the dog's mind and to predict the future. Clairvoyance! The gift of prophecy! Admittedly, it would be better to be able to foresee something really valuable or useful, like what the stock market is going to do next or whether saying yes to a marriage proposal means a half century of true love or six months of noisy desperation. But gifts are gifts, no matter how small, and surely it's better to be able to predict when dogs are going to vomit than to be unable to see the future at all?

To return to my original point, which concerns Anita Fairley, there's nothing psychic about my occasional flashes of insight about what my fellow creatures are thinking and what they're going to do next. Anita, I hasten to add, was not on the verge of getting sick to her stomach. Not that it would have mattered. We were outdoors, on the rocky shore of the ocean, not in the middle of a rug. Anyway, in a flash, I suddenly knew as surely as if Anita Fairley had spoken aloud that she just ate up being seen with this man. She gobbled it up with the ardor my dogs would've shown if they'd been turned loose on the raspberry pies. And how could I blame her? If I'd been with him, I'd have felt the same way.

Gabrielle made a great fuss about Anita's arrival. "Anita Fairley, of course, and Steve Delaney," she said, her tone hinting at what I already recognized as a characteristic desire to have everyone know and like everyone else. "And the rest of you can introduce yourselves." Gabrielle went on to offer lobsters and steamers to the latecomers, but Anita said that she and Steve had stopped for dinner. It seemed to me that at a minimum, Anita should have invented a white lie about heavy traffic or a flat tire. *We're late for dinner because we stopped to eat* didn't exactly sparkle with social grace. To make matters worse, Anita wasn't just an ordinary guest at an ordinary social event. Her father was the guest of honor. This was a celebration of the Pine Tree Foundation. And Anita was, as Tiffany had informed me, the foundation's attorney.

If my presentation of Anita seems ever so slightly biased in an almost imperceptibly negative direction, forgive me. My only excuse for the lack of objectivity is that I hated her on sight. Why? Not because of her good looks or her bad manners, but because of my violently overwhelming physical reaction to Steve Delaney, the man who was with her, meaning, of course, *not* with me. Let me cool down, step back, and relate the facts. The principal one is that as soon as I caught sight of him, blood rushed to surfaces of my skin I didn't even know I had, and my heart pounded so fast and so powerfully that the tachycardia must almost have been audible. As to the rate and quality of my respiration, I'll say only that recent head trauma hadn't destroyed my memory of what *that* meant and, worse, would mean to any adult listening in, and even though I was sitting, my knees went weak, and sparing you further details, I'd have made a god-awful public spectacle of myself if I hadn't been saved, as usual, by dogs.

Kimi deserves most of the credit. Popping up like a jack-in-the-box, she delivered a prolonged string of the *woos* and *roos* that malamutes link together to form what are unmistakably human sentences. Kimi belted out her dialogue so loudly that all on her own, she'd have drowned me out, but Rowdy did me the face-saving favor of adding his voice at an octave or two lower than hers, and then everyone broke into embarrassed laughter.

Tiffany, who was still making a pet of Kimi, controlled her canine charge better than I did mine. Unbalanced by the events of the day and now, suddenly, awash in this weird maelstrom of desire, I was no match for Rowdy, who made a headlong pull toward Steve Delaney. By accident, I think, I managed to hang on to Rowdy's leash and to stay upright. Ears flattened to his head, tail madly wagging, Rowdy dragged me straight to Steve Delaney, who bent down, took the big dog's head in his hands, and spoke to him in tones too soft for human ears.

"Well, of course!" Gabrielle announced to everyone. "I should have realized!" Explaining herself, she said, "Steve is a veterinarian. His practice is in Cambridge. I think we can take a wild guess that Holly uses him."

Her words echoed in my ears. *Holly uses him.* It's a common enough expression, isn't it? And a perfectly innocuous one. *What dentist do you use? What doctor? What vet?* And if I reply that I use so-and-so, there's no connotation whatever of exploitation. But suddenly, dear God, far from limiting themselves to nasty hints, the words now multiplied into a tirade of denunciation. *Holly uses him: She uses him to her advantage, exploits him, profits from him, preys on him, cashes in on him, imposes on him. Do you use him, Holly? Oh, do you ever!* The worst of the tirade was this: My muddled head had somehow left me with a clear heart. Every word of the tirade was true. This man I couldn't remember? I *had* used him. I had used him badly indeed.

"You're the last person I expected to find here," he said, speaking only a little more loudly than he'd spoken to Rowdy.

"Me, too," I said. "I mean, you're . . ."

"What are you *doing* here?"

The truth spilled out. "I have no idea. I really have no idea at all." Now I was on the verge of tears.

"You've hurt yourself," he said.

"I fell." Groping for dignity, I hastened to add, "I'll be all right. Really, I'll be all right."

"Steve!" Anita demanded. "Steve?"

Earlier that evening, it had been easy to identify her father's voice as the one I'd heard when I'd regained consciousness on the mountain. When Malcolm Fairley had spoken, I'd known instantly. Could Malcolm's companion on the mountain have been Anita? But Anita hadn't been on the island this afternoon, had she? She and Steve Delaney, *my* Steve Delaney, had been elsewhere. Headed here. Or had they started from here and taken a day trip? Had someone said? I couldn't remember. My hands made fists of themselves. I wanted to pound them hard on almost anything. My eyes teared up. I had to disappear before I made an utter fool of myself.

With what I recognized as freakish formality, I said to Steve Delaney, "You're going to have to excuse me. It's time for me to leave." Catching sight of Gabrielle, I led Rowdy to her and uttered some sort of formula for thanking hostesses for lovely evenings.

Instead of replying with another formula, she said, "Holly, you're woozy from that fall you took today. Do you want someone to walk you back to the guest cottage? Or help you with the dogs? Tiffany would be

92

glad to go with you. Or you could stay here. I think maybe staying here's the best thing."

"A crack on the head is nothing to fool around with," Malcolm Fairley agreed. "I learned the hard way. No pun intended! Gabbi will—"

"It's just cuts and bruises," I insisted. "Strictly superficial. I'll be fine. Thank you for the offer, Gabrielle, that's really kind, but I'll be fine on my own." Looking around, I saw no sign of Steve or Anita. Good! There'd be no need to wish them a pleasant evening or, worse, say that I hoped they slept well.

I retrieved Kimi from Tiffany, thanked her for her help, and, with a sense of tremendous relief, followed my dogs up the rocks, onto the lawn, and around Gabrielle's house to the parking area at the back. I *would* recover, I told myself, *if* I could just get away from all these people, get some sleep, and spend some time with my dogs. When it came to healing, one dog was worth a million doctors. Sleep was the second great healer. In the morning, I'd be myself again. When I was, everything would explain itself. The horrible sense of responsibility would shrink to a normal, perhaps even trivial, sense of minor obligation.

Amid the sport-utility vehicles parked behind Gabrielle's house was an old van that hadn't been there when I'd arrived. A panel door on the side stood open. By the door, almost stage-lit by the floods on Gabrielle's house and garage, was Anita Fairley. I could, of course, see her more clearly than had been possible on the dark beach. The illumination made everything worse, which is to say that she was even more striking than I'd realized. With her long, pale hair, rich green sweater, tan trekking pants, and fashionable boots, she belonged in an ad in an expensive sporting-

93

goods catalog. What really made her look like a model was that she posed, catalog fashion, with a dog on lead, a liver-and-white-ticked pointer bitch whose attention was directed toward the inside of the van. The pointer was, in fact, spoiling the shot. Instead of lovingly eyeing Anita or gazing self-confidently around in apparent search of upland game birds, the poor thing was trembling and issuing a soft, pitiful whine.

From inside the van came Steve Delaney's voice. "I'm ready for Lady now, Anita. Could you . . . ?"

Anita reached into the dark interior of the van with the hand that held the pointer's lead. Her hand emerged empty. The pointer started to climb into the van. Her tail was now whipping nervously back and forth. Anita was almost motionless. She could have given the animal a soothing pat. But she didn't. She didn't even bother to look around in case anyone was watching. In one swift, graceful, almost imperceptible movement, she swung a handsomely booted foot at the pointer's hindquarters. The pointer did not cry out. Anita hadn't exactly kicked her. She'd delivered a nudge, I suppose, a push, a poke, or a little prod. But she'd done it in a sneaky way. With her *foot*. And I don't like to see people use their damned booted feet on dogs.

"There you go, Lady!" Anita crooned. "There you go, sweetheart!"

I felt frozen in place. You *bitch*, I thought. *You insufferable bitch.*

94

Thirteen

AFTER LURKING IN THE SHADOWS UNTIL THE VAN drove off, the dogs and I followed its route down the road to the guest cottage. As we approached the door that led to the little kitchen, the dogs' hackles and ears rose. A fat, dark blob scuttled away from the big plastic trash barrel by the steps. The yellow bug light by the door cast almost no actual light, and I was too slow to catch the animal in the beam of my flashlight. My guess was a raccoon. The shadow had sped away a bit quickly for a porcupine. Maine has bears, and they sure will raid trash, but I somehow had the feeling that there were no bears on Mount Desert Island. Besides, although Maine's black bears are much smaller than grizzlies, the blob had been more raccoon size than bear size, and raccoons are notorious garbage thieves. If they'd neatly remove lids, sort through refuse, and deposit rejected items back in trash barrels in the fashion attributed to government investigators, no one would mind too much. As it is, they make a horrible mess. And Maine has lots of raccoons. Consequently, Maine trash barrels left in the open are always equipped with bungee cords, rocks, cinder blocks, or other marginally effective animal-proofing paraphernalia. If you locked your trash in a safe with a combination lock, a determined raccoon would eventually dial the numbers in their correct sequence. Still, when I noticed that the bungee cord on the barrel at the guest house was loose and that the cinder block on the lid was poised to fall off, I felt obliged to set things right.

I put the dogs in the cottage, went back outside, secured the bungee cord, and settled the cinder block squarely in the middle of the barrel lid. Just as I finished, the pale, bobbing beam of a flashlight appeared on the road in the direction of Gabrielle's house, and I heard people talking. Having spent the evening blundering my way through human social interaction, I felt desperately eager to avoid even the slightest contact with anyone of my own species, which should properly be known as *Homo palaver.* At the same time, I wanted to avoid making the blatantly unfriendly gesture of dashing into the cottage and shutting the noisy screen door. Consequently, I slipped around the corner of the cottage to wait until the passersby had become just that by passing by. Within seconds, I'd identified them as Quint and Effie. They must, of course, be walking home.

With the frankness of one member of a couple speaking to another in presumed privacy, Quint said, "Well, at least Gabbi won't be able to inflict Norman Axelrod on us from now on. Him and his goddamned needling. For Christ's sake! Any charitable donation, any charitable enterprise, has tax benefits. What did he think? That Gabbi could afford to just *give* all her land away? He knew damned well that this is not some shady tax dodge, but he would just not let up."

"What he was, was hostile," Effie agreed as they were directly in front of the cottage. "But we're still stuck with Wally and with that damned Opal the Snake. The next time that woman tells me that development is inevitable, I'm going to kick her. Don't think I haven't come close!"

"Opal is an old friend of—"

"I am sick of hearing that she's an old friend of

Gabbi's! So what? The fact is that Opal and Wally are nothing but philistines. *Business* types," she added damningly. "You know what Wally did before? Ran a chain of drugstores! And then he sold out so he could start ruining . . ." Effie's irate voice trailed off as she and Quint continued home.

Instead of feeling relief at my freedom from human company, I found myself listening intently for any overtones or undertones that might waft back toward me. Furthermore, once I was back inside the cottage, it seemed disquietingly clear that Rowdy and Kimi were in some peculiar mood that I couldn't fathom. As I wandered around turning off lights, straightening cushions, brushing my teeth, and trying to discover what, if anything, this Holly Winter person customarily wore to bed, the dogs followed me, but not in a peaceful, cozy way. In fact, zipping back and forth around me, their tails carried finlike above their backs, they moved with a distinctly predatory air, like furry gray sharks circling a victim in preparation for the kill. Not that I expected an attack. On the contrary, never for a second was I afraid of the dogs themselves. What disturbed me was my complete inability to interpret their behavior: And I somehow knew that if I had lost my ability to understand dogs, I had lost my comprehension of my mother tongue.

"What *is* it?" I asked them plaintively. "What's the trouble here? You *expect* something. Is that it? I'm so terribly sorry. I'm so tired. My head aches. I hurt all over. We just have to go to sleep. That's all I can do. Maybe in the morning, I'll know what you want. I am so, so sorry." I was again close to tears. Then, finding a king-size sheet folded neatly across the foot of the bed, I hoped for a moment that I'd deciphered the dogs' expectations. "Aren't you good dogs!" I exclaimed. "You sleep *on* the bed, don't you! Of course you do. And you know to wait until I spread a sheet over the comforter, so we don't get dog hair on it. Good dogs!"

It's now strange and rather wonderful to look back on what I took for granted. For example, I found nothing startling or ludicrous about the idea that preparing the bed for dogs was my way of turning down my own covers.

After I'd finished spreading out the sheet, however, the dogs were still restless. They zoomed out of the bedroom. Something clattered. I was too weary to investigate. The dogs zoomed back. When I patted the bed, both dogs leaped onto it, but then immediately jumped off, circled around, and eyed me with trust and mystification. So what did I do? Instead of sensibly ignoring the dogs, crating them, or even offering another apology, I burst into a crying fit. I sank to the floor, threw my arms around Rowdy's neck, and buried my scratched, stinging face in his thick, deep coat. Pushing her way into the mass of big, hairy dog and exhausted, sobbing person, Kimi nuzzled me, licked my face, and then gave Rowdy a monumentally rivalrous shove that bothered him not at all, but sent me sprawling.

So there I lie, fragile, addlebrained, aching, scared, and suffering from a maniacal crush on a stranger who must be my vet, but is another woman's lover. Also, I'm coated in dog spit and undercoat, and all of a sudden? I'm happy. For the first time since I awoke on the mountain, I have this sharp, clear sense that *everything*—in particular, who I am and the situation I'm in—has this magical quality that it seemed as if nothing would ever have again. And the magical quality

98

is, of course, *familiarity*. And it's not a creepy, déjà vu, malfunctioning-brain-cells kind of familiarity, either. Far from it! I really have been here before. Indeed, I have often been jolted by big dogs. I *recognize* the sensation. It is mine. I am happy.

And my nose is running. I'm thirsty. Lobster and clams? That ever-so-obvious explanation of my thirst entirely eludes me. I wash my face at the bathroom sink, but cannot find a drinking glass. With a stupid smile on my face, I make for the kitchen. The dogs follow. I choose a blue plastic tumbler from a shelf, fill it with cold bottled water from the refrigerator, and drink the entire eight ounces. Meanwhile Kimi picks up a stainless-steel bowl sitting empty on the kitchen floor. She drops it. It rings. Ah-hah! The clatter!

Rational thought emerges: Rowdy and Kimi are restless *because* they are thirsty. They are thirsty *because* their water bowl is empty. They have been asking for water.

Water! Helen Keller's first word, right? Magic! The key to everything else. I fill the dogs' water bowl. I congratulate myself: I am beginning to reacquire my native language.

Fourteen

AT TWO IN THE MORNING, WHEN LOUD BANGING dragged me from a stupor, I was in the thick of a guilt dream about forgetting the dogs' water. The source of the sound that awakened me could not, however, have been the metal water bowl. The bedside light revealed Kimi stretched on top of the covers and Rowdy on the floor in a sled-dog tuck, tail curled over his nose. I stumbled to the kitchen, switched on the bug light, and flung open the back door. The noise had stopped. The bungee cord and cinder block were securely in place on the plastic barrel. Still, I prayed aloud for divine retribution against every raccoon in the state of Maine. Back inside, I opened the refrigerator for some milk, and the dogs bounced into the kitchen. Alaskan malamutes are superb watchdogs, ever on the alert for the whisper of a refrigerator door. They watch you open it, they watch in case you accidentally leave it ajar, they watch you eat whatever you took out, they watch for crumbs you might drop. Watch, watch, watch! The bathroom cabinet yielded a bottle of ibuprofen tablets. I swallowed three and went back to bed.

Comforting reflections lulled me to sleep. This infatuation of mine with the vet? With Anita Fairley's boyfriend? If looked at in the right light, by which I meant, I suppose, the black of night, it could easily be seen as a sign of recovery. Love, romance, passion? The emotions of robust life! Furthermore, it wasn't as if my affections had fixed on some grotesque, repellent, or unsuitable object. On the contrary, Steve Delaney appeared to be altogether attractive and admirable. Women probably fell for him all the time. And it wasn't as if he were *married* to Anita Fairley, either, I reminded myself soothingly. That bitch! Bitch, bitch, bitch! I fell asleep.

The analgesic may be why I felt less horrible in the morning than I'd expected. After two cups of killer coffee, I felt almost human. Yesterday's aching and buzzing were nearly gone. What remained was localized physical soreness centered on the lump on my scalp. My only new symptom was so ordinary that it may not even count as a symptom at all. A song was running through my head. Over and over. Neurologists probably have a technical term for the irksome phenomenon, which is probably some sort of benign synaptic event. Anyway, what ran through my head wasn't just a tune, but a song with words, a line from an old hymn: *I love to tell the story of unseen things above.* Oddly enough, although I remembered the rest of the verse, melody and all, the running-through-my-head part stopped there. In the hope of ridding myself of this musical mental poltergeist, I caroled aloud:

> I love to tell the story
> Of unseen things above,
> Of Jesus and His glory,
> Of Jesus and His love:
> I love to tell the story
> Because I know 'tis true;
> It satisfies my longings
> As nothing else can do.

Trivial discoveries about Holly Winter: This poor woman really, really can't sing. She switches keys. Her timelessness makes a yowling cat sound like Maria Callas. Important discovery about Rowdy and Kimi: They love this woman so much that in their ears, she *is* Maria Callas.

After breakfast and a quick still-in-my-bathrobe out-and-in with the dogs, I felt seized by the impulse to return to Dorr Mountain. Sleep, far from alleviating fear, had sharpened it; obligation seemed to jab at my solar plexus. *Unseen things above,* I kept hearing. Meaning what? Forgotten things above? Things seen on

Dorr and now forgotten? Things I might now remember?

Floundering around on Dorr would accomplish nothing. I needed a plan. Hadn't I formulated one? Yesterday? If so, it had disappeared. Before dashing off to wander aimlessly in hundreds of acres of parkland, I needed to slow down.

Fighting the urge to *do* something, I made myself go over the material I'd briefly surveyed yesterday afternoon. My material possessions seemed to fall into two classes: dog gear and the printed word. I examined the contents of the large zippered bag I'd noticed yesterday: dumbbells, scent articles, a shoelace, an aerosol can of spray-on cheese, a box of liver treats. I even remembered the uses of some of this stuff. The shoelace, for example, prevented anticipation. You looped it unobtrusively around the dog's collar in place of a leash and, if need be, held on to it to stop the dog from bolting into an exercise in advance of your command. The aerosol cheese was handy for teaching the retrieve; a bit of the gooey stuff smeared on a dumbbell was a great motivator. You could also use it for the "go-out," as I knew the exercise was called; a cheesy daub could make a dog happy to leave you and go out to the far end of the ring. Every item in the bag was, in effect, a piece of sports equipment. The sport was dog obedience training. No clue there!

A close examination of my wallet showed that I was a card-carrying member of the Cambridge Dog Training Club and the Dog Writers Association of America. Ah-hah! My elusive profession. My checks were in my name only. I wore no rings. My father, Gabrielle's hero, was Buck Winter. I was Holly Winter. Single? Married and liberated? Separated? Divorced? Separation felt plausible. The idea meshed with a gnawing sense of loss.

A few novels piled on the night table by the bed had my name handwritten in the front. Stacked on the coffee table by the fireplace were the various guides and maps I'd noticed yesterday. A few of the books about Acadia National Park belonged to me. *Mr. Rockefeller's Roads* turned out to belong to my father. On the front page, he'd inscribed his name in oversize capital letters: BUCK WINTER. He had also, I discovered, defaced page after page with outraged marginal annotations. In a section about Rockefeller's commitment to preserving the land from the depredations of the automobile while encouraging the public to explore the beauty of the wilderness, my father had commented, "If it has ROADS, it isn't wilderness!!!!" A book called *Trails of History* was also his. On the pages about the paved road leading to the summit of Cadillac Mountain, he'd printed in vehemently emphatic capital letters, "PLOW THE G.D. THING UNDER AND PLANT TREES!!!"

Settling at the table with a cup of fresh coffee, I tackled the notebooks and the bulging manila folders that I, in my previous existence, had left by the answering machine. As I'd seen yesterday, the folder marked *Arsenic* was jammed with articles about the legendary poison. The amount of information was more than my feeble brain could process. Arsenate was less toxic than arsenite. What was the difference between the two? Arsenic deficiency caused death in lactating goats. The skin lesions caused by arsenic were easy to confuse with leprosy. And . . . ? The thousands of facts about arsenic gave no hint about why I'd amassed them.

Two other folders, however, explained my interest. One, uninformatively labeled *Coat*, contained copies of what I now effortlessly recognize as e-mail. In contrast to the folder of facts about arsenic, this one was crammed with claims, insinuations, and, as I soon discovered, conflicting reports and opinions. "Old-time handlers," one page informed me, "used to use the stuff all the time, including on coated Hounds, but especially on Poodles." Another person wrote that she'd been in dogs for forty years and had never heard of anyone using arsenic on a dog; the stories of its use as a coat enhancer were nothing but old wives' tales. On another page, someone said, "I've heard it's used by Poodle handlers to improve coat color in apricots." My head reeled. Apricots? Oh, apricot-colored poodles. Okay. Person after person said, in effect, *Well, I've certainly never heard of anyone with* my *breed dosing a dog with such dreadful, horrible, dangerous stuff* and went on to suggest that I ask handlers of *other* breeds, including shelties, bichons, Gordon setters, Pekes, and dozens more. A knowledgeable-sounding paragraph declared that arsenic had no effect on the color of a dog's coat; rather, the substance produced a desirable texture. Someone else claimed that it reliably caused thick, luxuriant growth. And where would a dog handler get the stuff? At any health food store, I was advised. At any pharmacy. At a shady pharmacy. At a feed and grain store. From any vet. From a disreputable vet. An obviously sensible person pointed out that years earlier, arsenic had been the principal ingredient in the medicine given to dogs to prevent heartworm infection. A scrap of memory came to me: Arsenic was still one of the drugs used to treat heartworm and certain other infections in dogs.

What should have been the really informative folder was labeled *Axelrod.* Unfortunately, its contents, two pages torn from a yellow legal pad, had been scrawled in Russian or Arabic. Furthermore, the pages seemed to have been chewed by dogs. At a guess, I'd taken notes on phone conversations with Norman Axelrod. I'd printed his name at the top of the first sheet in the folder. "Wants expose. Says handler dosing dog with arsenic." Here, I'd had the foresight to print the handler's name: Horace Livermore. "Mini poodle, apricot, Isaac. Says has proof, hair, nail samples. Dog on circuit with Livermore, finished, U.S., then Canada, etc. Contraband? Livermore smuggling to Canada. What?"

At the bottom of the page, I'd drawn a big, wobbly arrow that I had no trouble in deciphering as personal shorthand for a conclusion I'd reached or an action I intended to take. After the arrow, I'd scribbled, "Ask Buck re Livermore."

On the second page, I'd written, "MDI? Insists must go there, but not the soul of hospitality."

After the arrow on that page, I'd written, "Call Bonnie re hiking article, Natl Pk that allows dogs, exposé???"

Okay. Norman Axelrod had called to try to persuade me to write an article about his professional handler, Horace Livermore, who was supposedly dosing Axelrod's apricot mini poodle, Isaac, with arsenic. Axelrod maintained that he had proof obtained from samples of the dog's hair and nails. He also believed that Livermore was smuggling some kind of contraband into Canada. I'd made a note to ask my father about Horace Livermore. I'd also intended to ask Bonnie, the voice on the answering machine, about articles I might write: one about hiking with dogs, one about Acadia—the National Park that allowed dogs—and possibly—three question marks—the article Axelrod had proposed, an

105

exposé about a professional handler who had dosed a client's dog with arsenic.

I'd evidently acted on my own orders. Here I was, on Mount Desert Island. Yesterday my dogs and I had been hiking in Acadia National Park. I'd been reading about arsenic and gathering scuttlebutt about its use as coat enhancer for show dogs. As I'd intended, I must have spoken to the mysterious Bonnie about it. Hence the strange message she'd left on the answering machine. As to Horace Livermore, did I know him? Had I, in fact, asked Buck about him and about the supposed contraband? If so, exactly what had I asked Buck? *Have you ever heard of a handler named Horace Livermore?* Or maybe a question that assumed familiarity, something like, *Ever heard any rumors about Horace Livermore?* I knew Steve Delaney, and, as Ann's letter had informed me, I knew Gabrielle Beamon and Malcolm Fairley, too, and I hadn't recognized them, hadn't remembered them at all. Might I also know Livermore? Norman Axelrod had constituted a threat to Livermore. Axelrod had plunged to his death. Nearby, I'd taken a bad fall.

As I finally showered and dressed for the return trip to Dorr, the annoying hymn continued to pester me. Those "unseen things above"? Things I'd seen and forgotten? Could Horace Livermore have been one of them?

Fifteen

LIKE VISITORS TO THE BEAMON RESERVATION, ROWDY and Kimi confront a horrendous list of prohibitions. The dogs need not, however, be enjoined to enjoy themselves; except in the presence of noxious stimuli,

106

they always do. Now, for instance, while I am senselessly exposing myself to what Rowdy deems the most noxious stimuli of all—shampoo and running water—he and Kimi take advantage of the delightfully contingent nature of the rules that human beings impose on dogs. Human beings state these rules as moral assertions: Good dogs do not filch and devour greasy sponges from the sink, never think about hiking their legs indoors, and would not dream of chewing on junk mail and strewing the cottage with damp lumps of sweepstakes promotions and offers for overpriced software. Translated into dog, however, these rules are practical if-then statements about context, act, and consequence. Or so I suppose.

Kimi. If the human being does not have her eye on me, then the consequence of snatching the sponge from the kitchen sink is the ambrosial taste of rancid butter mixed with bits of fried egg. As to the consequence of regurgitation, if at first the morsels of buttery, eggy sponge refuse to stay down, try, try again! Flat on the floor, the sponge in her jaws, Kimi glares at Rowdy and, in a low growl, addresses him. *Mine! Mine, mine, mine, mine, mine!*

Rowdy. Ineffectively masked by the reek of furniture polish, one leg of the dining table radiates the almost irresistibly tantalizing scent of the aged urine of another male dog. Flirting with the urge to overmark, Rowdy executes a series of swift passes. No one is watching. Therefore, no one will yell, as has been yelled before, "Don't even *think* about it!" Thinking about claiming that table leg as his own pleases Rowdy mightily: *Mine! Mine, mine, mine, mine!*

Anthropomorphism? The sin of attributing human characteristics to animals. Well, if you don't think a dog can think *Mine, mine, mine,* then you don't know much about dogs.

Anyway, having savored the pleasure of *thinking* about lifting his leg indoors, Rowdy strolls to the weathered wooden basket next to the fireplace where Gabrielle and her guests dump newspapers, magazines, catalogs, and direct-mail junk to be used in starting fires or tossed into the flames. At home, Rowdy regularly noses through a somewhat different basket, a large wicker one filled with fleece dinosaurs, tug ropes, chewmen, and dozens of other canine playthings that usually emit the delicious reek of his very own household. Now and then, these items briefly disappear and mysteriously reappear stinking of Ivory soap. The contents of this away-from-home toy basket, in contrast, exude the bouquet of ink, the intriguingly sweaty scent of many pairs of human hands, and, best of all, a divinely animal aroma that induces olfactory visions of aged road kill and yummy, yummy leather. The unopened letter he selects from the pile would, if opened and read by Gabrielle, inform her that a local bank has preapproved her for a home equity line of credit. The printed word says nothing to Rowdy. What speaks to him is the glue on the envelope. *Chew me!* it urges him. *Tear, rip, and swallow! Bon appétit!*

Sixteen

IN CLICHÉD NEW ENGLAND CONTRAST TO THE DAY before, this one was sunny and dry. Consequently, the tourists who'd spent the previous day wandering through gift shops in Bar Harbor were getting to the real point of vacation by checking out the gift shops within Acadia's boundaries. Or so I decided when I tried to park the Bronco where I'd found it yesterday, in the lot near The Tarn on Route 3. The lot turned out to be full. The closest place to get indoors and spend money was near where I ended up parking, in the big lot serving the complex consisting of the Nature Center, the Wild Gardens of Acadia, and the Sieur de Monts Spring. Many of the cars, vans, and tour buses had undoubtedly transported people who would visit the Nature Center shop and, incidentally, stroll through the Wild Gardens of Acadia and glance at the Sieur de Monts Spring before resuming the wilderness-by-asphalt approach to seeing everything the park had to offer. The grandly named Sieur de Monts Spring is housed in a gloomy little building with dirty windows that allow visitors to peer down at a depressing puddle and ask, *This is the spring?* It is. According to a sign posted outside the Nature Center, the most common cause of injury to park visitors was falling on rocks. After Norman Axelrod's fatal fall, the warning felt like a timid and vaguely sick understatement, a bit like the fabled warning of the Fall River, Massachusetts, mother who told her children to stay away from Lizzie Borden's yard because Miss Borden "wasn't very nice to her mommy and daddy."

As Ms. Wilderness by Foot, I got off to an unpromising start. Yesterday, when the dogs had found me, Kimi had been wearing her two-piece pack, and although Rowdy had lost his saddlebags, he'd still been wearing his vest. When I'd removed the dogs' vests, I'd paid no attention to how they were fastened. Now, with Rowdy still in the car, I struggled mightily with Kimi and the pieces of her pack before finally realizing that I was trying to put everything on backward. This evidence of my incompetence unnerved me. I didn't even *remember* my lost competence; I'd inferred it from what my former self had written in her—my?—hiking diary, which I'd studied before leaving Gabrielle's cottage. According to the diary, the dogs and I had arrived at M.D.I. only four days before my fall. Kimi, I learned, had been carrying rice in her pack not because I harbored a morbid fear of starvation, but because I was conditioning the dogs for backpacking by systematically increasing the amount of weight they carried. The entries for all hikes, including quite a few in the Berkshires and in conservation land in Boston's western suburbs, specified how much weight each dog had packed and how far we had hiked. The main point to emerge from my notes was my considerable experience in hiking. The final entry, made the day before yesterday, was for an eight-mile hike that had taken us to the summits of Sargent, Cedar Swamp, and Penobscot mountains and down something called the Deer Stream Trail, which I'd described as a "damned steep riverbed of rocks." I'd added, "Rough footing, but more unpleasant than challenging. No blisters."

A few days ago, I'd hiked down a steep, rocky trail. If I'd commented on my escape from blisters, wouldn't I have noted any problems I *had* encountered? *Rough footing, fell twice?* Throughout the diary, the only remarks about anything remotely like injury or discomfort were tediously frequent complaints about hot weather: "Great hike except for broiling sun. No shade! Sweat bath! Goddamned global warming!" And on and on. Furthermore, several entries made within the past six months contained positive reports about a new pair of Fabiano hiking boots: "Weigh a ton, but *excellent* on rock." Yesterday, hiking in the cool weather I liked and

110

wearing those excellent-on-rock boots, I hadn't just skinned a knee or twisted an ankle, but had taken a fall that might have proven fatal. How had it happened?

"We're going to find out," I told Kimi. "And we're also going to find Rowdy's pack and pick up the bags of rice we left, and we're going to see . . . Well, we're going to see what's to be seen, that's what!" In case we did find Rowdy's pack, I had him wear his yoke, but my right arm and both shoulders were so sore that I carried nothing myself. Before the dogs and I had even left the sidewalk that ran between the parking lot and the Wild Gardens of Acadia, a tourist shook an only half playful finger at me, then at Kimi, and said, "No fair making him do all the work!" Two seconds later, another tourist echoed the first. "What'd that one do to get stuck carrying everything?" About two seconds after that, a pair of adorable children just *had* to pat the dogs, and their parents naturally *had* to take pictures of the adorable children with the adorable dogs, and so forth and so on—*Thank you, actually they're malamutes, they're not* supposed *to have blue eyes, and no, she doesn't mind carrying the pack, she likes it, and yes, she's a girl, her name is Kimi, the other one is a male, Rowdy, and . . .*

And if I didn't bolt, we wouldn't get on a trail until sunset. Whistling to the dogs to rev them up, I sped past the Wild Gardens and had just cleared the Nature Center building when I all but collided with Steve Delaney, who was standing near the entrance looking bored. The brief encounter nearly began with a dog fight, which would have been Kimi's fault. Neither of Steve's dogs did a thing to provoke her, unless you count the involuntary act of radiating female scent. One of the two was the pointer I'd seen the previous evening. The other

111

was a shepherd—a German shepherd dog. Kimi gave me no time to collect my thoughts. At the sight of the shepherd, she raised her hackles, emitted a low growl, and yanked on her leash, and believe me, a malamute yank is not some light tug. It's a massive wham designed to break an ice-encrusted sled from the tundra or to free a stubborn human arm from the shoulder socket. The dog doesn't give a damn which. This kind of behavior is hideously embarrassing under any circumstances, even when you manage to terminate it within seconds by pretending that you're God dictating the Ten Commandments. Instead of wordily commanding that *Thou shalt not . . .* , you boom NO! at the top of your lungs, but you boom it with Old Testament wrath.

"I hear you took a serious fall yesterday," Steve said flatly. He looked older than he had in last night's darkness. Hollows and lines showed under his blue-green eyes.

"I told you last night. I just got a few scratches."

"You're in no shape to go hiking alone."

"In case you haven't noticed, I'm not alone." I nodded at Rowdy and Kimi.

He almost smiled. "Your theme song."

"My what?"

" 'You'll Never Walk Alone.' "

I didn't even recognize the phrase, never mind catch the allusion. Still, with utter nastiness, I said, "Damn straight!"

Instead of the violently erotic response to him I'd had at Gabrielle's party, I now felt overwhelmed with grief compounded by a humbling and even humiliating sense of my own stupidity. To prevent him from seeing me cry, I stomped away, hauling the dogs with me. Before

112

long, we were on a wooded footpath. As some intact part of my brain must have known, it took us to the end of The Tarn and the trailhead for Kurt Diederich's Climb, which I was able brilliantly to identify as such because, as one of the tourists had pointed out yesterday, *Kurt Diederich's Climb* was carved in one of the risers of the stone staircase that rose sharply upward. With better judgment than I'd had yesterday afternoon when I'd practically flown down the stone trail at the end of the dogs' leads, I felt intimidated by the steepness of the stairs and by the word *Climb.* Putting one foot in front of another was within my capacity. A climb was beyond me. What if I fell again? Or lost control of the dogs? Or *lost* the dogs? Or got all three of us lost in the woods? "We will *not* get lost," I told the dogs with sudden resolve. "We will not even *think* about loss. Loss has nothing to do with us. It does not exist."

It does, of course. So do climbs. As climbs go, however, Kurt Diederich's isn't one. Its beautiful stone steps rise upward, but they are *steps,* and Dorr Mountain is more a hill, as in "anthill," than it is a mountain, as in "Everest." For a hill, Dorr is steep, but the point of Acadia isn't difficulty; it's beauty. Kurt Diederich's Climb has that in abundance. It wound upward, flattened into sections of stone-lined trail, passed beneath cliffs, and, after a half mile that felt like more, ended at the T-intersection and cedar post where the dogs had paused yesterday. Consulting the hiking guide I'd stowed in Kimi's pack, I figured out that the trail marked in the book as the Emery Path was the one the wooden arrow called the Dorr Mountain East Face Trail. After watering the dogs and then myself, I set off to the left, toward the scenes of my fall and Axelrod's death.

The route took us up yet more flights of cleverly constructed steps that seemed designed and built by supernatural beings with the aid of natural forces: elves, perhaps, assisted by glaciers, or magically animate granite working with gravity to split itself into slabs and fall into artful patterns of wondrous convenience. A typical section of the narrow, stone-paved trail ran below a ten-foot wall of rock on the uphill side and, on the downhill, a long row of boulders arranged in curbstone fashion to protect against falls while providing seats for hikers to use while catching their breath, retying their boots, picnicking, or admiring the view. The postcard vista of the valley below and the rocky hills beyond it was, I regret to mention, hideously scarred by the evil-looking sprawl of what I assumed was a medium-size factory. Even in a mill town or industrial park, these graceless buildings would have stood out as architectural blights. Here, the ruinous ugliness felt obscene. On one of the maps in my hiking guide, this pockmark on the face of the island was labeled Jackson Lab.

I diverted my eyes from it by scanning in search of Rowdy's lost saddlebags, which had to be the bright red of the part of his pack that remained and the same bright red of Kimi's pack. As we continued upward, the oaks, pines, huckleberry bushes, and other vegetation gradually took on the dry, stunted look of plants adapted to life on exposed rock. Now and then, lone hikers and vigorous couples passed us heading swiftly to and from the summit of Dorr or the Ladder Trail. We came upon families resting by the side of the trail or progressing along it while pep-talking lagging children. Despite the wholesome friendliness of everyone we encountered (*What beautiful dogs! Oh, look! That one's wearing a*

114

backpack! Isn't that cute! Are they brother and sister? Aaron and Alison, look! Huskies!), my sense of fear rose with the altitude. In the increasingly barren, earth-toned landscape, the bright primary red of Rowdy's discarded saddlebags should have leaped out and shrieked at me. The only reds, however, were the soft, natural hues of leaves. Worse, the closer we drew to the scene of my fall, the more sharply I remembered the pain of regaining consciousness. Nothing triggered the slightest memory of the events preceding my injury.

Feeling weak, I not only let the dogs charge ahead of me, but felt grateful to hang on to their leashes and let their power haul me along. At the well-marked fork where the right-hand trail led upward to the top of Dorr, the left-hand path downward to the Ladder Trail, Rowdy and Kimi unhesitatingly moved left. Given a choice, a malamute will almost invariably take the familiar route. I was mystified. Still, it was now bafflingly clear that Rowdy and Kimi had at least started down toward the Ladder Trail. Furthermore, from everything I could piece together from the guidebook, its maps, and my pitifully defective memory, the Rock of Ages where I'd landed was somewhere below the path toward the Ladder Trail. What in God's name had I been thinking? What in God's name had happened here?

Seventeen

EAGER TO EXAMINE THE AREA WHERE NORMAN Axelrod had met his death, and where I'd perhaps come close to meeting mine, I started along the gentle

115

beginning of the upper portion of the Ladder Trail. To my annoyance, the dogs and I had covered only a short distance when we came upon a lone hiker taking a break just off the stretch of trail that, according to my estimate, ran directly above my Rock of Ages. The hiker, a man I guessed to be in his late twenties, had the admirable combination of dark skin, dark hair, and vivid blue eyes. It's a combination admired by *me*, anyway, especially, as in the case of the hiker, when the guy has attractive, somewhat exotic features and is altogether the picture of muscular perfection. His short-sleeved white T-shirt and khaki shorts revealed lean, strong arms and legs. He had on woolen socks and heavy leather hiking boots. The shorts and boots had a comfortable, broken-in look, as did the unzipped black day pack that rested next to the hiker, who was sitting on the ground drinking from a plastic bottle. As maybe I need to spell out, this wasn't some fleshy tourist who'd just finished expensively costuming himself at one of the outdoor outfitters' shops in Bar Harbor. This was the kind of fanatic who trains for through-hiking the Appalachian Trail, speeding along the Pacific Crest, or frisking on the glaciers of Denali by dashing around Acadia making everyone else feel fat, slow, and morally inferior.

The hiker smiled and said a pleasant hello that included the dogs as well as me. When I'd returned his greeting, he eyed the dogs and said, "The steep part begins ahead. You don't hit the first ladder until below some steps."

"Thanks," I said. "We don't do ladder trails, or at least the dogs don't. I just wanted to see what the beginning of the trail was like."

To my relief, he did not admire my "huskies," ask

116

why they didn't have blue eyes, or joke about making Kimi do all the work. Instead he asked, "You show them?"

Normal enough question, to which there must be a hundred normal answers, such as Yes, No, Sometimes, Once in a while, All the time, Not anymore, and I retired them after they took Best of Breed at Westminster in successive years. The only idea that came to mind was the grossly abnormal truth, namely, that if I did I had no memory of it. Before I had a chance to say anything, normal or abnormal, however, the hiker made it clear that he'd been stating the obvious rather than asking a question. He rose gracefully and tucked his right hand into the pocket of his shorts. As any show dog knows, that's where the liver lives. Rowdy and Kimi shifted into show mode: Tails wagging over their backs, ears up, eyes sparkling, they posed for an invisible judge. With no recollection of how I knew anything about anything, including the dialect of the dog fancy, I felt pleased to watch them free-stack so beautifully. Without asking my permission, the hiker produced bits of what was obviously dog-appealing food from his pocket. Catching the dogs' eyes, he lightly raised and lowered his hand.

"Not every dog baits for trail mix," he commented with approval.

I said, without thinking, "These dogs bait for dirt."

After tossing each dog a few pieces of what I could now see was a mixture of nuts and raisins, he stowed his water bottle in the black day pack, zipped it, and slipped it onto his shoulders.

"Have a good hike," he said innocuously.

Before I could return the banality, he'd taken long, easy strides in a direction that surprised me. His gentle warning about the Ladder Trail had made me assume that he'd just ascended it and was taking a water break before heading to the summit of Dorr. Instead of making for the trail, however, he moved rapidly in the direction the dogs and I were headed, and then suddenly bounded to the right, uphill and off the trail.

"Bushwhacking," I told the dogs. "He should've worn long pants."

As I did not tell the dogs, the hiker's sudden disappearance unsettled me. For the first time, I was sharply aware of reenacting what must have been the events of the previous day. Somewhere nearby, maybe just below the ledges, was my Rock of Ages. Wasn't it? Or was it farther to the right? As if the secure footpath might transform itself into a steep, unheralded, unavoidable ladder that would send us on a terrifying downward plunge, I shortened the dogs' leads and took careful, one-at-a-time baby steps. Even at my foolishly slow rate, I soon reached the spot where the lone hiker had unexpectedly vanished upward. There, the trail turned left and headed abruptly downward. What appeared was not the nightmarish, fun-house ladder I'd feared, but another of the many narrow stone staircases that ran up and down the little mountain. This stretch of stepped trail was, however, exceptionally long and steep. Even more than the similar trails we'd already traversed, it created the artful impression of natural or even supernatural construction. Rather than switchbacking left and right along what, on reflection, would reveal itself as an artificial, if credibly naturalistic, route, this section of the Ladder Trail followed the steep downward incline of the base of a cliff. The dramatic rise of the rock wall to the right somehow made the stones of the steps look narrower, sharper, and more treacherous than those of the other stone trails. Cutting sharply between the cliff and an area of smooth ledges and stunted vegetation, the stairs had none of the quaint, inviting charm so notable on the nearby trails. Although the morning was sunny and dry, a humidly sinister aura seemed to hover over the staircase, as if some nasty woodland sprite took perverse delight in coating the rock treads and risers with the unexpected danger of slippery dampness.

It was presumably on these steps that Norman Axelrod had taken his deadly fall.

Standing safely above the top tread, I tried to envision the mechanics of the fatality. A man makes his way down to the topmost step. He is out of shape; he moves slowly. In today's sun, the stones looked damp; in yesterday's fog, they must have appeared even more slippery than they did now. Therefore, he moves with great care. He places one tentative foot on the first step. Then the other. And then . . . ?

And then all of a sudden, slipperiness gives way to the heart-jolting sensation of feet sliding out from under, arms flailing, body twisting in a futile, reflexive struggle to regain hopelessly lost balance, and in a split second, indeed in a kaleidoscopically shattered second, stability flies upward and vanishes into the fog, and the body plunges downward, bouncing off rock after cruel rock until a vicious twist of gravity seizes the vulnerable head and, with fatal force, hurls cranium onto granite in a coup de grâce.

Oh, really? My imagination balks. In the absence of the late Norman Axelrod, I envision myself in his place, and when I send myself, strictly in fantasy, of course, running lickety-split down the long, narrow flight of swiftly descending stone stairs, the vivid scenario that

119

presents itself is a double picture of terrifying illusion and harmless reality. If, in fact, I sprinted down this ever-so-picturesque staircase, I might trip and tumble. But far from cannonballing off the rocks or plummeting off a precipice, I'd soon grab or bump into the smooth ledges and vegetation that act, I now see, as a subtle safety wall while sustaining the tantalizing illusion of danger. It is easy to imagine how someone could fall *on* the stairs. It is almost impossible to imagine a fatal plunge *down* them.

The morning's tune returns. *I love to tell the story,* it sings. *Of unseen things above.* With a definite *above* to look toward, I run my eyes up the face of the cliff. Seventy feet? Yes, from the top of this cliff down to the sharp rocks of the staircase is a drop of a good seventy feet, and unlike a knee-skinning topple down the trail, a plunge off that cliff could only mean a dive to death.

So Norman Axelrod died here, on these stone steps. Why here? Because he fell from above. And I'd been nearby. *Unseen things above:* things I had seen? People? Events? Norman Axelrod, inexplicably standing atop that cliff. Alone? And then . . . ? And then plummeting from it? Witnessed. Witnessed by me.

I was suddenly in a great hurry to see everything unseen, to scramble up the cliff and then down or over to my Rock of Ages, to find where Axelrod had stood the second before his plunge, where I'd fallen from, where I'd landed. Driven by the conviction that I was, at last, actively pursuing this wretched, forgotten mission, I hastened up the trail and found the spot where the handsome hiker had set off uphill in what I'd assumed was confident bushwhacking. A second's pause at the spot revealed what now seemed the obvious signs of an old trail: a narrow and overgrown but beaten path up through the scrubby huckleberry bushes, and flat stones set in the ground stair-tread fashion in the wonderfully as-if-by-nature style of every other trail on this little mountain. Hampered more by my concern for the safety of my dogs than by the dogs themselves, I glanced eagerly around for a place to hitch them while I made a quick dash up the abandoned path. As if operating all on their own, my eyes sought out a tiny moss-carpeted clearing just off the main trail with two oak saplings that could serve as temporary hitching posts. Clambering the short distance uphill to the area, I said to the dogs, "I'm only leaving you here for two minutes, okay? Two minutes maximum. I don't know what's up the old trail, and I don't want any surprises, so you're going to wait here for practically no time. Got it? What no one needs is another fall on anything. I'm going to reconnoiter and be right back and—Jesus. Déjà vu."

But *vu* was wrong. *Vu* is *seen.* What was the French word for *hitched?* Not as in marriage, of course. Well, déjà whatever it was, when we got close to the two little oaks, the damage to both was obvious. Each displayed a recent, raw band where the young bark had been worn away. Leaves and branches had been torn. Worse, both little trees were bent as if by a violent hurricane. Beyond one of the oaks, a patch of brilliant red peeked out from behind a small boulder: Rowdy's saddlebags. He'd dumped his pack the last time I'd tied him here, either before or after he'd freed himself by almost uprooting the tree. Kimi had loosed herself without losing her backpack. Déjà hitched. I'd tied the dogs here before. Yesterday. Before my fall.

I'd left the dogs. And look what had happened! Leaving Rowdy's saddlebags where they were, I ripped Kimi's from their Velcro fasteners and dumped them in the clearing. Then I headed for the abandoned trail, the dogs eagerly bounding with me. Like the lone hiker, the three of us climbed the slope. What opened up here above the main trail was a large area of wide, broad rocky ledge stretching ahead of us and to our left, in the direction of the cliff. The trails up Dorr that we'd traversed so far were, of course, stone-paved trails and staircases, and paths worn hard and flat by the feet of millions of hikers. Here, on the great stretches of ledge, cairns marked the trail: In place of a visible footpath or blazes of bright paint, piles of stones directed the hiker across the granite surface and, I assumed, toward the summit of Dorr. Moving slowly, speaking calm words to Rowdy and Kimi, I headed away from the cairn-marked trail and to our left, toward what had to be the top of the cliff. I soon stopped. I'd seen enough. Yes, Norman Axelrod could have climbed up here. Easily? No. But only because he'd been unfit. The entire climb up Dorr must have been difficult for him. Malcolm Fairley, his companion, had said so. This last stretch would have been no more difficult than the steep staircases. To reach the edge of the cliff, he'd have had to do no more than amble. So, he could have reached this spot and gone beyond it. He'd obviously done so. No wonder Fairley hadn't found Axelrod! This abandoned portion of the Ladder Trail appeared on none of the maps I'd studied. Even my detailed hiking guide said nothing about it. If I hadn't seen the lone hiker leave the main trail, I'd never have guessed it existed. So why had Norman Axelrod taken this abandoned trail, veered left, and made his way to the top of the cliff?

I reversed direction. I'd seen what was to be seen up here. What would obviously not appear no matter how much prowling I did was the answer to the big question:

Why? Why had Axelrod taken the abandoned trail? Why had he left it to go to the edge of the cliff?

Descending to the upper stretch of the Ladder Trail, I was once again tempted to hitch the dogs so I could search for my Rock of Ages without having to worry about safe canine footing. The previous day, of course, the dogs, after liberating themselves, had galloped loose for God knows how long without hurting themselves at all. Common sense should've suggested that I was the one whose agility and equilibrium were not to be trusted. Addlepate that I was, the thought never crossed my mind; it simply didn't occur to me that in hunting for my Rock of Ages, I might once again collide with it. The possibility that did present itself was that Rowdy and Kimi, inspired by the appearance of a squirrel, a fox, or an off-leash dog, might make an unexpected bolt. If they did? They wouldn't, I told myself. They just wouldn't.

"You are to be *good* dogs," I informed them. Useless! But we lucked out. Again moving slowly and carefully, keeping my eyes on the ground and on the dogs, I left the trail and headed downhill over the rocky ledges. "Easy!" I cautioned the dogs. "Easy does it!" Luckily, Acadia's wildlife chose not to reveal itself, and no rival dogs appeared. In almost no time, we'd inched our way across lichen-covered boulders and come to a drop-off. Only ten feet or so below lay the cleft boulder where I'd regained consciousness. Now that I stood on the spot from which I must have fallen, I wondered what, besides discarded bags of rice, I'd expected to gain from returning to the scene of my injuries. Had I nourished some secret hope that the sights, sounds, and scents of the place would magically restore me? I took a deep breath and looked around. Below, Route 3 carved a swath through the woods in the valley between Dorr and what the guidebook and maps had informed me was Huguenot Head, directly opposite, and Champlain Mountain, to the right.

With no warning, a voice sounded from what felt like no distance at all. "Charlie!" a woman demanded. "Would you mind waiting for Tucker? He is doing his best to keep up, but his legs are simply not as long as yours, and as I have had to tell you more times than I care to remember, this is a *family* expedition! And furthermore, we need to wait for your father. You stop right where you are and wait for the rest of us!"

"Tucker always spoils everything," a boy whined.

"I do not! Mommy, I don't, do I? Charlie does."

An adult male, sounding dangerously out of breath, snarled, "Tucker, enough of that! Charlie, you wait for the rest of us, or you stay in the car when we get to Sand Beach, and that's that."

Reflecting on the superiority of big dogs to small children—absence of whining, presence of strength and motivation to carry heavy packs—I waited mutely until the family expedition had made its way up what was obviously the nearby Ladder Trail. The ledge on which the dogs and I now stood and, below it, my Rock of Ages were far closer to the trail than I'd imagined. I'd heard every word spoken by young Charlie and Tucker, and their parents. Looking up, I had an unimpeded view of the high cliff above the trail. The cliché about New England weather? It changes from hour to hour, minute to minute. If there'd been thick fog, I'd have seen nothing from here. If the fog hadn't arrived when I stood here yesterday, or if it had cleared even briefly, I'd surely have been able to see Norman Axelrod at the edge of that cliff. What's more, he and anyone with him would have had a clear view of *me*.

The grimness of my situation hit me. On his own, Axelrod, the notorious tree-hater, would never have left the beaten path. He wouldn't even have known that the abandoned section of the Ladder Trail existed. Something or someone had lured him upward. And sent him on a lethal plunge. I toyed with the fantasy that by weird coincidence, Stephen King had been hiking in Acadia and that Axelrod, the celebrity seeker, had spotted the novelist and trailed after him. *We'll leave your name out of it,* Malcolm Fairley had promised. *Anonymity is anonymity.* Fairley had known of the abandoned Homans Path. Had he also known of this abandoned trail? I had a clear vision of the lone hiker vanishing upward; *he* certainly knew that trail. Just as clearly, I saw him skillfully baiting my dogs; he'd done it like a pro. Oh, Jesus! *Like* a pro? Or because he was one? Because my lone hiker *was* Horace Livermore?

I didn't bother to retrieve the rice, but I did return to the clearing for the dogpacks. Spurred by panic, I set a speed record for the canine-accompanied descent of Dorr. Miraculously, Rowdy, Kimi, and I somehow managed to avoid colliding with the families, couples, and solitary hikers trekking up and down the little mountain. In a manner entirely uncharacteristic of me, I brushed off all admiring comments about the dogs, refused requests to pat them, and answered not a single question about their ever-so-cute packs. Then, having avoided smashing into anyone on the way down, I got all the way to my car only to run into Anita Fairley.

The dogs and I were on the blacktop next to my old Bronco. They were slurping up water from their folding fabric bowls, and I was swigging spring water from a bottle, when Anita appeared out of nowhere and said,

125

"Ah, the ghoulish impulse to witness the scene of a death! Have a nice hike?"

I said nothing to her, but right now I feel an uncontrollable compulsion to comment that no one has the right to be *that* beautiful. The previous night, in the flattering illumination of the campfire and of the floodlights, I'd assumed that Anita's hair was artificially blond and hoped that daylight would reveal its roots. With luck, it would look brassy, dry, and cheap. Now, in sunlight, her tresses looked naturally pale and naturally wavy. Her skin was flawless, and although a collection of rags would've looked fashionable on her, she was dressed in the kind of voguish, earth-toned outdoor clothes I wouldn't even know where to buy.

"My idea of a nice hike," she purred, "is a drive to the top of Cadillac. And here I am about to be stuck on my father's trail crew with Wally and Opal, grubbing around in the dirt on the Homans Path. Not that I volunteered. I prefer to limit my contributions to the Pine Tree Foundation to nice, clean legal work. But my father had the sense to ask Steve instead of me, and Steve said yes, so what could I do? All for love!"

I longed to smack her.

"I'm just dying to meet your father." Her tone was confiding, but her expression seemed snide. "I've heard all about him. He sounds like quite a character!"

Before I could say anything—what I had in mind was *Oh*—the rest of Malcolm Fairley's volunteer crew arrived: Steve Delaney; Opal and Wally Swan, the developers; and Malcolm himself. With Steve were his dogs, whose names I knew better than my own: India, the shepherd, and Lady, the pointer. Opal. Wally, and Malcolm carried long-handled loppers.

"Is Anita recruiting you?" Malcolm Fairley asked me.

126

"We could use an extra hand. Zeke, our other volunteer, won't be joining us today. Dogs are welcome!"

I offered some sort of excuse.

Anita, standing safely behind both her father and Steve, made a face. "Leave the dogs," she told Steve.

Malcolm said, "If you change your mind, Holly, you'll know where to find us. Just get on that path and look up into the woods for a lot of felled trees. When the Park Service abandoned the path, they cut them down to block it off, but you won't have any trouble getting past them, and when you get to the steps, you'll see that the stonework is in remarkably fine shape. A shame that trail was ever closed! It's a treasure. Off we go!"

With that, Malcolm Fairley headed across the parking lot toward the Wild Gardens, with Wally and Opal following. Steve's face was almost impassive; only a hint of pain showed. Nodding lightly to me, he handed Lady's leash to Anita and then led India toward his van, parked six or eight spaces away from my Bronco. Eager to be with Steve, Lady tried to forge ahead of Anita, who dealt with the behavior by slamming a booted foot on one of the pointer's forepaws. Lady, of course, yelped. Steve and India glanced back.

"Is there a problem there?" Steve asked.

"No," Anita told him. "I accidentally stepped on her foot, and she's being a sissy."

India, I noticed, was silently lifting her lip at Anita. Steve looked miserable.

Approaching Anita, I whispered, "I'm warning you. Don't you ever dare to hurt Lady again when I'm around, because the next time, I'm going to scream bloody murder about it. Is that clear? And let me also warn you that India knows exactly what you're up to,

127

and she is very protective of Lady, and she won't tolerate this kind of thing forever. India doesn't like you, and she doesn't trust you."

Anita's beautiful face flushed.

"Neither do I," I added.

Eighteen

EXAMINING HIS FACE IN THE CRACKED MIRROR ABOVE his bathroom sink, Buck Winter endures a hideous, exciting rush of self-consciousness he has not known since adolescence. His literal inability to see himself clearly is his own fault. Buck, however, blames the crack on global warming, a phenomenon he takes not only seriously but personally. Indeed, so serious and so personal is his resentment of the climatic ruination of the state of Maine that one morning last July when the battered, duct-taped transistor radio propped on his bathroom radiator had the gall to forecast temperatures in the nineties for the next four days, he vented his rage by hurling his razor to the floor, grabbing the damned radio, and slamming it into the first object to catch his eye—namely, the mirror. In Buck's view, a heat wave represents an infernal violation of Natural Order. Maine, for Christ's sake, is supposed to be *cold!*

When Buck *believes,* he does so with evangelical fervor. Maine is one of his two religions. Whenever he drives north across the bridge from Portsmouth, New Hampshire, to the sacred ground, he creates a traffic hazard by bowing his head and intoning loudly, "Entering God's Country, the beautiful State of Maine!" When heading south on the bridge, he regretfully announces, just as loudly, "Leaving God's Country, the beautiful State of Maine!" By "God's country," he means, among other things, a place where the temperature damned well stays down where God intends it to remain. Buck assumes that he and God have identical likes and dislikes. After all, if God can't be expected to show some common sense, who can?

God is of little help to Buck right now. The problem is the Deity's total lack of experience with human romance. Although it's been decades since Buck's last heady infatuation with a woman—Marissa, in fact, his late wife—by comparison with God, Buck is, by definition, a man of the world. Buck's other religion, dog worship, is of disappointingly little practical help. Bending his massive frame downward to study his face in the uncracked sections of the mirror, he wishes, not for the first time, that he were the kind of creature he knows how to groom and present to best advantage. But he is not and is never going to be a golden retriever.

Speak of the angel, at that moment, Mandy wanders into the bathroom in the hope that Buck will turn on the shower. If he does, she will exercise her prerogative of leaping into the tub, standing under the water until she is drenched, flying out of the tub, and shaking dog-scented water all over everything. Neither Buck nor Mandy realizes that the cracked mirror perfectly suits the decor of the rest of the bathroom and, indeed, the rest of the house. But today Buck does not turn on the shower. Instead, he addresses Mandy, who is a beautiful and intelligent young bitch, sound of mind and body.

"Know thyself, Mandy!" Buck advises her. "In the Great Show Ring of Life and Love, see yourself as the judge will see you! And if you don't like what you see, hire yourself a professional handler!"

Buck has done so. Although his neglected house and well-kept kennels in Owls Head, Maine, are a mere hour and a half north of Freeport, home of that esteemed Maine institution, L.L. Bean, Freeport has become a shopping mecca that bewilders him. Consequently, he relies largely on Bean's catalogs and the Bean site on the World Wide Web. An old customer, he pored over the many catalogs mailed to him within the last six months and selected a remarkably suitable gift for Gabrielle Beamon. No one could ever accuse him of stinginess. On the contrary, he gives generously, if eccentrically and often inappropriately: expensive firearms to pacifists, costly fishing tackle and elaborate hunting knives to vegetarians. In contrast, an L.L. Bean dog bed is an outright normal selection. Yes, but which dog bed? Round? With a green fleece top? Rectangular? Rectangular and therapeutic? Blue? Tan? Forest green? With or without a pattern of dog paws? Close study of the chart on page 220 of the Holiday catalog simplified matters: Rectangular dog beds were unavailable in size small. Therefore, round. Tan he rejected as bland. Faint heart never won fair maid! Bright blue. Like Gabrielle's eyes.

"Monogrammed," he told the customer service representative, a competent-sounding woman with sweet voice. " 'Molly,' M-O-L-L-Y. Not I-E. Y. Twenty-five-inch round dog bed, denim blue cover, no paw prints, monogrammed 'Molly.' "

Having taken the information about the dog bed, the service representative made what she could not have known was the mistake of asking, "And your next item?"

"Whatever you like!" Buck cheerfully bellowed.

Unruffled, she replied, "And what sort of thing did

130

you have in mind? A gift? Sporting goods? Something for the home?" After persistent questioning, she narrowed the field to men's clothing. "Could you give me some idea of . . . ?"

"Whatever you like!" repeated Buck, slightly annoyed.

"It's a matter of what you want, isn't it? What your preferences are?"

"It says here, 'Discover all the ways L.L. Bean makes shopping easier for you.' *That's* my preference. Now, what would you think about these chino pants?"

Once she understood the customer's request, the representative dealt capably with it. Skillfully inquiring about where he planned to wear the proposed wardrobe, she elicited plentiful information not only about Mount Desert Island, but about Gabrielle Beamon and the number of years that had passed since Buck had set out to court a woman. After a friendly discussion of the beauties of Acadia National Park and the pain of love, the Bean representative consulted her computer listings of items this customer had previously ordered, asked whether he'd gained or lost weight recently, and suggested garments suitable for creating a positive impression on a woman of taste during a fall weekend on Mount Desert Island. It soon became apparent that Buck wanted choices rather than suggestions. Therefore, she chose. Instead of having the order shipped, he arranged to pick it up. He hates paying shipping costs.

"Hire a professional!" Buck trumpets to Mandy. The thought of a professional handler reminds him of Horace Livermore. And this image leads, as does everything these days, to Gabrielle Beamon. "Nothing wrong with a little friendly competition! And if you want to win, hire a professional!"

Instead of driving directly north from Owls Head to Bar Harbor, Buck therefore heads south, reaches Freeport, swears at the traffic, and finally finds a place in the L.L. Bean lot. Ignoring such temptations as brightly colored canoes and kayaks in which he pictures Gabrielle gracefully paddling, he follows the friendly L.L. Bean representative's instructions for finding the customer service desk, where his order awaits him: the monogrammed dog bed, shirts in chamois cloth and Royal Stewart flannel, a fleece anorak, chinos, lightweight hiking boots, and a piece of soft-sided luggage to replace his army-green duffel bag, which appears moth-eaten but has actually been chewed by mice. He bears left and looks upward at the familiar moose head mounted above. He pauses a moment. Several customers observe him. They smile at the sight of this craggy moose of a man gazing happily upward an apparent replica of his own head.

Nineteen

THE ENCOUNTER WITH MY FATHER FELT LIKE ANOTHER head injury.

But I have leaped ahead. Before I bounce back, let me point out that these sequencing problems are well documented in cases like mine. Actually, I'm lucky. The persistent sequelae could be far worse than they are.

Anyway, my reaction to Buck was perfectly normal; my father has a concussive effect on everyone. Take Quint and Effie, who hailed me as I slowed to a crawl before turning left at the Beamon Reservation parking lot. Effie had a dazed look. "Your *father's* here!" she exclaimed, her manner suggesting the breaking of astounding news, as if she'd located a supposedly dead birth parent for me and wanted to prepare me for the shock of an imminent reunion.

Cracks on the head or no cracks on the head, memory is an unreliable faculty, so maybe I'd better remind you that Effie was not an adoption-reunion professional, but the young potter and weaver married to Gabrielle Beamon's nephew, Quint O'Brian, both of whom I'd met at Gabrielle's clambake. By sunlight, they still radiated New Age wholesomeness. What I could see now was that although Effie's long, French-braided hair was a deep chocolate brown and her husband's curls cherubic blond, the couple had identical skin, fair and dewy. The sameness of skin may, of course, have been a meaningless coincidence or a minor source of their initial attraction to each other. Still, I found myself seeing that moist freshness of countenance as the result of a shared regimen of whole-grain loaves, exotic vegetables, and dietary supplements with unpronounceable names in combination with the use of peppermint-scented health-food-store liquid soap.

Quint and Effie were apparently engaged in fulfilling one of their duties as caretakers of the Beamon Reservation: Both had binoculars slung around their necks. If you work for a wildlife preserve, then birding isn't just the relaxing pastime it is for everyone else, is it? No, it counts as *work*, not exactly as *hard* work, if you want my opinion, but work all the same, even though Quint was, of course, Gabrielle's nephew. A cushy job gained through nepotism is still, after all, a job. Did I want the O'Brians to collect welfare instead? Furthermore, in contrast to most of the activities pursued by the guests at the clambake, looking at native fauna through binoculars at least didn't violate any of the reservation's multitudinous don't-you-dares posted nearby.

"I have to tell you," Effie said breathlessly, "that if that bumper sticker of his is supposed to be a joke, well, violence is not *my* idea of a suitable subject for humor. And it's not Quint's either." She'd stuck her head through the window of my car and almost into my face. Up close, she actually did smell of peppermint. Understanding the significance of odor is rather primitive, even doglike, but maybe I'd eventually progress to figuring out the implications of spoken language. My father? A bumper sticker? Violence as a suitable subject for humor?

Quint looked embarrassed. "It's more a matter of Opal and Wally. And the Pine Tree Foundation." He had that stiff politeness of prep school graduates. You know what I mean? The kind that makes you think they're lying and that the minute your back is turned, they'll be running around committing all kinds of dirty, illegal proletarian sins, but with upper-class flair.

Removing her face from mine, Effie turned to Quint. "Well, so far as *I'm* concerned, the foundation has nothing to do with it. This is a matter of principle. It's not about Pine Tree Foundation politics. The point is, violence or nonviolence? And speaking for myself, I couldn't care less if Opal and Wally *are* offended, and if they are, they've brought it on themselves. Nobody made them become developers. The same goes for Anita. If she didn't want to be the butt of lawyer jokes, she shouldn't've gone to law school. And if Wally and Opal wanted to be part of an environmental organization, they shouldn't've become developers in the first place. So if they take offense, it's a personal matter between Opal and Gabbi. As far as the Pine Tree Foundation goes, good riddance!"

"Effie," Quint said pacifically, "people *can* change. Malcolm is always saying that, and he's right. He has Opal and Wally volunteering on the Homans crew, and if that experience isn't enough to persuade them, there's nothing wrong with offering an economic incentive to invest in the environment instead of to destroy it. In part, that *is* what the Pine Tree Foundation's about. And I know you think it's hypocritical to combine charity and self-interest, but the only rational approach, Effie, is to focus on the enlightened contributions people *do* make. Standard Oil is an excellent example. Now, there's a history of extreme economic and environmental exploitation and violence, but if it weren't for—"

Effie cut him off with a warning glance.

Shrugging off her concern, he persisted. "It's because of John D., Jr., that this island isn't covered with theme parks and blacktop and ticky-tack. Is that what you'd prefer?"

"Of course not, Quint, but Opal and Wally are a far cry from being philanthropists, and you know it."

"So are the other investors," he said. "Gabbi, for one. There's no reason why Opal and Wally shouldn't be invited, too. For all we know, they already have been."

"I know that Opal is an old friend of Gabbi's! I've heard it a thousand times. And you're right. For all we know, Opal was one of the first people Malcolm invited, after Gabbi, which is, if you ask me, a totally undemocratic and elitist policy, anyway."

I'd reached the limit of the bewilderment I could endure. "What is?" I asked.

"Investment by invitation," Effie replied. "Word of mouth. The old-boy network."

"Effie, among other things, Gabbi and Opal are not old *boys*. And Gabbi is no snob. If she were, she'd hardly—" Red-faced, Quint broke off.

Tactfully ignoring what was clearly going to be a reference to my father, Effie shook her head. "Unfair is unfair. Privilege is no better if it's based on class instead of sex. It's still exclusionary. It's the same old rich-get-richer."

"My wife, the radical," Quint said amiably. "So if the Pine Tree Foundation is strictly a rich-get-richer scheme, why didn't Norman Axelrod invest? The more elitist the foundation was, the better he should've liked it."

"Because even though he saw everybody else making money, and even though, yes, he would've *paid* to be able to say he was involved with the, uh, benefactors, he did *not* want to do anything to promote conservation and save the environment, that's why! And since everyone else saw that the foundation was obviously a good thing, as usual, he had to decide that it wasn't. You *know* how oppositional he was, Quint. Wasn't he, Holly?"

"I suppose so," I said.

"Speaking of opposition," Quint began hesitantly. "It's awkward, but . . ."

"The bumper sticker," Effie told me. "Is there something you can do about it?"

"I don't really know," I said.

"I was hoping he might listen to you. Not that we want to interfere with freedom of expression."

"Of course not," I said.

"Advocating violence," Effie informed me, "is, uh, incompatible with the goals of the Beamon Reservation."

"And impolitic," Quint added.

After issuing a vague promise to see whether I could do something about whatever was upsetting Quint and Effie, I continued my interrupted drive to the guest cottage. Parked next to it I found a white Chevy van with a bumper sticker that proclaimed, KEEP MAINE GREEN. SHOOT A DEVELOPER! Pacing slowly near the trees at the edge of the lawn, as if preparing to browse on the vegetation, was a human moose.

Twenty

"WELL, WELL, WELL!" BELLOWED MY FATHER. "HOW'S my girl?" Kimi, memory intact, knew instantly which girl he meant. She gave him the reply he wanted. "*Ah-woooo-wooooo!*"

My father then addressed Rowdy, who was already wooing an almost uncontrollably enthusiastic greeting. "And how's my boy?" Buck demanded. "Hey, big fellow! How's my boy?"

Raising his arms to simulate a rack of antlers, he easily persuaded both dogs to leap up and rest their forepaws on his massive shoulders. With no visible encouragement, they scoured his grinning face with their big pink tongues.

I might as well not have been there. Assuming— falsely, if naturally—that my father's preoccupation with the dogs was temporary, I took advantage of what I imagined to be a brief opportunity to study him while his mind was elsewhere. Having since come to my senses, I now recognize *elsewhere* as the permanent residential address of Buck's mind. What I observed then, however, in addition to his obvious wackiness about dogs and his striking resemblance to a moose, was . . . But perhaps I am taking a knowledge of moose for granted. Anyone who knows anything about moose will tell you that moose are always bigger than you expect them to be. Like camels and giraffes, they are improbable, ungainly, and fascinating, as if they didn't turn out quite as the Creator intended, but got kept anyway for reasons no one has been able to fathom. In other words, although the recent crash of my biological hard drive had impaired my ability to expect anything terribly specific, my father was, paradoxically, bigger than I expected, with craggy features, an oversized head, and thick, dark hair. In fairness to moose, I should add that in their own way, they are quite handsome, as was Buck, whose face radiated boyish joy at the pleasure of fooling around with my beautiful dogs.

"Looking good! Looking good, there!" His voice was deep and smooth, with a hint of a roar. He did not, of course, refer to me.

"Thank you," I said. With irony? Not at all! Given a choice of looking good myself or having my dogs look good, I'd go for the dogs any day. "You're looking good yourself." I really was glad to see him. He was, after all, my father, as well as a person with dogs on the brain, therefore someone in this untrustworthy new world of mine whom I plainly could trust. What's more, my remark was perfectly ordinary; people go around saying it all the time without regard to its truth, falsehood, or immediate relevance. In other words, especially since I had no recollection of how Buck usually looked and consequently no standard of comparison, I was not actually complimenting him on his appearance. For all I knew, he'd aged ten years since our last meeting. For all

I knew, he always dressed entirely in brand-new clothes.

"Off," he told the dogs, who obediently returned to the ground. "Drove to Freeport this morning," he confided. He looked abashed. "Took a little detour. I was going to stop at the outlet in Ellsworth, but I didn't want to take a chance of not finding the right kind of thing." With an apologetic glance at Rowdy and Kimi, he brushed dog hair off his medium-brown jacket, which coordinated pleasantly with his plaid shirt and khaki pants. The gesture was awkward, as if he were performing it for the first time. "Not that Gabrielle cares," he said defensively. "But she's a class act. It wouldn't be right to disgrace her." He added proudly, surveying his finery, "Head to foot." With that, he raised what I guessed was a size 13 foot to display a shiny hiking boot in brown leather. "Kicking up my heels lately," he explained.

"So I understand," I said with a smile.

Can moose blush? Yes. This one regarded me through narrowed eyes. "Met her at a show," he said, without bothering to specify the variety. Addressing the heavens, he added, "What the hell's happened to good sportsmanship these days? That's what I'd like to know." The demand didn't seem rhetorical. On the contrary, my father listened and waited so attentively that I found myself sharing his hopeful expectation that God would then and there deliver a full explanation of what the hell *had* happened to good sportsmanship and how He or She intended to restore it. The Divine Restoration Plan, I now realize, would have hinged on the official appointment of Buck as God's Emissary to the Dog Fancy, a position he already considers himself to fill, albeit in an unofficial capacity.

"It was a disgrace to the Fancy," Buck declared,

making the capital letter audible: *Fancy*. "There was Gabrielle, the kind of fine, upstanding individual we should be knocking ourselves out to attract to the Sport, and what kind of welcome did she get? Worse than none! To begin with, Horace Livermore failed in his professional responsibility to his client. Left *her* to wander around looking for him! Hah! And until I straightened him out, he had no intention of taking Molly into the ring himself and every intention on God's green earth of charging Gabrielle his top-dollar fee for the incompetent services of one of his damned lackeys." He added definitively, "Nice bitch," meaning—I think—Molly, not Gabrielle. He then launched into a history of the bichon frise followed by a description and critique of the breed standard with particular reference to Molly's strengths in that regard, especially when compared with the deplorable bichons bred and shown by a woman named Yvette Sommerson, who turned out to be Gabrielle's dragon, the villain in the humiliating episode of Molly's eviction from the private canine restroom. "Horace and Molly beat the pants off her," Buck concluded with satisfaction.

I said, "Horace Livermore. He handled a mini poodle for Norman Axelrod."

"Course he did. He did until Axelrod fired him. Stupid thing for him to've done. Should've known what was going to happen. They all do it at that level, you know. I don't know why he called you. He should've asked me. I'd've told him it happens all the time."

Yes. *Who? What?* And so forth. Greatly understating matters, I ventured, "I'm not sure what you're talking about."

"Arsenic. Not that it's right. Another instance."

"Of poor sportsmanship," I ventured.

Buck nodded. "But at that level, of course, it's common enough. And at least it's not *new,*" he said damningly. "Professional handlers've been using arsenic for years. You almost have to feel sorry for the poor bastards. Their income depends on winning, and the stuff produces *luxuriant* growth. Intense color. Beautiful to see if you don't know what's causing it. Axelrod shouldn't have been surprised. The dog's all right?"

"Yes. Isaac. He's fine. Gabrielle is taking care of him."

At the sound of Gabrielle's name, my father burst into what I was somehow able to identify as an effort at song.

"It wasn't across a crowded *room,*" I pointed out sourly. "It was across a crowded dog show. And if Horace Livermore is *that* kind of handler, why were you so eager for him to handle Molly?"

"Best there is," Buck declared. "And that's what Gabrielle deserves."

I remember the lone hiker's graceful, athletic movement and his skill in baiting my dogs. "And Molly? Is that what Molly deserves? A handler who uses arsenic?"

"Long-term low doses on the specials dogs he's campaigning." Buck said it dismissively. "Molly's never out of Gabrielle's sight. But you've known Horace Livermore for years." If so, Buck looked less puzzled than my responses warranted. Who and what I'd known for years was a jumbled mess, at least to me, but at least I hadn't revealed my weakness by asking what Horace Livermore looked like. Interestingly enough, the language-processing centers of my brain remained unimpaired: I retained perfect comprehension

141

of my native dialect, which is to say, the jargon of the dog fancy. *Specials:* entries in the Best of Breed competition, limited to champions, as opposed to *class dogs* and *class bitches,* the ones competing in the classes—Open, Bred-by, and so on—for championship points, *Bred-by,* meaning, incidentally, Bred by Exhibitor.

"Of course," my father conceded, "you knew his sister Candace a lot better, back in the old days. That Border collie of hers, Finn, used to beat you and Vinnie on a regular basis. Candace hasn't been around here for years, not since she came down with that chronic whatever-it-is. She still shows in Canada. Matter of fact, one of her dogs was in the last issue of *Front and Finish.* Young Border collie. Now that I think of it, that's a breed you ought to consider." And he was off again, this time on a sermon about Border collies in relation to the mental and moral benefits of what he called "a little healthy competition." By this he meant, I soon deduced, placing consistently in the ribbons at the top levels of dog obedience, a sport at which I'd evidently excelled before switching from golden retrievers to Alaskan malamutes. Eventually, he said, looking hurt, "Some reason you haven't asked about Mandy?"

Because I have no idea who Mandy is? And find myself inexplicably unable to tell you so?

"No reason at all," I assured him. "How *is* Mandy?"

"In season!" Buck was triumphant. You'd've thought that Mandy, whoever she was, had invented the estrous cycle. "Speaking of Mandy, you remembered not to mention the rest of the pack to the lilies of the field. Not that I'd ever ask you to tell a lie, Holly."

"The lilies . . . ?"

"That's what I call them. The yellow-bellied pacifist granola nephew and his wife." He quoted, " 'Consider the lilies of the field, how they grow: they toil not, neither do they spin.' "

"Quint and Effie," I translated. "But Effie *does* spin, doesn't she? She's a weaver. And a potter. I met them last night, at Gabrielle's clambake. And in fact, I just—"

"Sponges, the pair of them." With yet another abrupt switch of metaphor, he said, "Parasitic tofu. Not that Gabrielle sees it that way. For a sophisticated woman, Gabrielle is remarkably naive. If you don't keep your eye on her, she lets herself be used by people." He then cited a canine example. "Take Molly. It's a manipulative breed. Too cute for its own good. But that one's conned Gabrielle more than most. Never walks on her own four paws if Gabrielle's there to carry her. Picky eater. Spoiled rotten. Same goes for the nephew and the wife. Spoiled rotten." He paused to survey his new attire yet again. "So, is the old man going to pass muster with them?"

"Yes," I said, "but given what you think of them, I don't know why you care. Besides, it's not your clothes they're worried about. It's your bumper sticker. Effie feels that violence is not to be taken in jest."

"Who the hell said it was?" Buck was outraged.

"You, according to Effie. 'Shoot a developer'?"

"Nothing wrong with keeping Maine green," Buck countered.

With that, he bade prolonged goodbyes to Rowdy and Kimi, and then opened the door of his van. Prominently mounted on a rack inside was a deer rifle. He climbed in, slammed the door, waved cheerfully to me, and drove off toward Gabrielle's.

My father had, of course, failed to notice that there

was anything wrong with me. I had to wonder what, if anything, I'd have had to be missing to make my father take note. An arm? A leg? The power of speech?

The answer: a dog. If Rowdy or Kimi had been missing, he'd have noticed the absence right away.

Twenty-one

"MY FATHER," I TOLD THE DOGS, "MAY HAVE BEEN Gabrielle Beamon's rescuer, but he's obviously not going to be mine. Have you ever in your lives seen one human being more blatantly uninterested in another? Was I supposed to *confide* in someone who doesn't even say hello to me? Was I supposed to trust a person who has known me for my entire life and fails to notice that all of a sudden there is something horribly *wrong* with me?"

As if to demonstrate their radical difference from my father, Rowdy and Kimi eyed me with delighted fascination. We were now indoors, where I'd made myself a cup of sweet, milky tea and treated each dog to a chunk of cheese. Thus the rapt attention. As an aside, let me mention that it's a damn shame that food training doesn't work as well on parents as it does on dogs.

"But you know what?" I continued. "The difference is still there. Food or no food, it's still real. When you found me freezing to death out on the miserable rock, *you* noticed me! *You* were glad to see me! And even though I didn't have a clue who you even were, you knew you were *my* dogs!" Running my eyes over Rowdy's and Kimi's thick, stand-off wolf-gray coats, admiring their heavy bone, smiling at the over-the-back wagging of their white tails, looking into the deep chocolate of their almond-shaped eyes, I added, "Not that I blame him for paying attention to *you*. Love me, love my dogs, love my dogs, love me. One and the same. And I am hardly in a position to blame him! This dog thing is obviously hereditary. And if he is totally infatuated with Gabrielle, wonderful! If he has any sense, he'll marry her *now* while he's still her hero and before she comes to her senses, and you'll *woo-woo-woo* at their wedding, because he will definitely make sure you're there, and I might or might not dance, depending on whether he remembers to invite me, which it is painfully clear he might very well not because he might completely forget my entire existence. After all, *I've* forgotten most of it! Why shouldn't he?"

Dogs take everything personally. When I quit ranting about how my father failed to pay attention to me and finally noticed the dogs' bewilderment and hurt, I promptly apologized. In tones of sweet comfort, I said, "*You* are good dogs. You have not done anything wrong. I am very sorry that I got carried away." I bent down, pulled their two big heads together, and nuzzled. "We will get through this," I promised them. "We just aren't going to get the help I thought we were, that's all." My brain tickled in a familiar-feeling way. "As the saying goes," I said, "Dog helps those who help themselves."

Not that it was the most hysterically funny thing anyone has ever said, although Rowdy and Kimi pranced appreciatively. No, the important thing about the bit of foolishness was that it felt *familiar* in a new and splendidly specific way: As soon as I spoke, I knew I'd just said the kind of thing I *would* say. Reveling in the unfamiliar sensation of feeling even a tiny bit like

145

myself, I exclaimed, "In Dog we trust!" Carried away, I cried, "Dog is my copilot! A mighty fortress is our . . ." I stopped there. Sacrilege wouldn't offend my canine listeners, who wouldn't hear it as such. But when you're on the brink of horrifying yourself, it's time to quit.

Fired up by my anger at Buck and the renewal of my normal religious fervor, I dumped the tea remaining in my cup into the kitchen sink and even remembered— remembered!—to wash the cup to discourage the dogs from filching it, licking off the traces of milk and sugar, dropping it on the floor, and breaking it, thereby leaving sharp pieces that might cut their pads. Then, incredibly, I also remembered, if rather belatedly, to investigate the contents of Rowdy's saddlebags, which I'd carried into the cottage and left on the table. With one exception, the contents of Rowdy's pack were uninformative. Instead of weighting his pack with rice, as I'd done with Kimi's, I'd padded his pack with hand towels and loaded it with bottles of spring water. In a zippered bag clipped to the top of the pack, however, were a green steno pad and a ballpoint pen. Oh, Lord! Was I the kind of obnoxious writer who is always prepared in case inspiration strikes? If so, the muse had barely whispered. Only the first few pages of the pad had been used, and what I'd written on those was not writing, properly speaking, but indecipherable scrawl culminating in a rebus that I must have used as a form of idiosyncratic shorthand.

It had three elements: two hopelessly inartistic efforts at pictures linked by a remarkably clear equal sign. The rudely triangular image on the left, short scratches emanating from a vertical line, was a childish rendition of an evergreen tree. The figure on the right was a sort of wobbly diamond with two interior lines connecting the opposite points. A kite? Possibly a kite with no tail and no string. Maybe not? By comparison, the tree was an obvious tree. And the meaning of my rebus? Maine is not the Pine Tree State because it's thick with coconut palms; I wouldn't have written myself a shorthand note about the presence of pines in Acadia National Park. A *pine tree is . . . ?* The Pine Tree Foundation! The kite, however, stumped me. *The Pine Tree Foundation can go fly a kite?*

The Pine Tree Foundation, Gabrielle Beamon, the late Norman Axelrod, Horace Livermore, arsenic, Anita Fairley, Steve Delaney, and my father could all go fly kites! With an excess of energy that I see as symptomatic of a new phase, I scurried around creating order in the cottage. I scrubbed the kitchen and bathroom sinks, took out the trash, vacuumed dog hair, and neatly stacked some ratty-looking magazines and Acadia brochures that Rowdy and Kimi had used as chew toys. To keep me company while I did housework, I turned on the radio, which must have been set to an N.P.R. station. An educated voice expressed gratitude for grants from the Ford Foundation, the Pew Charitable Trust, the John D. and Catherine T. MacArthur Foundation, the Joyce Foundation, and the Geraldine R. Dodge Foundation, for reporting on biological resource issues, but not to the Pine Tree Foundation for Conservation Philanthropy. Did Pine Tree make grants? What exactly *did* it do, anyway?

I'd just finished showering, drying my hair, and changing into clean jeans and a navy T-shirt with a dog

147

team racing across the front when the call of the paternal moose *("Aaarrrg!")* sounded at the kitchen door. Before I'd even managed to shove past the dogs to open it, Buck charged in and, without even greeting the dogs, demanded to know why I'd rolled belly-up for that goddamned ambulance chaser my vet had taken up with.

"If you mean Anita Fairley," I said, carefully avoiding the point of his roaring, "she isn't an ambulance chaser. So far as I know, she doesn't do personal injury law. She must do corporate law, taxes, real estate, uh, that kind of thing. Conservation law. She's the Pine Tree Foundation's attorney. Admittedly, I don't like her, but she's perfectly respectable. She's Malcolm Fairley's daughter."

Raising his thick eyebrows, my father said, "It's not like you to try to weasel out of something, Holly." He didn't go on to say that he was disappointed in me; he didn't need to. "When I ask you a direct question—"

"I have other things to think about right now," I interrupted. "And Steve Delaney isn't *my* personal property." I paused. "Obviously."

"He was yours, last thing I heard."

"Well, your knowledge is out of date. And people are not each other's property, anyway. We're all free to—"

"Cambridge!" he groaned.

"It's only dogs who are forever. If you want a permanent bond . . ."

"Get a dog," he finished. "And get married."

"Which of us are we talking about?" I demanded. "It must be you, because there's no one I'm about to marry, and so far as I know, there's no one interested in marrying me."

"How many times you turn him down?"

148

"Who?"

"Your vet!"

"I don't know," I answered truthfully. "Maybe I never turned him down at all. Maybe he never asked."

That drew another groan.

"You've seen Anita Fairley! She's beautiful!"

"When've I seen her?"

For the second time within minutes, I reminded my father of something I assumed he already knew. "Anita is Malcolm Fairley's daughter," I said irritably. I'd presented that family credential once, hadn't I? But Buck evidently hadn't paid attention.

"I've never even met this goddamned Malcolm Fairley, and when I do, he's going to be—"

"We've known him for years. You have. And I . . . *I've* known him . . ." My voice trailed off. "Or at least *he's* known *us*." The question popped out. "Hasn't he?"

Buck stared at me with fierce alarm. "What the hell is wrong with you? You haven't been using drugs, have you?"

"Of course not." Aside from addiction to dogs in general and the Alaskan malamute in particular, this was true.

"You know, Holly," Buck said sadly, "the last thing I ever want to do is pry into your personal life."

In retrospect, I have a monosyllabic comment to make about the claim: *Hah!* But the anxiety in his face and voice touched me.

"I have not been using drugs," I assured him. As if announcing comparatively wonderful news, I added, "I cracked my head on a rock."

As I have learned by observing other people's families, normal fatherly behavior in this kind of situation consists of doing whatever it takes—

requesting, cajoling, insisting, or even applying physical force—to get the child, including the adult child, to a hospital as fast as possible.

Buck, in contrast, assumed that my injury was attributable to my having switched to an unsuitably strong breed of dog. "With goldens, it never would've happened," he asserted before going on to suggest several other breeds, the Border collie, for example, that I had the bulk and muscle to handle. In conclusion, he said, almost in passing, "You did get the vet to take a look." The remark was ludicrously perfunctory. He sounded exactly, and I mean *exactly*, as if the first thing any sensible human being would do in response to a crack on her skull would be to rush to the nearest veterinarian. It is hideously possible that in the forgotten days of my infancy, my doting parents immunized me against numerous dog diseases that people can't catch. Of course, if my relationship with Steve Delaney had been different from what it was, I'd naturally have had the common sense to get him to check me out.

"I'll be all right," I said evasively.

"How bad was this crack on the head?"

I shrugged.

"Where did this happen?"

"Dorr. Near the top of the Ladder Trail. And no, I didn't take the dogs on the ladders."

"I'm not worried about the dogs," he said, probably for the first time in his life. "Are you seeing double?"

"No. My vision is fine."

"No bones broken."

"No."

"How bad is this memory loss?"

The relief of having someone else recognize and acknowledge it was so tremendous that I couldn't help smiling. "I can't even remember what I've forgotten," I said lightly.

"This slimy bastard," he said. "Malcolm Fairley."

"If he's a slimy bastard," I said, "it's news to me."

"Everything about him ought to be news to you, young lady. You just met him. He just met you."

"No. That's not so. We have, uh, friends in common."

"What friends?"

"Gabbi. And Ann. I have a letter from Ann that says how sweet Gabbi is." I omitted the *bossy* part. "Ann thinks Malcolm is difficult. And charming. They miss him."

Buck's expression was frighteningly serious. "No mention of Bentley?"

I was smug. "You see? We do know Malcolm. Yes, Ann says that a Trophy Edition is a Bentley. I didn't quite get that part."

"Jesus Christ!" Buck exclaimed. "Why didn't you tell me?"

"I just did."

"Holly, let me see the letter."

When I'd found it and given it to him, he skimmed it and said, "Why'd you think you'd written this in the margin? *God spelled backward?*"

"I had the feeling it was a, uh, family saying."

"It is. But why'd you think you'd written it *here?*"

"Force of habit?"

"Oh, Christ, you poor kid. Holly, you wrote it there because this letter's *not* about Gabbi Beamon and Malcolm Fairley. It's from your friend Ann Ratcliff, and what it's about is her *malamutes!* You never even knew Malcolm. He died before you met Ann and Bruce. The ones you know are Gabbi and Bentley."

"I thought maybe I drove one," I said pitifully.

151

"Drove what?"

"A Bentley. Never mind. But I see what you mean. New people with the names of my friends' dogs. God spelled backward." The rest of the world, of course, would've said, *Weird coincidence.*

"So, what else have you forgotten?"

I burst into tears. "Everything! I read the dogs' tags, and I didn't even recognize my own name. I forgot Rowdy and Kimi! Daddy, I didn't even know they were my dogs."

I always call him Buck. Always have. But not now.

Twenty-two

I DID MY BEST TO TELL BUCK EVERYTHING I'D observed and discovered since I'd awakened yesterday on the mountain: my injuries; my sense of mission; Malcolm Fairley's account of Norman Axelrod's fatal fall; my fragmentary recollection of Fairley's conversation with someone; Bonnie's message and my notes about arsenic; Axelrod's belief that Horace Livermore was not only dosing the show dogs he handled with arsenic, but was smuggling some unknown contraband to Canada; the dead man's antagonism to the Pine Tree Foundation and to environmental causes in general; the almost universal gratitude to Malcolm Fairley for combining charity and profit in satisfying the Pine Tree Foundation's investors; Axelrod's habit of needling Gabrielle about using the Beamon Reservation as a tax dodge; the flouting of the rules at the Beamon Reservation; Gabrielle's friendship with everyone, including Axelrod and even Opal and Wally Swan, the developers; Fairley's recruitment of Wally and Opal as volunteers on the Homans Path reclamation project; Quint and Effie's mistrust of Wally and Opal; my evidently false impression of acquaintance with Malcolm Fairley; Anita Fairley's nasty behavior to Steve's pointer, Lady; and on and on. I even dug out the steno pad and showed Buck my shorthand hieroglyphics that seemed to equate the Pine Tree Foundation with a kite.

He whacked the steno pad against the table. "And you don't remember a damned thing about this?"

"Nothing. I'm sorry."

"You never could draw," he said. "Or sing," he added unnecessarily.

"I've discovered that. Could we get to the point?"

"Which one?"

"Any. It isn't just that I can't remember things. I also can't make sense of what I know. I can't put things together."

"Look," he said, "you got dragged into this because that goddamned Norman Axelrod wrote a letter to *Dog's Life,* and Bonnie—that's your editor—didn't want to publish it. What'd happened was that Axelrod had been using Horace Livermore, and he fired him. You know that. Axelrod said he had proof. About the arsenic. Maybe he'd had some samples analyzed. Bonnie had the sense not to go and publish the letter because, first of all, she knew Axelrod was a crank, and second of all, she didn't want Livermore suing for slander."

"Libel," I corrected.

"Jesus. You may have lost your memory, Holly, but you haven't lost your personality."

"Thank you," I said.

153

"So Bonnie handed everything over to you. You were supposed to be working on an article about dosing dogs with arsenic. She told you to start with Axelrod. You talked to him on the phone, and you decided there was something in it, because you wanted to meet him. That's how I heard about it. Truth is, you wanted to get out of Cambridge. And you wanted to know if I knew a place you could stay near Bar Harbor."

"So you asked Gabrielle."

"Yeah."

"And I decided to work on some other articles, too. I have notes about that. Backpacking with dogs. That kind of thing. Okay. I write about dogs. I've figured that much out. Is that it? *That's* what I write about?"

Buck looked mystified. "What more do you want?"

"Malcolm Fairley seemed to have the idea that I was a, uh, journalist."

"You are!" Buck proudly informed me.

"Well, what do I write about *besides* dogs?"

"Shows," Buck answered promptly. "Judges. Breeders. Training. You wrote a book about Morris and Essex."

I shrugged my shoulders.

"Mrs. Dodge," he prompted. "Geraldine R. Dodge." He waited.

"Foundation," I said. "The Geraldine R. Dodge Foundation. I just heard that on the radio."

"America's First Lady of Dogs. Geraldine Rockefeller Dodge."

"It's not ringing any bells," I confessed. "I know who the Rockefellers are. But I don't remember writing a book. I don't *yet*."

"That's my girl." He might have been praising a puppy for a nice straight sit.

"Malcolm Fairley seems to think . . . I got the impression from him that . . . I'm trying to remember. It was last night, at Gabrielle's clambake. You know about that. She had this clambake for the Pine Tree Foundation. And for some reason, she invited me. I went. I was pretty disoriented. I'm trying to remember. Okay. Malcolm Fairley or someone else was talking about the benefactors. The Pine Tree Foundation has these benefactors, philanthropists, who just donate to it, I guess, to support conservation. They're not investors. They're donors who give money, and that's what makes it possible for the investors to get such high returns. Anyway, the point is that the benefactors want to remain anonymous, but they're obviously from the old families that have been giving money to preserve land on Mount Desert for years and years. And even for me, it wasn't too hard to guess . . . I mean, the book is here in the cottage. *Mr. Rockefeller's Roads.* It's your copy. It has your name in it. But I do remember, uh, background information, I guess you'd call it. It's the foreground that's all gone."

"And?"

"And? Oh, someone was about to say a name, Rockefeller, probably, and Malcolm Fairley started half joking about not naming names of the foundation's benefactors because I might publish them, and the benefactors had to be kept anonymous. It was the same thing he said to whoever was with him on Dorr. One of his benefactors, probably. But at the clambake, he made it sound as if I was in a position to—"

"Axelrod was a jackass," my father said. "Did anything to feel important. Built himself up. He probably told Fairley you were from the *New York Times.* Axelrod sucked up to celebrities, not that he

155

knew any, but according to him, he did. He'd drive by Stephen King's house in Bangor, and the next thing you knew, he'd tell you they were best friends. Easier than admitting he didn't have any, best or otherwise. Axelrod, of course, not Stephen King."

"So, you knew Norman Axelrod?"

"Christ, everyone in the state of Maine knew him, or knew who he was. And bolted at the sight of him."

"Except Gabrielle."

Buck flushed. "Gabrielle is an exceptional person," he said glowingly. Then the flush turned from warmth to anger. "What else do you know about Fairley?" he demanded.

"Everyone sings his praises. Everyone. Gabrielle. Quint and Effie. And they're real purists. Last night, Effie didn't like it one bit that people were breaking the rules of the Beamon Reservation. And for all that Quint has this job as caretaker because he's Gabrielle's nephew, he still knows a lot about environmental issues, nature, all that kind of thing. Effie thinks that Malcolm shouldn't have anything to do with Opal and Wally, because they're developers, but Quint obviously admires Malcolm. And the guests at the clambake were grateful that they'd made so much money from the Pine Tree Foundation. No one said it quite like that, but if you want to be blunt about it, the clambake was really a thank-you party for Malcolm Fairley for making everyone lots of money."

"Nothing else fishy about him?"

"About Malcolm Fairley? No. Except what I overheard on Dorr. But I was barely conscious. And this business about knowing him. But that was me. Because of Ann's letter. I might have missed something about him, though. I wasn't myself. I'm still not."

Buck caught my eye.

"*Yet,*" I said dutifully. "And besides doing all this financial wizardry, he does hands-on work. He's organized a volunteer crew to restore the Homans Path, which is this old, abandoned—"

"I know what the Homans Path is."

"Well, Malcolm Fairley has Wally and Opal, and, today, his daughter, Anita, and Steve Delaney working on the trail. Some other people, too, I think. When Malcolm Fairley talks about preserving Acadia, M.D.I., you can tell from his voice that he's absolutely genuine. About the rain forests, too. He has some involvement with Guatemala. Anita Fairley is a whole other story. She's the Pine Tree Foundation's attorney, but she doesn't necessarily do the work pro bono. Or maybe she does. For all I know, she does it out of dedication or maybe loyalty to her father. And she must be an investor, and in that case, she's making plenty. So her motives could be strictly economic. If she has some commitment to conservation, it's strictly to conservation at a distance. Her father apparently put the pressure on her to spend a day working on the trail, and she was anything but happy about it. She isn't the outdoor type. But you can tell to look at Malcolm Fairley that he's in great shape, and he spends a lot of time in the park."

With no warning, Buck gave an abrupt, military-style salute and headed for the door.

"Where are you going?" I asked.

His smile was sly. "Off to keep Maine green."

157

Twenty-three

"YOUR FATHER," GABRIELLE BEGAN, "IS REALLY extremely angry.

Despite the peculiarity of my mental circumstances, I was already starting to get sick of hearing about *my* father. Did people imagine that Buck's behavior was under *my* control? I was happy to notice, however, that the sensation of being tackled about Buck was vividly familiar.

"He came charging in," she continued, "asking all sorts of questions about Malcolm." An essential component of Gabrielle's beauty, I decided, was her obliviousness to it. Objectively speaking, she was too plump to wear jeans, and the plaid flannel lining visible where she'd turned up the cuffs added to her natural bulk. Although the day was still dry and sunny, she had on ugly, muddy rubber duck boots and a frayed yellow oilskin jacket that had probably cost a fortune forty years ago. If she wore makeup, it didn't show. The flaws in her skin did. Her silver-blond hair was wild. She must have noticed that I was staring at her. "I've been digging clams," she explained.

My father, I somehow knew, would admire a woman who digs her own clams. Molly the bichon had evidently not gone clamming. Her curly white coat was unmuddied. As usual, she was fastened almost umbilically to Gabrielle's middle. With what I immediately recognized as a flash of memory, I felt surprised that Buck hadn't yet severed the cord that kept Molly off the ground. Distant memories came to me of his lectures about small dogs as real dogs, creatures who should damned well stand on their own four paws.

"What did he want to know about Malcolm Fairley?" I shooed Rowdy and Kimi away from Molly. They'd moved from sniffing her paws to rising up in what might become obnoxiously rough efforts to dislodge her from Gabrielle's arms.

"Where the quote s.o.b. unquote lives, where he is right now, and how quote he got his clutches into me unquote." Speaking more to Molly than to me, Gabrielle added, "Clutches! Not that I haven't noticed a gleam in Malcolm's eye, but there's none in mine. There's something too *nice* about him. I can't imagine where your father got the idea that the attraction was reciprocated. And I told Buck that. You didn't say anything to him to suggest . . . ?"

I shook my head. "Not a word. Not that I can remember. We mentioned the Pine Tree Foundation. I talked about the clambake. I did say it was in honor of Malcolm, but . . ."

"Well, it was, of course," Gabrielle said, "but it isn't as though I'd given a party for Malcolm. The investors did. I do have reason to be especially grateful, because thanks to Malcolm, I *was* one of the original investors, and I've taken advantage of the opportunity to reinvest."

"Does Buck know that?" I asked. Whoops! "Not that he cares . . ." What's a gracious way to tell your father's inamorata that he would never marry for money?

Gabrielle spotted my dilemma. "Of course not," she assured me. "Buck isn't the gigolo type."

I smiled in relief. "Anything but."

"Yes. He does have a competitive streak, though. Maybe there's a little rivalry going on there because of what Malcolm and the foundation have been able to do

159

for me. For many others, too, of course. That's why *we* wanted to celebrate. It isn't as if I, personally, had given a party for Malcolm," she said again. "Still, the fact is"—Gabrielle's husky voice dropped—"that the celebration was for Malcolm and not for him. Men get their feelings hurt about things like that, you know. Well, enough! What's happened now is that Buck has gone charging off like a . . ." Gabrielle left a sort of fill-in-the-blank gap.

"Moose," I supplied.

"In mating season," she finished, flushing a little at the indelicacy. A second later, however, she burst into beautiful laughter.

I didn't join in. The idea of an enraged bull moose in rut struck me as very dangerous and not in the least bit funny. "Gabrielle, does Buck know where Malcolm Fairley is? I told Buck about the work on the Homans Path, but I'm . . . I think I told Buck that I'd seen Malcolm there today. But I just can't remember."

"Of course he knows," Gabrielle said blithely.

"How?"

"He asked me. I told him. This is the crew's regular day on the Homans Path. Where else would Malcolm be?"

"You told Buck that? When he looked like a bull moose in mating season?"

"That was just a figure of speech," Gabrielle replied. "And a coarse one at that. Forget I said it. But after I told Buck, when I realized *how* angry he was, I had second thoughts. So I thought I'd better stop in here and pick you up instead of just going there myself. Buck needs to be mollified a little, that's all, Holly. He's misunderstood *something*, and once we find out what he's misunderstood, we'll get it straightened out. With

160

both of us there to talk to him, I'm sure he'll listen to reason."

If I'd been in my right mind, I'd probably have mouthed a cliché: *There's always a first time for everything, isn't there?* What frightened me, however, was not a conviction about what my father would or wouldn't do; on the contrary, it was a deep, sure sense of Buck's utter unpredictability. My most powerful feeling astonished me: I felt frantically compelled to protect my father from himself.

"Let's go," I told Gabrielle. Then I told Rowdy and Kimi the same thing in the same tone of voice. Gabrielle didn't seem to mind. Maybe she and my father really did have a future together.

The five of us—two people, three dogs—piled into Gabrielle's white Volvo. Molly, as usual, was glued to Gabrielle's tummy. Rowdy and Kimi were loose in the back. Twisting around to remind them to stay there, I missed seeing the approach of another vehicle until Gabrielle had pulled to the side of the dirt road and *yoo-hoo*ed through the open window to Quint and Effie, who'd been heading toward her house. Effie was at the wheel of an adorable green pickup so small and so cute that it looked like a magnified toy truck.

"Were you coming to see me?" Gabrielle asked. Without waiting for a reply, she went on to report excitedly that her hero was off to fight a misguided duel in her honor and that she and I were rushing off to intercept him. "We can't talk now!"

Her eyes gleaming, Effie said, "There! I told you so, Quint! We saw Buck Winter tearing out of here, and I told Quint, but he didn't want to believe me. *Someone*"—Effie glared at me—"must have told him about how Wally and Opal are trying to get their hands

161

on that land of Norman Axelrod's that abuts the reservation! Is he really going to *shoot* a developer?" Her face and voice exuded horrified delight.

"Effie, don't be foolish!" Gabrielle replied. "We'll discuss it later." With a little wave of her hand, she drove off.

"Shoot a developer!" I exclaimed. "Honestly!"

"Well," remarked Gabrielle, without taking her eyes off the narrow road, "he does have a gun. But Effie couldn't possibly know that, could she? She's just worked herself into a fit of excitement about that bumper sticker. Effie takes everything to heart, you know."

"He has a rifle in his van."

"Oh, not that one," Gabrielle said brightly. "It's some kind of *little* gun."

"A handgun?"

"It's in a holster." Gabrielle said it reassuringly, as if the holster somehow rendered the sidearm inoperable.

"What for?"

"Buck always carries a gun in the woods. The first time we went for a walk together, I asked him about it, and he said you never know what you're going to run into. I assumed he was thinking of snakes."

"There are *no* poisonous snakes in Maine," I pointed out. "Certainly not this far north, anyway. And in Acadia? What is there to shoot in Acadia National Park?"

"Tourists!" Gabrielle joked.

Her lightheartedness was grating on my nerves. I wished I could think of some way to impress the seriousness of the situation on her. "Carrying a handgun in a national park? I'm sure it's illegal. I hope he doesn't get arrested."

162

"Anita will get him out if he does. Besides, his jacket covers it. At worst, he'll just pull it out and *show* it to Malcolm," Gabrielle insisted. "But I don't think he'll even do that. What I'm afraid of is that they'll end up in a fistfight and that one of them will get hurt. Your father is really *very* angry, you know."

"I believe you," I said, still with no precise idea of what Buck was so angry about. By now, we were speeding along Route 3 past The Tarn, almost at the turn for the Sieur de Monts Spring area. Glancing back to check on Rowdy and Kimi, I caught sight of the cute little pickup, which was no distance behind us. "Oh, damn it!"

Gabrielle flicked her eyes to the rearview mirror. "You didn't know?"

"No, I didn't know. I wasn't paying attention. I suppose Effie just couldn't stand to miss seeing Buck take potshots at a developer."

As Gabrielle cruised around looking for an empty space in the big parking lot by the spring, the Nature Center, and the Wild Gardens of Acadia, I noticed Buck's van, bumper sticker and all. Steve Delaney's van, its window lowered to provide air for his dogs, was still parked where I'd seen it earlier.

"Oh," Gabrielle said cheerfully, "Opal and Wally *are* here! That's their Land Rover!"

You'd have thought we were arriving at a cocktail party. With no hint of frivolousness, however, Gabrielle hopped out of the Volvo and set off toward the abandoned Homans Path. Even on the flat terrain, I had a hard time keeping up. My injuries were beginning to reassert themselves; my shoulder hurt, and my head was swimming. At the ends of their leashes, Rowdy and Kimi trotted behind Gabrielle on the sidewalk by the

163

Wild Gardens and then along a broad dirt road. I let the dogs drag me.

"We turn left somewhere around here," Gabrielle said. "There it is! And now we have to keep our eyes open. To your right, up there on the hill, you'll see where the Park Service cut down a lot of trees. That's what they do when they officially abandon a trail. You should hear Malcolm on *that* subject! And it really is outrageous. They just chop down tons of trees at the top and bottom, and that's that. No more trail. You have to look carefully for a little track leading to it. The trail phantoms keep it open. Unauthorized people, you know, who sneak around keeping abandoned trails open. I've wondered whether Zeke might be one of them."

"Who?"

"This nice young man who suddenly turned up here and volunteered for Malcolm's trail crew. There's something . . . I don't know how to put it. Something *unsaid* about him, if you know what I mean. Malcolm doesn't think so, but he—Zeke, not Malcolm—was fishing for an invitation to the clambake, and it made me wonder. Here's the trail!"

For once, Molly belonged in Gabrielle's arms. The narrow track soon gave way to an area of felled trees that we had to scramble over. The logs were the remains of tall trees. Dozens and dozens had been cut and left to rot. It seemed almost impossible that the Park Service had been guilty of such savagery against the natural resources it was supposed to protect. When I said as much to Gabrielle, she made the obvious reply: Malcolm Fairley felt the same way. That was the whole idea of the reclamation project.

"Wait till you see the actual path!" She scrambled over a big log with surprising agility. "The excuse for abandoning it was there was no money for maintenance, but it's held up remarkably well with almost no upkeep."

From behind us, Effie's voice sounded. "Gabbi! Gabbi! Wait up!"

"Oh, no! I thought we'd lost them," Gabrielle grumbled. "We do not need Effie complicating this situation. I suppose we'd better wait. They'll catch up with us in no time, anyway."

Quint and Effie reached us in less than a minute. They glowed with pink-cheeked youth. Neither was out of breath. I expected Gabrielle to greet them with a request that they turn around and go away. It was, however, as contrary to Gabrielle's nature to make anyone ever feel unwelcome as it was to Rowdy's or Kimi's. Both dogs issued their usual *woo-woo-woos*, and Gabrielle hailed her nephew and his wife with an ordinary "Hi there, you two!" and then informed them that they were to let her go first. "And Effie, it would probably be best if you were to leave the talking to me. And to Holly. We just need to straighten out a little misunderstanding. A certain bumper sticker would be *outside* the scope of the discussion."

It took us what seemed to me like forever to navigate the big logs and reach the beginning of the Homans Path itself, another stepped trail similar to Kurt Diederich's Climb and in almost equally good condition. By now, I was feeling too sore and weak to take in the clever beauty of the steeply rising stone stairs. Quint and Effie charged ahead of me, thus inspiring Rowdy and Kimi to forge up the damned steps far too fast for me. I hung on to their leashes and concentrated on keeping my footing. Last in line, I was also the last to hear the shouting that bounced downward over the rocky stairs.

My father's unmistakable bellow reached me. Delighted to hear his voice, the dogs put on speed. I scrambled and gasped until the dogs came to such an abrupt halt that I crashed into them. No one noticed. At a wide, flat landing where the stepped trail paused before resuming its upward course, Buck and Malcolm Fairley faced each other. They stood about a yard apart. In back of them, near a pile of newly cut brush and small tree limbs, Wally and Opal, Steve Delaney, and a cranky-looking Anita Fairley silently observed the confrontation. Amazingly, Buck didn't even seem to see Rowdy and Kimi, never mind Gabrielle or me. He and Malcolm Fairley stared at each other with locked eyes. In dogs, that's the signal of an imminent fight.

My father had stopped roaring. Now, his voice was frigidly calm. "If something sounds too good to be true," he said to my amazement, "then it probably is."

I had no idea what he was talking about.

As if he'd read my thought, he broke eye contact with Malcolm Fairley and turned to me. "You never could draw," he reminded me. "That picture you showed me? That's not a kite. It's a pyramid. That's what you meant it to be."

I was still lost.

"A pyramid!" he suddenly roared. "*A pyramid scheme!*"

Twenty-four

AS WAS HER HABIT, EFFIE SPOKE UP. "I HAD A FRIEND who got caught in one of those. It had to do with food supplements. There was some disgusting yellow powder you were supposed to mix with water and drink for breakfast, and cookies that tasted like gravel. Anyway, somebody recruited her to be a distributor for all this stuff, and supposedly, her main job was to recruit other distributors. That was how she was supposed to make money, getting commissions from the people she recruited. Only, to get started, she had to buy this humongous inventory, which she was stupid enough to do, and then she couldn't talk anybody into distributing it for her, and she was stuck with the whole mess."

"Effie," Gabrielle said, "does this have anything to do with anything?"

"It does, you know," said Quint, eyeing Wally and Opal.

At the clambake, I remembered, Opal's hairdo—the long brown-and-gray hair swept into a ponytail on the crown of her head—had looked jarringly childish on a woman in her mid fifties or so. Now the ponytail seemed no more than a sensible way to keep her hair from interfering as she cut brush on a stone trail. She wore jeans, a faded blue sweatshirt, rough pigskin gloves, wool socks, and hiking boots. The sensible work clothes, combined with the exercise-induced pinkness of her face, made her look prettier than she'd appeared the previous evening. A pair of loppers hung from her right hand.

"Quint! Why are you looking at me like that?" Opal demanded. "To the best of my knowledge, I've never even *eaten* a health food supplement in my life. The whole idea that I would get swept up into some pyramid scheme to distribute food supplements is preposterous."

"Food supplements have nothing to do with it," Quint said. "Forget food supplements. That was just an example. The content is immaterial."

"I should hope so," Wally said pompously. "You won't catch any of us selling any of those powders. Or cookies! Do we look like Girl Scouts?" He guffawed. No one else did. At the clambake, poking at the coals and rocks and, as Gabrielle had phrased it, murdering lobsters, Wally had been in his element. Today, he stood out as the only physically unfit person on the trail crew. His round, almost hairless head dripped with sweat; his face was deep red and squishy looking, like a baked apple. His yellow polo shirt was soaked, and his big, soft gut poured over the waistband of a pair of khaki shorts. His bare arms and legs were as puny as most of the saplings that lay in the brush pile.

"The point Effie was beginning to make," Quint continued, "was about pyramid schemes. In this case, the content isn't food supplements. It's land grabbing and property development."

"Exactly *who* are you accusing of land grabbing?" Opal shrieked, incensed. "That is the most ridiculous thing I have ever heard!" She pointed the loppers at Quint. "Every piece of property Wally and I have acquired we have bought in a perfectly legal, ethical way, and we are far and away the most responsible developers on this island. Land grabbing! I don't like the sound of that one bit, Quint!"

"Land grabbing." Gabrielle repeated it, as if practicing a foreign word. "Land grabbing. I'm not sure I know what it means." She looked down at the bichon in her arms almost as if she expected Molly to explain the term.

Effie hastened to supply a definition. "It means rushing in to snatch up land from people who don't understand what it's really worth or what you intend to do with it." After only a moment's hesitation, she

168

added, with victory in her voice, "Like Wally and Opal moving in to grab Norman Axelrod's land so they can *desecrate* it with awful condominiums that will pollute the Beamon Reservation!"

Opal opened her mouth, but Wally spoke first. "*Land grabbing* suggests deliberate misrepresentation about the purpose the land is being bought for. In case no one here realizes it, some of the worst offenders in that regard are conservation groups."

"Oh, that's ridiculous," Effie charged. "How could anyone not want land to be preserved?"

"Conservation groups," Wally informed her, "do not, contrary to popular opinion, hold on to all the land they buy. Among other things, they resell it to the government, which can then sell it again, or they sell it directly or indirectly to developers, and that's a fact. Furthermore, some property owners *want* their land developed."

"Norman Axelrod, for example," Opal supplied.

"Obviously," Effie countered, "Norman was no friend of environmentalism, but he wasn't about to sell out to you and Wally while he was *alive,* was he?" Before Wally or Opal could respond to the veiled accusation, Effie unveiled it. "Quint and I have discussed the matter at length. We cannot believe that Norman climbed up Dorr just because he felt like it. We think he was deliberately led up there."

"Not led," Quint corrected. "Lured."

"Thank you," his wife commented. "*Lured.* And we do not think that on his own he would've gone anywhere he was likely to fall. And the question we keep coming back to is, *Qui bono?*"

"For Christ's sake," my father bellowed, "speak English!"

169

Rowdy's and Kimi's ears went up: *Does he mean us?*

"You wait and see," Effie warned. "With Norman Axelrod dead, Wally and Opal are going to find some way to get their dirty hands on his property. They'll *murder* every living thing on it, just the way they got their hands on Norman Axelrod!"

Wally was now sweating with rage. "That," he shouted at her, "is libel!"

"Isn't it slander?" Gabrielle asked innocently. "I always have a hard time remembering which is which."

"If something is *true,*" Effie informed her, "then it isn't either one. So what Quint and I would like to know," she said, turning to face Wally and Opal, "is just exactly where the two of you were when Norman Axelrod *supposedly* fell."

"This is absurd," said Gabrielle, the peacemaker. "Effie, we have known . . ."

"Anita!" Wally demanded. "Anita, Opal and I have just been libeled . . ." He broke off. "Slandered. Which is it?"

"Slandered." Anita looked disheveled and hot. A scratch on her right hand was oozing blood. She raised the hand to her mouth and, with odd sensuousness, licked the wound. "If it's spoken, it's slander."

"Well, in that case," Wally said vehemently, "Opal and I are suing for slander. *This* woman, Effie O'Brian, has just damaged our reputation in the presence of witnesses. Not only in the presence of ordinary witnesses! In the presence of our attorney! Anita, aren't you an officer of the court? Well, you heard her! And we are suing!"

As if to underscore the power of the threat, Wally bent to retrieve a crowbar that lay at his feet. It occurred to me that if Buck was, in fact, carrying a handgun, at

170

least he wasn't the only armed person in the group. A hatchet rested near Malcolm Fairley's feet, and Steve held a pair of loppers heavier than Opal's. Lightweight pruning shears dangled from Anita Fairley's left hand. Now she tightened her grip on them, transferred them to her injured right hand, and ran her left hand idly through her lovely blond hair.

Malcolm, her father, was staring at her. He had the kind of solid-looking New England face and Yankee jaw that seem designed by Nature and trained by Nurture to reveal almost no emotion. The only visible change was in the color of his weathered skin: The tan drained away, leaving him white and haggard. Then red splotches surfaced on his cheeks. Facing his daughter, he asked quietly, "Anita, can this statement be true?"

"Am I an officer of the court?" she replied. She was expressionless.

"Wally," said Malcolm, his voice cold with shock, "has referred to the presence of *his* attorney." He waited. Anita said nothing. "You," Malcolm told her, "are the only attorney present."

"My practice is my own business." Anita's face was sullen. Impatiently, she brushed invisible dirt or dog hair off her pants. "There's such a thing as client confidentiality, you know."

"*My daughter,*" Malcolm said incredulously, "is representing *developers?*" It was almost as if a mist had magically appeared to surround him as he spoke words of private horror to himself. "Property developers? *Here* on this island? *My* daughter? The Pine Tree Foundation's attorney? Impossible."

Opal glared at her husband. She spoke softly, but her voice quivered. "Wally, how *could* you be so stupid!"

With what struck me as genuine obliviousness to

171

Malcolm Fairley's shock at the revelation of Anita's betrayal, Wally ignored his wife. He directed himself to Malcolm. "Let's get something straight here. No one has done anything in the least bit fishy. Swan and Swan is the most environmentally responsible corporation in the state of Maine, and—"

"Hah!" Effie interjected.

"And Opal and I personally are committed to the preservation of the natural environment where, it just so happens, we live. Why else would we be out here sweating in the woods, for Christ's sake? Opal can speak for herself, but I, for one, am not standing around listening to slurs and digs. There's never been any reason why Anita shouldn't represent us, and I never have liked this keep-it-quiet attitude on her part or on yours, either, Opal. It's insulting. You'd think we were criminals."

"You said it, Wally," Effie told him. "I didn't. And there certainly are about a million reasons why everyone here but you is reeling at the news that Anita represents you, and the main one is conflict of interest. A lawyer can't represent an organization dedicated to saving the environment from developers and at the same time represent the developers! That's conflict of interest! Never mind that everyone who knows Malcolm understands his total dedication to conservation, given which, he would hardly want his daughter acting for the enemy, would he? Would he, Anita?"

"Leave me out of this," Anita said.

"How?" Quint asked. "How are we supposed to leave you out of it when you put yourself in the middle? If you wanted to stay out of it, you could've declined to work for developers. And if you and Wally and Opal all thought that it was ethical and aboveboard for you to represent Swan

172

and Swan at the same time you were representing the Pine Tree Foundation, why keep it a big secret?"

"For the very good reason," answered Opal, with a swish of her high pony tail, "that we thought it might be misunderstood, particularly by Anita's father. The situation was perfectly simple. Wally and I needed a good attorney. Anita is one. Furthermore, she passed her bar exams in Maine and in Massachusetts, and Swan and Swan has some interests there, too. On top of which, we know Anita. Therefore, it made perfect sense. So far as telling people, we decided to be considerate and discreet. We did not lie. Anyone who was interested could have consulted any number of public records."

"Why would anyone have done such a thing?" Effie demanded. "Why would Malcolm or anyone else have gone digging into records to find out that Anita was doing something that all of us thought in a million years she'd never do? Does anyone go around trying to make sure that Quint and I aren't secret agents of the military-industrial complex? Of course not! You don't check up on people unless you have some reason to be suspicious in the first place."

Quint turned unobtrusively to his aunt and asked, "Gabbi, did you know about this?"

As if testifying in court, Gabrielle answered solemnly, "I did not."

Anita finally spoke up for herself. "This whole matter is being blown all out of proportion. Anyone would imagine that Wally and Opal intended to build a skyscraper in the middle of Bar Harbor or open a chemical factory and turn Northeast Harbor into Bhopal. What no one, including you, Daddy, wants to admit is that development is inevitable. Better Wally and Opal than someone else."

Malcolm Fairley looked so crushed that I wished Anita had said nothing. With heartbreaking bitterness, he echoed her. "Development is inevitable." His eyes were filled with tears. "Anita, how could you have done this to me? To the Pine Tree Foundation? What if the benefactors find out? What if they discover that my daughter, the foundation's attorney, is representing the interests of *any* developers? If they find out, they may immediately withdraw the support on which all our efforts rest. Didn't you realize that the foundation must be like Caesar's wife? It must be *above reproach* and *seen to be* above reproach. My own daughter! How *could* you have betrayed me?"

"Daddy," Anita replied unprettily, "cut the shit.'"

Twenty-five

MY FATHER STOOD APART. EXCEPT TO OBJECT TO Effie's lapse into Latin, he'd said nothing. Uncharacteristically, he hadn't even caught the eye of any of the dogs or snuck them treats from the supply he always carried in his pockets.

Always. Buck always carried dog treats.

That piece of trivia was as accessible to me as if my memories of my father had never vanished; all of a sudden, the memory was in its proper place again. In fiction, the recovery of the forgotten past is notably gauzy, nebulous, insubstantial. Veils lift. The victim blinks away mental cobwebs. *One by one, the membranous curtains of oblivion heretofore draped over our heroine's eyes drew apart, revealing mist-shrouded visions to her startled gaze.* In real life?

Wham! I collided with a rock-solid object that had gone missing and was inexplicably back where it belonged. My reaction may, of course, be idiosyncratic; not everyone's father is a gigantic ruminant mammal. One thing to be said for Buck is that he is a solid figure in my life. Hence the collision?

As I was starting to say, my father stood apart from the recriminations and nastiness, as did Steve Delaney, who had distanced himself by unobtrusively ascending four or five steps of the Homans Path. Malcolm Fairley, I remind you, had just accused his daughter, Anita, of betraying him, and in response, she'd told him to cut the shit.

Once again, it was Effie who spoke up. She seemed a peculiar person to assume the role of Anita's defender. What fitted her for it, I suppose, was her willingness to give voice to opinions that other people kept to themselves. "Anita is not the only one who's been fraternizing with the enemy," Effie announced.

Gabrielle took her to task. "Effie, you have said more than enough! If you are referring to me, I want you to know that I do not believe in letting politics dictate my friendships, and that includes the politics of conservation. And if your remark is directed at Malcolm, you know perfectly well that ten minutes of hands-on experience is worth a million hours of being subjected to diatribes about the environment. If there's anyone here who really does think globally and act locally, it's Malcolm! He is deeply involved in efforts to save the rain forests, and we know what he does here! Furthermore, I might remind you of the old saw that you catch more flies with honey than you do with vinegar."

"Flies!" Opal flung the pair of loppers to the ground. My dogs eyed her with interest. Her arms flew upward.

"*Flies?* So much for friendship, Gabbi! Wally and I are *not* flies! We have *not* done anything wrong, and we do not need to be *caught!* Gabbi, I am very hurt by that remark."

"I did not intend to call you a *fly*," Gabrielle responded, "or Wally, either. I simply meant that in general, if you want to persuade people of something, it's more effective to be nice than it is—"

"Who says we need to be persuaded of anything?" Opal interrupted. "What arrogance!"

Quint said, "Opal, please do not—"

"Quint," Gabrielle told him, "leave this to me! We're among friends here, and—"

"Friends," Opal insisted, "do not refer to friends as *flies!* Flies in the ointment, I suppose! Gabbi, I knew you were a hypocrite, but I never dreamed—"

Quint again tried to defend his aunt. "Who is calling *whom* a hypocrite?" That's a direct quote. Quint was the kind of person who, even in rage, gets the cases of his pronouns right.

"I don't know who you're calling a hypocrite, you miserable little parasite, living off your aunt instead of getting a real job," Wally charged, "but if you want my opinion, I'm sick to death of listening to this holier-than-thou horseshit about the goddamned charitable purposes of the goddamned Pine Tree Foundation, which I know goddamned well everyone else invested in for the same reason Opal and I did, except that *we* never said we did it for anything but profit. And Gabbi, I don't know where you think you get off calling us flies, for Christ's sake, and hypocrites—"

"I didn't!" Gabrielle protested, so vehemently that Molly's white curls shook.

"When," Wally fumed, "you and your family and

176

your guests can hardly wait for your personal nature preserve to close for the day so you can swarm all over it breaking every one of your own rules. You know, Gabbi, that's one thing Norman Axelrod was dead right about! The whole setup is a tax dodge, and you know it's a tax dodge and a royal opportunity for nepotism, just like Norm always said."

Gabrielle was regal. "Wally, you have time and again accepted my hospitality, my lobster, my champagne, and my friendship, not to mention *my* personal invitation to Opal, and incidentally to you, to invest in the Pine Tree Foundation, and now you *dare* to turn on me! You barbarian! I have never understood why Opal married you to begin with! Wally, in accepting hospitality and then turning on the person who offered it, you are breaking the most fundamental and ancient rule of civilized conduct. You . . . You *lout!*"

"You see?" Effie said quietly to Quint. "They *are* investors, just the way we thought. This is disgusting! Greed is everywhere."

Wally ignored Effie. "Wrong!" he fired at Gabrielle. "The fundamental rule isn't some crap about etiquette, for Christ's sake, it's *Thou shalt not kill*, and you knew damned well, Gabbi, and Quint, and Effie, that Norm Axelrod was systematically keeping track of what went on at your precious Beamon Reservation after hours. He was building a case against you, which was that your tax dodge was operating in violation of every legal agreement you ever made about it, and that it wasn't a nature preserve at all. If Norm had lived, you know, he'd have put an end to this horseshit, so what I want to know is, where were the three of you when he supposedly *fell?* Gabbi? And you, Quint, and you, Effie, you lazy lumps of snotty granola! Where were *you?*"

"Wally, shame on you!" Gabrielle's low, husky voice was as seductive as ever even when she was furious. "You made that up. Norman was doing no such thing. He was just a tease, that's all. He didn't really mean it." She gently stroked Molly's throat.

"He wasn't a tease. He was a troublemaker," Quint said.

"Why would Norman have wanted to make trouble for *me?*" Gabrielle was incredulous. "We were friends! Quint, let me finish! Now, I know he could be a very difficult person, but he was like a difficult relative. A cranky uncle. The trick was just not to take him too seriously."

Quint's preppie WASP vocabulary left him without the response he really needed: *Oy vey!* Lacking it, he said with infinite patience, "Gabbi, I'm not the first person to point out the possibility that *someone* took Norm Axelrod seriously enough to push him to his death. You didn't do it, and I didn't do it, and Effie certainly didn't, but someone did. What you have to appreciate, Gabbi, is that Norman Axelrod had a mean streak. He actively wished people ill."

"*Some* people, I grant you," Gabrielle replied. "Horace Livermore, for instance. Norm really did have a grudge against Horace. How can you blame Norm for that? Now, I have no complaints about Horace in terms of Molly. Horace is a wonderful handler. But Norm paid Horace a great deal of money to campaign Isaac and presumably to take the best possible care of Isaac, and Norm was just as sick as I'd have been in the circumstances when he realized what had been going on." She lowered her voice. "Horace had been giving arsenic to Isaac, you know. To make Isaac's coat pretty. Professional handlers do that sometimes. Not all of them, of course. And it really isn't as dangerous as you might imagine, but when Norman found out, he was livid. He wasn't content with just firing Horace. He really did want to make more trouble for him. He intended to! He wanted revenge. That's what Holly's doing here."

Effie looked frantic. "Gabbi, stop talking about dogs!"

Rowdy and Kimi perked up at the word *dogs*. For once, I ignored them. "Gabrielle," I asked quietly, "what does Horace Livermore look like?"

"Oh, Horace is—" Gabrielle started to say.

Effie had had enough. "Gabbi, this has nothing to do with dogs! Nothing, nothing, nothing! Why do you always have to relate everything to dogs?" Quint tried to hush her. She barreled on. "It has nothing, nothing, nothing to do with dogs!"

My mind silently collided with yet another solid object. This one was a personal axiom: a self-evident truth. *Everything*, I thought, *has* something *to do with dogs. Everything!*

Self-evidence is, however, more a matter of self than of evidence. "Norman Axelrod," Effie raged at Gabrielle, "wished you ill, and he wished a lot of other people ill, and one of his *grudges,* which is a gross understatement, was against the Beamon Reservation and against everything else that had anything to do with protecting the environment in general and Maine in particular. In case you've forgotten, Gabbi, he went out of his way to buy *Idaho* potatoes! He made a big point of it!"

In Maine, that's a heretical act.

"You know," Wally commented, "one thing I noticed about Norm was that he was a pretentious, name-dropping, celebrity-seeking blowhard, and he *was* a troublemaker, but if you kept your eye on him, you'd notice that often enough, he was right. Take Idaho potatoes. I prefer them myself."

"You *would,*" Effie told him fiercely.

As Effie and Wally engaged in this stupid interchange about spuds, my father caught my eye. Having done so, he turned his head to the side, stuck one arm in front of him and the other in back, bent his elbows, and stuck out his flattened hands at some weird angle. Another collision: My father was not just embarrassing. No such luck! No, he was outright mortifying. I couldn't imagine what he doing this time. His face wore an odd little smile. Reading my look of incomprehension, he exaggerated the peculiar posture. Just as I finally decoded his ludicrous effort to pantomime an ancient Egyptian, he quit. Now, still looking at me, he rapidly used both hands to sketch something in the air. Buck, I should note, loves charades. I hate the game. Still, I understood: What he meant was *pyramid.*

It seemed to me that Buck's foolish performance would kill his romance with Gabrielle; he might just as well have pulled out his handgun and shot Cupid dead. I was wrong. As it turns out, Gabrielle *adores* charades.

Politely ignoring the potato dispute and Buck's lunacy, Quint said, "The point Effie was starting to make is that although Norman was deliberately oppositional, he genuinely did not support environmental causes. And he did not believe in charitable giving."

"He didn't even understand it," Effie said. "Entirely lacking the philanthropic impulse himself, he simply couldn't identify it in other people. All he saw were reflections of his own selfishness and spite." She paused. *"Honi soit qui mal y pense,"* she finished.

With no hint of playing charades, Buck took a mighty step forward. Effie had broken his command to speak English. He wasn't actually going to shoot her for it, was he? *Honi soit qui mal y pense,* I thought. *Evil unto her who evil thinks.*

Twenty-six

BUCK DIDN'T EVEN DRAW HIS GUN. EFFIE WAS, I suppose, as disappointed as I was relieved. I am convinced that she longed to see him shoot a developer or, failing a developer, almost anyone else. Still, my father shot from the hip. He had the advantage of being bigger than everyone else. Everything about him, from his oversized skull to the deep resonance of his voice, made him the kind of dominant presence that Rowdy is in the show ring, at least on the days he wins. My dogs, I might note, had been taking an interest in the human snarling and growling, but neither had shown a sign of feeling or wanting any personal involvement. The Alaskan malamute, the most hierarchical of breeds, is, however, exquisitely sensitive to the emergence of an alpha leader in any pack, canine or human. When Buck took that step forward, Rowdy's and Kimi's ears alerted, and I could almost feel surges of strength radiate from their bodies. Suddenly, the action had something to do with them.

Perhaps the shift in power did. The content didn't. "Let me get this straight," my father said. "Norman Axelrod never invested a cent in the Pine Tree Foundation."

No one replied.

"Did he or didn't he?" Buck demanded.

Now everyone answered all at once. For a change, everyone agreed. *Certainly not!*

"A ninety percent return in six months," Buck said.

Malcolm Fairley smiled proudly. Heads nodded.

Buck said, "So here's Axelrod, surrounded by people who were getting rich quick."

"That's not how we prefer to think of it. Our primary purpose is charitable," Malcolm Fairley hastened to correct him.

"God Almighty," Buck said, whether to God, himself, or no one, I don't know. Then he addressed Fairley. "But he could've gotten in on it."

"Norm?" Fairley asked.

"I didn't mean God," Buck said. "His rate of return is half decent without your help."

"I invited Norm," Gabrielle said. "So did Malcolm."

"You didn't!" Effie exclaimed. "Gabbi, how could you?"

"It doesn't matter now," Gabrielle said in self-defense. "I knew that he didn't share the beliefs and goals of the Pine Tree Foundation, but his investment would still have benefitted the environment. And it didn't seem fair to leave him out."

"Norman Axelrod was outright uncharitable!" Effie spat. "*And* he hated trees!"

"That's something I don't understand." My voice was weak and timid. "Everyone agrees that Norman Axelrod hated the outdoors, hated exercise, and was not exactly physically fit. So, *what* was he doing on a hike? And not just a hike, but a hike that goes straight uphill?"

"We've discussed this already. There's hope for everyone," Malcolm Fairley said inadequately. Then he seemed to gather his forces. "And for all that the stepped trails blend with the natural landscape, they *are* man-made structures, as Quint reminded us. They aren't trees, and at the same time, they're a powerful, persuasive argument for conservation and preservation."

"But they're already *in* a national park," I pointed out.

"Conservation and preservation have many facets," Malcolm Fairley countered. "Here, where we stand right now, solidly within the park, this beautiful trail was deliberately left to deteriorate, but thanks to the generous volunteers who are donating their time and labor, we are saving what is, in effect, a magnificent symbol of man's ability to live in harmony with the wilderness in a give-and-take relationship with universal benefit."

I wished Buck would speak up. He didn't.

"What's special about Malcolm's approach," Gabrielle told me, "is that he sees positive opportunities everywhere. Who else would've imagined that Wally and Opal would throw themselves into working on a trail?"

"At the Pine Tree Foundation," said Malcolm, as if reading from a piece of promotional literature, "we believe in conservation from the ground up."

Instead of what? I wondered. Conservation from the ground down? From the air up? Down? The slogan was, I decided, meaningless. Fairley, however, seemed to like it. In fact, he repeated it. "Conservation from the ground up! And from that point of view, you see, no one is a lost cause. There's always something out there that someone can relate to in a personal, meaningful way. Even Norm Axelrod. If you want to make progress, you have to act on that assumption. That was the idea of inviting Norm to come and see the stepped trails for himself. To tell the truth, I was surprised myself when he accepted. If I hadn't mentioned the inconsistencies in the trail signs, he wouldn't have. In retrospect, I can see that I was wrong, not in terms of the general principles, but in terms of the specifics. In hindsight, it's clear that Norm was more unfit than I realized. I've had to ask myself whether he was outright unwell."

Others murmured in agreement. "Vertigo," someone suggested. "He'd never have admitted to it," someone else said.

"Whatever it was," Fairley said, "I should never have suggested the hike to him in the first place. And once we were up here, I should never have let him out of my sight. I blame myself for taking too much for granted. The rain. We're all used to hiking in rain. Norm wasn't. Wet stone. We're all used to it. Norm wasn't. And the trail was slippery. I came close to slipping myself once or twice. It's the most common accident in the park, of course, falling on rocks." How many times had he said that? Hundreds! "Most of all, we take our own strength for granted. We've all learned a hard lesson from this."

Buck moved in again. "Nothing weak about Holly," he said. "Nothing unfit about her."

"As I said," Fairley replied evenly, "I came close to falling myself."

"Holly learned to crawl on the rocks on the coast of Maine," Buck proclaimed with the kind of parental pride that makes any sane human being cringe. Had I really? If so, what on earth had my parents been thinking? The rocks on the coast of Maine are slippery and treacherous. Furthermore, they're thick with barnacles. And I'd been allowed to crawl on them? "She's been handling big dogs since she took her first steps," my father went on. I said silent prayers that Buck

184

would not, please, please not, launch into stories of my childhood. "In and out of the ring," Buck bragged, "there's never been a damned thing wrong with her footwork." Gabrielle and Steve, of course, understood him. Malcolm, Anita, Wally, Opal, Quint, and Effie, I'm sure, had no idea what he meant by either *ring* or *footwork*. They probably thought that we were a family of trapeze artists and that I'd grown up in a circus. Oblivious to their bafflement and my embarrassment, Buck elaborated by comparing me to a champion in a sport entirely unknown to most of his listeners: dog agility. "As lithe as a Border collie whipping through the weave poles," he proclaimed. "As swift and surefooted as Jean MacKenzie's Brownie on the A-frame."

"Does he mean you were a Girl Scout?" Effie whispered to me.

"No," I whispered back. "Brownie is a dog."

"This story of how Holly lost her footing and cracked her head? Holly didn't trip and fall on a tourist trail on this glorified anthill!" After a brief pause, Buck concluded with one of his favorite expletives. "God's balls!"

"What a peculiar expression," Effie muttered to me. "I didn't know you'd hurt your head. Are you all right?"

I shrugged my shoulders. After Buck's paean, I didn't know whether to cry or bark. Everyone else was as silent as I was, probably because of universal puzzlement at what, if anything, Buck was driving at. Eventually, Gabrielle spoke. "Buck, are you suggesting that Holly was pushed? Deliberately? Holly, if that's the case, why didn't you say something? You could've—"

"Because she doesn't remember," Buck said. "Yet. But she will." Having made an appropriate, supportive, hopeful, and confidence-building remark, he reverted to

185

normal, which for Buck means knocking himself out to win an eccentricity contest without realizing that he's the only contestant. Glancing up at the clear sky, surveying the trees, and running admiring eyes over the admittedly beautiful landscape, he announced, "Perfect day for a hike in the park! A few steps up, cut to the left, bushwhack no distance at all, and we'll hit the Emery Path, and then it'll be no distance at all to the top of the Ladder Trail."

Peculiar though the proposal was, it came as a relief to me, mainly because I was starting to suffer from an irrational sense of being trapped on that small stretch of the Homans Path. The sense of entrapment stemmed, I suppose, from the recognition that Buck was leading up to something. I felt increasingly impatient to have him stage his finale and be done with it.

Malcolm Fairley, however, objected. "We have work left to do here. This is, after all, a trail crew, not a hiking club. But don't let us stop you."

"Stop me? I'm just getting started. You know," Buck told him, "unlike you, I'm just a regular guy."

"We're all regular guys here," Malcolm said condescendingly.

Buck smiled in a way that alarmed only me. "A regular guy's idea of good return on an investment is like this: You pay a hefty stud fee, and in return, you get a litter of pups that get out there and win for you."

"Oh, is that so?" Fairley replied.

I wanted to kick Fairley. Of course, I wanted to kick Buck, too. *And* Steve Delaney, who kept his distance so effectively that he might as well not have been there.

"But if a regular guy's got some extra cash sitting around even after he's paid the stud fee," my father continued, "he knows better than to sink it into something that sounds too good to be true. Sound investment strategy for anyone. Norman Axelrod for example. He subscribed to it." Like a dog persistently returning to the same half-buried bone, he said, "You invited him to invest in the Pine Tree Foundation. *Invited him.* And he turned you down."

"The more fool he," Opal muttered.

Buck went on. "I'd've done the same thing. You see? I'm a regular guy."

Even Gabrielle was losing patience. "Buck," she said sternly, "those of us who *invest* in the Pine Tree Foundation are just like the next person. There is positively nothing *irregular* about us, as you know perfectly well. What's special in this situation is that the benefactors are *not,* uh, regular guys. And that changes everything."

"Outside the scope of most people's experience," Malcolm Fairley agreed. "Well put, Gabbi. Regular guys is precisely what they are not. Wonderful human beings, of course. Generous almost to a fault."

"Anonymity," I said. "Keep your name out of it."

"What was that?" Fairley asked.

Ignoring Fairley's question, Buck asked one of his own. "Has anyone ever *met* these wonderful human beings?"

The foundation's investors were quick to repeat the usual explanation: The benefactors preferred to remain anonymous.

"People in high places," Malcolm said. "Let's leave it at that."

"Malcolm, don't be silly," Gabrielle said. "It's not too hard to guess. We all know, after all. Just who's been generous to the island? Think of the carriage roads! For a start."

"Rockefeller," Buck said. "You know, that's not the name that keeps ringing in my ears. The name that does is Ponzi. Charles Ponzi, was it?"

187

Very softly and alluringly, Gabrielle whispered to him, "Buck, please! Let it go!"

"Stand by and watch you get fleeced?" he shot back. "Not on your life! Fairley? You! Hit the trail!"

Weirdly enough, Malcolm Fairley obeyed. In fact, he led the way. My father stomped at his heels. The rest of us trailed after Buck. To my surprise, Opal and Wally were directly ahead of me; I'd expected them to go stomping off instead of risking further insult.

"Who on earth is this Ponzi person?" Opal asked Wally. "Have I met him?"

"I hope not," Wally answered. "I hope I haven't, either."

"Who is he?"

"Was he," Wally corrected her.

"Stop being mysterious! You are getting on my nerves!"

"A Ponzi scheme," Wally grimly told her, "is a scheme to bilk investors out of their money. The man is suggesting that we've been taken for a ride. That's why he was talking about pyramid schemes."

"Oh, that's ridiculous," Opal said. "If the Pine Tree Foundation is sound enough for the Rockefellers, it's sound enough for us."

Twenty-seven

THE STEPS OF THE HOMANS PATH ABRUPTLY ENDED. Ahead lay the sad and ugly remains of slaughtered trees. If bushwhackers, trail phantoms, or animals had beaten a path around or through the extensive barricade of thick trunks, Malcolm Fairley and my father took another, tougher route. In describing this steep, miserable trek, Buck had been blasé; *no distance at all,* he'd promised. Sweating from the exertion, I belatedly realized that, as usual, he'd spoken from the viewpoint of big, strong dogs. In that sense, he'd been right. Rowdy and Kimi longed to bound through the obstacle course. I clung to their leads and cursed. "Easy!" I ordered the dogs. "Easy!" Ahead of me, Wally struggled to keep up with Opal, who scrambled energetically over and under the felled trees. At first, I tried to match the pace of those ahead. I could hear Wally gasping for breath. He and Opal began quarreling about whether to turn back. He wanted to; she refused.

I resigned myself to being a straggler. The dogs were far too strong and eager for me, and the combination of restraining them while bushwhacking uphill over rough terrain was more than I should have tried to manage. If we ever reached the damned trail, I'd let Rowdy and Kimi haul me along; here, they'd send me crashing into a log or decapitate me as I crawled under one. Before setting out, I should have turned one or both dogs over to Buck, or even to Steve, damn him, but I was now too far behind to make the request without screaming for help, something I absolutely would not do. Not in front of Anita Fairley! Buck had accused me of rolling belly-up, hadn't he? He'd been wrong. I didn't intend to prove him right.

Occasionally, when voices rose in anger, the sounds of bickering and grumbling drifted down to me. "The proof is in the pudding! I have done very, very well!" Gabrielle exclaimed. Closer to me, Opal said, "We did get complete reports, you know, Wally. Tiffany is diligent about sending complete reports." Later, from far ahead, I heard a man's voice, perhaps Quint's, saying, ". . . satisfied enough to reinvest . . ."

After what felt like hours, the group ahead finally veered left, and before terribly long, I heard my father announce something about having found the trail. I hoped that once having reached smooth ground, Buck or Fairley or someone else would declare a rest stop that would give me the chance to catch up. Evidently, no one did. When Rowdy, Kimi, and I finally stepped onto a blessedly smooth, open trail, Wally and Opal were visible far ahead of us. Since I now knew more or less where we were, I made no effort to hurry. My mental map of the area clearly displayed this trail as a line running horizontally across the east face of Dorr, parallel to the trail that skirted the bottom of the little mountain, thus also parallel to Route 3. Many of Acadia's old trails, I remembered, had a variety of names used in a bewilderingly interchangeable fashion on maps, in guides, and on signposts. The trail that wound by The Tarn began as the Kane Path, I thought, or The Tarn Trail, but was sometimes marked as the Canon Brook Trail, also known as Canyon Brook, which ran past the beginning of the Ladder Trail. We were now on the Emery Path or Emery Trail, also called the Dorr Mountain Trail or Dorr Mountain East Face Trail, which would take us past the turn for Kurt Diederich's Climb, then to the split near my Rock of Ages, where the right fork led to the top of Dorr, the left to the upper stretch of the Ladder Trail. The mental map was sharp. So were my memories of visiting the area this morning and of regaining consciousness there on the previous day. Of the events preceding my fall I still remembered nothing.

I spoke to Rowdy and Kimi. "So far. So far, I remember nothing. I can't remember. I can't *yet* remember. Not quite yet."

190

The contrast between the nasty climb through the barricade of logs and this unimpeded hike along the trail and up the stone steps was so great that the distance to the crucial fork really felt like almost nothing. When the dogs and I arrived, the group had already gathered near the cedar signpost, which was prominently located right at the fork. The trail widened to become an open space with natural-looking, smooth rock flooring. Slabs of granite surrounded the base of the signpost. Even in fog, the signpost would have been all but impossible to miss. The three wooden arrows nailed to it pointed, respectively, toward the summit of Dorr, the Ladder Trail, and the Sieur de Monts Spring. No one could possibly have misinterpreted the arrows. Dorr was unambiguously to the right; the Ladder Trail, to the left. Before my fall, I must have passed these signs. I'd known where I was going. From my observations this morning, I knew we had started toward the ladders and that I'd hitched Rowdy and Kimi to the trees from which they had subsequently freed themselves. Norman Axelrod, I was convinced, hadn't fallen down the stone steps. No, from the high cliff above the top of the Ladder Trail, Norman Axelrod had plunged to his death on the stone stairway. Bruised and unconscious, I had ended up only yards from where he had landed.

No one, however, was discussing Axelrod's death or my own fall. Rather, I had walked into the midst of another outraged argument about the Pine Tree Foundation.

"If this were some scheme to bilk us," Gabrielle was indignantly pointing out, "we'd have *lost* money. In fact, over the course of more than two years, we have consistently *made* money."

Addressing herself to Buck, Opal said, "The point

that's escaping you is that this is a very personal arrangement. Not just anyone gets to participate. Take Zeke, for example. He didn't show up today, but when he works on our crew, he works hard, and he's a nice guy, but he isn't really one of us."

"If anything were amiss with the foundation," Quint said, "we'd be the first to know. If there'd ever been a hint of anything not quite *comme il faut,* we'd hardly have *reinvested.*"

"And," Opal told Buck, "you have to understand that although you are in the dark about the workings of the foundation, *we* receive regular quarterly reports, which are, you have to understand, to a very large extent, *financial* reports. The whole thing seems mysterious to you, and too good to be true, because you have no way of knowing what's going on."

"If we were in your position," Effie said gently, "we'd probably feel the same way."

I assumed that she meant financial position. Although she was trying to be tactful, her condescension irked me. Buck, however, responded with a sort of sinister joviality. "No question about it!" he boomed. "I'm in no position to be fleeced in a Ponzi scheme."

"Oh, for heaven's sake, let's stop it!" Gabrielle urged. Catching sight of a family of hikers emerging from the trail to the top of Dorr, she paused. Everyone remained silent until the people had moved off. "Among other things," Gabrielle resumed, "I'm not even sure I know what a *Ponzi* scheme *is.*"

Steve Delaney broke his long silence. "There's an easy way to see the basics of how that kind of thing works." He bent down and filled both hands with fistfuls of the pine needles that formed a natural mulch at the edge of the granite-paved clearing. In the tone he'd have used to explain a veterinary condition to a pet owner, he said, "Now, we're going to let this be money. Gabrielle, you have some to begin with." He placed a small pile of pine needles in front of her. "And you, Effie. And you, Quint." He doled out two more mock supplies of cash. Then he gathered some small stones, lined them up, and gave each of them a supply of pine needles. "And these people have some ready cash, too." His hands were now empty. He brushed them off. "To start with, I've got nothing."

"And who are you?" Gabrielle asked. "In this game, I mean."

"Ponzi," Steve said. "I'm Mr. Ponzi. And have I got a deal for you! Gabrielle, Quint, Effie, I'm offering you a special investment opportunity. The three of you give me some money, and I'm going to double it for you."

"Why should we trust you?" Quint asked.

"Because you know me. And I've explained what a great deal this is. It's special. It's not open to just anyone. All the same, because you're cautious, you want to test the waters. So, you don't invest everything. Not to begin with. You try this deal out. You invest a little."

"Why not?" Gabrielle gestured to her pile of pine needles. "I'll start."

Steve took her up on the offer by removing about a fourth of her capital and placing it on the ground in front of him. "Quint and Effie, you can pass up the opportunity for now, but all these other investors"—he pointed to the stones—"are going to take advantage of it." He removed greater and lesser amounts of play money from the stones, and added it to his own pile. Then he gathered and lined up more stones and supplied them with fresh pine needles from the nearby woods.

"Now these people are investing, too." He took some of the fresh investment material and added it to his own pile, which was now quite large. "Now, Gabrielle, it's time for you to get the return on your investment." He paid her from the big pile. "Double your money?" he asked. "Satisfied?"

"Yes," she said, "except that . . ."

"Exactly," Steve said. "Except that I paid you with the money I took from these other people." He pointed to the new row of stones. "But what do I care? There are more stones where they came from. More investors. Take Effie and Quint. You two were careful before. But now you've seen the results. Gabrielle invested. She doubled her money. So, why not you, too?" He removed half of Effie's pine needles and half of Quint's. His own pile was now big again. "What about you, Gabrielle? The investment opportunity is still open. What are you going to do about it?"

"I'm going to ask where all this money is coming from," she said.

"And Mr. Ponzi is going to tell you," Steve said. "It's all invested in this special deal. Everything's going great. You've seen for yourself, haven't you? You doubled your investment in no time. Why not do it again? Where else can you get that rate of return? And are you going to leave your friends out? Opal is an old friend of yours, isn't she?"

"Of course," Gabrielle said.

"So, let's share a good thing with her. And with Wally, too." He removed some of their pine needles. "Let's not forget the other initial investors!" He distributed some of the growing hoard of pine needles in front of the first row of stones. "And you, Gabrielle, are going to reinvest." He removed most of her stash.

"But there's no actual investment!" Gabrielle protested. "It's just other people's money."

Steve wore the satisfied smile of a teacher who has gotten the point across. "You said you weren't sure what a Ponzi scheme was. Now you understand it."

"But it can't go on forever," Gabrielle objected. "Yes, I got paid, but . . ."

"Initial investors do," Steve agreed. "If they don't, it's not a Ponzi scheme. Or it's one that never got off the ground."

Gabrielle was still concentrating on Steve's demonstration. With the exception of my father and Malcolm Fairley, everyone else, however, was shifting around uncomfortably.

Waving a hand over the display of stones and pine needles, Gabrielle said, "Fine! I understand. It's all a house of cards. But this has nothing to do with anything . . ." She hunted for a word. "With anything real. With anything *relevant!* This kind of thing couldn't go on for long. You can fool some of the people some of the time, or whatever it is, but eventually, the whole thing would collapse." Her voice now carried a hint of desperation.

Steve nodded.

"So, what happens then?" Gabrielle demanded. "When it collapses?"

Steve bent down, swooped up as much as he could hold of the big pile of pine needles, and made a show of striding off.

Gabrielle was suddenly angry. "Stop that! This is ridiculous!"

Steve let the pine needles fall to the path. As he did, Malcolm Fairley broke into appreciative laughter. "Well done, Steve! You really had Gabbi going there for a while. Excellent! Never let it be said that we can't take a joke at our own expense. Right, Anita?"

Anita had taken a seat on the big rocks around the base of the cedar signpost. She could have been posing for a photograph intended to illustrate the joys of hiking in Acadia National Park, except that her expression was more placid than joyful. In response to her father's bid for support, she did nothing but dip her chin.

Looking confused, Gabrielle produced a token, mirthless smile. Wally, however, was furious. "What's this *we?*" he demanded. "I don't hear anyone laughing but you, Malcolm, because the rest of us don't see the joke."

"Of course you do, Wally," Malcolm said amiably. "Steve has picked out a few points of superficial similarity to have a little fun with us. The pine needles were a nice touch, Steve." Malcolm chuckled. No one else did. Malcolm resumed. "The rest of you aren't taking this seriously, are you? There's *no* real comparison, you know. Ours is, among other things, a charitable undertaking. The Pine Tree Foundation for *Conservation Philanthropy.* And the Pine Tree Foundation is as solid as . . ." He paused. "It's as solid as . . ." With relief, he finally said, "As solid as where we stand right now! It's as solid as Dorr Mountain!"

"Malcolm," Gabrielle observed, "below where we're standing right now? From here down, it's all rock slides. All the way across, and all the way down to The Tarn."

Buck produced one of his moose noises: *"Arrggh!"* It took even me a second to realize that he was laughing appreciatively. When he looked at Gabrielle, his whole craggy face crinkled into hundreds of separate little smiles.

"A poor choice of image," Malcolm Fairley
196

conceded. "But you know what I mean! The foundation is as solidly constructed as the carriage roads! There! Haven't we been overlooking a crucial point?"

The famous roads are, in fact, well constructed. Besides paying for the project, John D. Rockefeller, Jr., supervised the construction himself. The carriage roads are synonymous with Rockefeller. Malcolm had no need to refer explicitly to the foundation's anonymous benefactors. If I caught the allusion, everyone else must have, too.

Catch it I did: Wham! Another jarring collision with a rock-hard memory. My whole body jerked, and my head recoiled as suddenly and sharply as if I'd slammed full speed into a high rock wall. *When I'd been following Malcolm Fairley and Norman Axelrod, I'd overheard Axelrod complaining about the steep ascent. He'd sounded out of breath. "Why the hell* here?" *he'd wanted to know. "Why the hell* here? *When the carriage roads would've made more goddamned sense?"*

I repeat: On Mount Desert Island, the carriage roads are synonymous with Rockefeller.

"Carriage roads!" Wally shouted at Malcolm Fairley. "Carriage roads! For all we know, you've bamboozled the Rockefellers, too!"

Twenty-eight

"NO NAMES!" MALCOLM FAIRLEY WAS ADAMANT. "The strictest anonymity is one of the conditions, and I fully intend to see that it's respected."

"I heard you say that," I told him. "After I fell. You were talking to someone, and that's what you said."

Wally started to reply to Fairley, but his wife cut him off. "Wally, please! These people operate on another level! They obviously have a whole staff of accountants and financial advisors and so forth who do nothing but check these things out. For that matter, so does Gabbi, more or less. Not on *that* scale, but she has people in Boston who—"

Quint was, for once, less than the little gentleman. He interrupted Opal to address his aunt. "Gabbi, you *did* run all this by your people, didn't you?"

The appearance of more park visitors gave Gabrielle a good excuse not to answer. Even after the hikers had passed by, however, she evaded the question. Tenderly stroking the bichon in her arms, Gabrielle said, "Molly is thirsty, and Rowdy and Kimi must be, too. I don't have any water with me, and Holly doesn't, either. And does someone have something we could use for a bowl?"

Her observation was accurate; all three dogs did need water. Still, Quint wasn't fooled. "Gabbi!"

"Quint, family matters are something we discuss in private. I'm surprised to have to remind you of that. Enough said! Holly, do you have a folding bowl with you? Because I don't. This was quite careless of us."

"Pardon me, Gabbi," Opal said sternly, "but this is not just a family matter. Wally and I took *your* word—"

"I personally assure you," said Malcolm Fairley, "that—"

"You *personally* assure us?" Wally cut in. "Let me tell you that I for one don't give a sweet shit about *personal* assurance. What we assumed we had was *impersonal* assurance, and we assumed that Gabbi had gotten it. Now, did you or didn't you, Gabbi?"

My father did not seize the opportunity to shoot a

198

developer. Wally's profession had nothing to do with it. As Buck later told me, Wally could've been "a seaweed-gumming ecologist, for Christ's sake." Furthermore, Buck didn't shoot anyone, even—here I quote—"the stinking son of a bitch who had the fucking balls to talk to Gabrielle like that. Did the little bastard think I was going to stand there and listen to that horseshit?"

In brief, with no warning, Buck lunged toward Wally and delivered one ferocious blow to the solar plexus. My father is violent, but not stupid. If he'd allowed gravity to drop Wally to the granite, the result might have been a serious injury. As it was, Buck caught Wally on his way down and, with remarkable gentleness, lowered him to the ground. Meanwhile, Effie descended, or maybe ascended, into frenzied ecstasy. "He *hit* him!" she cried out. "He hit Wally! He hit him, he hit him, he hit him!"

Hysterics is bad enough in a man. In a woman, it's intolerable. Ugh. Still, I couldn't help wondering whether Effie's husband ever made her feel that good.

"Effie, we saw what happened," Gabrielle told her, "although I think Wally's just had the wind knocked out of him. That's right, isn't it, Steve?"

With the prone Wally glaring up at him, Steve was checking the man's pulse and palpating his rib cage. In almost no time, however, Wally caught his breath, sat up, and declared that there was nothing wrong with him. Furthermore, he insisted with shameful ingratitude and blatant inaccuracy that he didn't want to be examined by a horse doctor. Steve is a small-animal vet: dogs, cats, birds, and, of course, lizards and other household pets, not horses. Rudely dismissed by his human patient, Steve rummaged in his fanny pack, produced a fabric dog bowl, and handed it to Gabrielle, together with a bottle of water that he had removed from the waistband of the pack. Driven by the absence of a third arm, Gabrielle put Molly on the ground and watered her. Then, as I watered Rowdy and Kimi, who exchanged rivalrous growls about having to share a single bowl, the human bickering threatened to resume.

"So the truth is," Quint said to Gabrielle, "you didn't have your people check it out."

"They aren't *my* people, Quint. I don't own them! Their services are not free. And I saw no need."

Buck intervened. "Here's the situation. Fairley here offers Gabrielle the chance to invest in this foundation. They're both involved in conservation on the island. Here's a way Gabrielle can support a cause she's committed to anyway, and make money at the same time. The foundation's lawyer is Anita here, and Gabrielle knows her. Gabrielle hears about these philanthropists. No names! Just hints. The carriage roads. So Gabrielle doesn't do the usual research. She assumes it's been done. By someone else. By the carriage roads, let's say. Out of the kindness of her heart, she lets her friends and relatives in on the deal. Wally and Opal. Quint and Effie. Lots of other people?"

"Oh, yes." Gabrielle nodded. "Naturally, all the investors wanted to share the opportunity with their friends and relatives, too."

"Norman Axelrod must've just eaten this up," Buck commented.

"On the contrary," Effie said. "He couldn't have been more hostile. We've already said that."

With an evil grin on his face, my father clarified his meaning. "Axelrod must've eaten up the prospect of blowing the whistle on this whole scheme. Profit motive masquerading as charity? Keep Maine green! The color of money. And the Rockefellers. Let's not forget them. And Fairley, don't give *me* this anonymity crap. Axelrod must've been drooling over that one, especially if Wally here is right. Axelrod would've loved blowing the whistle on a con that took in the Rockefellers." Buck paused. "So, why didn't he? What stopped him? Why didn't he go ahead and blow the whistle?"

"He died," I said.

"Good girl!"

Kimi wagged her tail.

"Axelrod hates trees," Buck resumed. "He's in lousy shape. He goes for a hike. On a slippery day, he hikes with the head of a foundation he's going to expose as a Ponzi scheme. Why? And Fairley, no one's asking you."

"To discuss things," Quint suggested. "Take a walk together and talk things out."

"Oh, Quint!" Effie said. "That's what you'd've done. You know perfectly well that it's not what Norm would've done. And even if Norm had wanted to ask Malcolm some questions, or go ahead and confront him, he could've done it over the phone. Or at the foundation. Or anywhere else."

I said, "Norman Axelrod expected to meet one of the Rockefellers."

No one asked whether I was hypothesizing or reporting.

"He'd've climbed Everest for that," Effie said. "Never mind Dorr."

"Norman did have a weakness for celebrities," Gabrielle agreed. "But maybe what happened was that Norm expressed his, uh, doubts about the Pine Tree Foundation to Malcolm."

201

"Threatened to expose the whole scheme!" Wally amended.

"So," Gabrielle continued, "Malcolm must have arranged a secret meeting to assuage Norm's suspicions."

Everyone, of course, turned to Malcolm Fairley, who promptly said that he was not at liberty to reply. "I'm a man of my word," he said.

I again tried to report on the fragments of conversation I'd overheard, but Gabrielle was determined to confront Fairley. His smugness probably annoyed her as much as it did me. "Malcolm, really!" she exclaimed. "Being a man of your word doesn't mean refusing to answer straightforward questions about what's obvious anyway. We have taken your word for a great deal, you know, including the finances of the foundation and the support of the benefactors and your hike with Norm. Now, stop being mysterious!"

Buck beamed at her. "Cut to the chase," he said. "Fairley sets up this Ponzi scheme. Axelrod gets suspicious. Fairley lures him up here by promising him he's going to meet a Rockefeller. Hah! Poor sucker! Axelrod dies."

"I was not there!" Fairley protested. "For some reason, Norman wandered off, and I was, in fact, hunting for him in the wrong place when he fell. I was near the top of Dorr and nowhere near the Ladder Trail. The person who was, in fact, nearby when poor Norman died was your daughter!" He glared at Buck.

"If we're going to start trading accusations about daughters," Opal said, "let's not neglect yours, Malcolm. If the foundation is, God forbid, a Ponzi scheme, then Anita is in on it, too. For all we know, she murdered Norm to save her own skin. And yours, too!"

202

"Anita's a proven sneak," Effie pointed out. "She snuck around behind Malcolm's back to do Opal and Wally's legal work. Maybe she snuck up behind Norm's back and—"

"Anita was with me," Steve interrupted.

"Sir Galahad," Buck commented.

"He'd say anything for her," Effie agreed. "Lawyers and developers! The scum of the earth!"

I was about to remind her that Steve was a veterinarian, not a lawyer or a developer, but before I had the chance, Opal spat out, "Effie O'Brian, I'd like to give you a good swift kick and send you tumbling down this mountain! Your holier-than-thou attitude makes me want to puke! In case you wondered, everyone knows that before you married Quint, you didn't have a plug nickel, and if you had to work for a living like the rest of us instead of living off the Beamon money—"

"If there's any left," Gabrielle said glumly.

"Maybe your *hero* stepped in to make sure there was," Opal said nastily. "He certainly seems to believe his own conspiracy theory. He probably killed Norman Axelrod to give you time to get your money out before Axelrod was supposedly going to blow the whistle."

"Wish he'd warned us," Wally said.

"You seem to have missed the grand finale that Steve outlined for you," Anita said. "He showed you how a Ponzi scheme begins, and he showed you how it ends. You have overlooked the last act. When the house of cards begins to collapse, the organizer absconds with the goods, whereas my father is right here and has shown no indication whatever of going anywhere. I, however, have had enough of this

203

performance. I cannot imagine why we allowed ourselves to be dragged up here in the first place by some paranoid buffoon!"

"We're jogging," my father responded.

"Jogging?" Anita demanded. "Oh, *please!* Gabbi, if you want my advice—"

"I've taken too much of your advice already," Gabrielle snapped.

"What we're doing here," said Buck, as if no one else had spoken, "is jogging Holly's memory."

I looked blankly at him and shrugged my shoulders.

"I am leaving!" Anita announced.

"Head toward the Ladder Trail," Buck ordered her, "because that's where the rest of us are going. We're going to set the scene, and—"

Anita radiated scorn. "This is the corniest thing I've ever heard of, and I'm having no part of it. I was nowhere near here yesterday, and I can prove it. I'm leaving. Steve, let's go!"

"Jogging," Steve said quietly, "strikes me as not a bad idea." Our eyes met. He looked heartbreakingly sad.

Imitating my father, Anita said, "Sir Galahad! Well, Holly Winter, there's a little something Sir Galahad hasn't told you yet."

"What would that be?" I almost whispered.

"Aren't you curious about how I can prove where I was yesterday?"

"Not very," I said.

"You should be," Anita said vindictively. "Because as Steve told all of you, he and I were together yesterday morning. What he didn't tell you is that we have the marriage certificate to prove it."

Twenty-nine

FAINTING IS A PHYSICAL PHENOMENON THAT RESULTS from a lack of blood supply to the brain. One minute, you're in full possession of consciousness. The next, you're out cold. Why? Because, as Science in Her Wisdom used to tell us a few hundred years ago, a hard whack to the head disrupts the flow of vital fluids to the Seat of Reason. So far as I know, explanations have not improved greatly since then, probably because there's been no public demand. For zillions of years, people have had a perfectly satisfactory understanding of what happens when you discover that your true love loves someone else. Thus was born, of course, the partnership between *Homo sapiens* and the genus *Canis:* the unspoken *Till death us do part,* unspoken because it goes without saying. Who exchanges rings with a dog? If love is absolutely permanent, who needs a gold band? Who needs a symbol? Dog love is never *token* love. It's always the real thing.

I have digressed. My father has a good excuse for transporting me from the scene of my swoon to a clearing near the top of the Ladder Trail. According to Buck, his original aim in dragging everyone up the little mountain toward the scene of Axelrod's death was to reawaken my memory of the events preceding Axelrod's fatal plunge. When I passed out for the second time, he decided that I should regain my senses in more or less the same place I'd been when I first lost them. For all I know, he thought they'd been hanging around waiting for a brain to reinhabit. I see no excuse, however, for the method he used to revive me, which consisted of upending a water bottle on my head. I had, admittedly, awakened yesterday with my face in a puddle, but Buck didn't even know about the water and the blood. Furthermore, our companions had used their jackets, sweatshirts, and sweaters to make a soft pallet for me on the rock slab, and in applying his primitive first aid, Buck had dampened other people's clothing. I don't buy his crummy excuse, which is, "What did you expect? Smelling salts?"

I shouldn't complain, though. And it's hard to argue with someone who turns out to have been right.

This time, Rowdy and Kimi were there to nurse me back to sentience, which is to say that when I awoke, I was coughing up water and dog hair. As I work it out, Kimi stood above me on all fours scouring my eyelids with her maternal tongue, and Rowdy was sprawled on the ground at my head with his forelegs wrapped protectively around my skull. When Kimi finally let me see anything, I stared up into Rowdy's toothy jaws. Not everyone would have found the sight as cozy as I did.

Before I had the chance to orient myself, Buck started asking questions. "Is this where it happened? You left the dogs near here? Why'd you do that?"

Gabrielle had to force him to give me a minute to recover. I'll never forget how sweet she was. No wonder I'd been confused about Ann's letter. This Gabbi, too, was sweet *and* bossy. "Leave her alone!" she ordered Buck. "Dogs, out of the way! Let me in here!" As I struggled to sit up, she helped me, and then she produced a welcome wad of clean tissues, dried my face, and commanded me to blow my nose. I did. Unlike my father, she had the courtesy to ask whether I was all right. I was. I should have lied.

"So, is this where it happened?" Buck repeated.

I was slow to reply. The old hymn was running through

my head again: *I love to tell the story of unseen things above.* This time, however, I knew what that line meant to me. I had the sense not to blurt out my knowledge. "Are we near the top of the Ladder Trail?" I asked.

Buck said that we were. Hauling me to my feet, he told me to show him where I'd left the dogs. I glanced around to take stock of our exact location. The faces distracted me. Steve Delaney's eyes sometimes turn from blue to green. Now it was his face that bore a chartreuse tinge. Anita Fairley—Delaney? Fairley-Delaney?—was as beautiful as ever: thin, blond, *soignée.* Her father, Malcolm, looked distant and embarrassed, as if he were witnessing some tasteless public display that had nothing to do with him. He busied himself by retrieving his damp canvas jacket from the head of my makeshift pallet, brushing dirt off its sleeves, and draping it on a large rock to dry. The couples, Opal and Wally, Quint and Effie, stood in twosomes a few yards from the rest of the group. I wondered whether anyone had congratulated Steve and offered felicitations to Anita. Molly the bichon was, for once, scurrying around on the ground. Noticing that Anita had her right hand casually tucked into the pocket of her pants, Molly pranced up to her and yipped. Anita rolled her eyes, removed her hand from her pocket, and absentmindedly brushed imaginary contaminants off her thighs. Gabrielle called to Molly, who zipped to her. As Gabrielle was about to hoist the little white dog, Anita muttered, "Christ! Here we go again. Kanga and Baby Roo." No one replied, but instead of picking up the dog, Gabrielle settled for retrieving the end of Molly's leash.

"Over there," I said, pointing to the torn saplings I'd identified that morning. "I hitched the dogs to those trees."

"So she'd have her hands free for Norman Axelrod," Anita said.

Again, no one responded to her. During my blackout, the group had evidently decided to ignore Anita's existence. The agreement must have been tacit; Steve Delaney would never have concurred aloud with the policy of pretending that any wife of his, even Anita, wasn't there. Doglike loyalty befits a veterinarian. My violent and unwelcome physical passion, I might mention, had vanished. All that hullabaloo about the intimate connection between love and death? *Sex* and death? My knowledge of mortality is limited, but I swear that there's a deep tie between lust and the death of memory.

"You ever see those movies where they reenact the crime?" I am tempted to say that Buck asked the question rhetorically, but I can't get the adverb to jibe with my father's attitude, probably because Buck is more dictatorial than oratorical. Also, Q.E.D., as people actually say viva voce in Cambridge, Massachusetts, Buck can be hopelessly corny. Cambridge? Where, as I now remembered with startling clarity, the dogs and I lived. In case you wondered, my Latin is on a par with Rowdy's and Kimi's. In communicating with some of our vernacularly challenged Ph.D. neighbors, we point and gesture. I have picked up a few phrases of academic pidgin. Q.E.D. Viva voce. The dogs wag their tails.

Speaking of that eternal subject, perfect dogs, Buck led Rowdy and Kimi to the saplings they'd damaged in breaking free. I followed. "Do what you did yesterday," he instructed. In typical Buck fashion, he said nothing about the injuries I'd suffered, but allayed my fears by promising that the dogs wouldn't get loose this time. "They won't have any reason to worry about you," he added encouragingly.

208

Considering what Cambridge would call my "family of origin," it's a miracle that I ever progressed from barking to speech. To give my parents the credit they earned, however, they did continue to obedience train me even after they made the horrid discovery that I was not a golden retriever. My parents' child, I compliantly hitched Rowdy to one tree, Kimi to the other. "That's it," I told Buck. "Except that they had on their packs."

Under Buck's direction, I made my way past the silent people and took a few steps beyond the trail, onto the ledge. There I paused.

"And then she pulls out her camera and takes ghastly tourist snapshots of the vista," Anita narrated.

My camera had, of course, remained in my day pack, where I'd later found it, completely smashed. There'd been fog; it had been a bad day for photography. As to tourist shots of vistas, the most prominent feature in the otherwise spectacular view was the hideous sprawl of the Jackson Lab. Now I remembered exactly what those ugly buildings were. I'm not an animal-rights lunatic, but I am an animal lover. Research facilities that experiment on animals are not my prime choice of subject for vacation photos.

"Move away," Buck ordered me. "Head down the ridge, closer to where you fell from. You remember where that was? Because I don't know."

I nodded and took a few steps. My heart pounded. I looked uphill to my tethered dogs. Both stood alert, their eyes on me. I'd glanced back at them yesterday, too. They wore the same expressions of watchful curiosity.

"The parade of suspects," Buck bellowed. "Isn't that what they call it in the movies?"

Anita groaned. Still, when Buck herded everyone a

209

few yards down the path toward the Ladder Trail, she stayed near Steve.

"Me first," Buck volunteered.

"Big of you," Anita said.

Ignoring her, Buck made a foolish show of striding up the path. Where the trail passed between the ridge where I stood and the trees where the dogs were hitched, he made a needless display of marching as if he were leading a parade. Kimi whined for his attention. Rowdy *woo-woo*ed. Gabrielle came next, with Molly bouncing merrily on lead at her side. Wally went by. Then Opal. Then Steve. My heart pounded. Anita. Effie took her turn. Quint took his. As I waited for Malcolm Fairley, I felt suddenly giddy.

"Just walk on by?" Malcolm asked unnecessarily.

"Like the song says." Buck assumes that everyone is a country-and-western fan.

Fairley looked puzzled. As he approached, I said, "You offered Norman Axelrod a lure. That's what you told us last night. At the clambake. People wanted to know how you'd persuaded Axelrod to hike up Dorr. And you told them you'd offered Axelrod a lure. You did."

Fairley halted, blocking my view of Rowdy and Kimi. Rowdy has possibly the most beautiful malamute head in the world: correct shape, ideal ear set, lovely small ears, blocky muzzle, dark pigment, gorgeous bittersweet-chocolate-brown almond-shaped eyes with the sweet, soft expression that's perfection in his breed. Kimi looks tougher than Rowdy does, mainly because her black mask hints at her willingness to obey no one's laws except her own. At the moment, I didn't want or expect either dog to do anything but serve as an emboldening sight for my frightened eyes. Regardless of how sweet or tough the appearance, an Alaskan malamute doesn't back down. Ever. In contrast to my dogs, I am only an honorary malamute. Fortified by the sight of them, I could be tough. With their gaze on me, I'd be ashamed to back down.

But I couldn't see them. Without their strength, I felt paralyzed. As I've said, however, dog love is the real thing. Both dogs shifted, and catching their eyes, I did, too, until our views were unobstructed.

"You offered a positive lure," I told Fairley. "Axelrod confronted you with his suspicions about the Pine Tree Foundation. You offered the ultimate reassurance. At the same time, you offered him a lure he couldn't resist: the chance to meet a celebrity. Bigger than Stephen King. Legendary! A household word! The magic name you keep warning everyone not to say aloud."

"Rockefeller," my father boomed.

"Anonymity!" Fairley pleaded with unmistakably genuine distress.

"Tiffany," I said, "your secretary, told me that she prepared agendas for your meetings with the benefactors, meetings at your house. Not at the foundation. She said that sometimes you went to see them, or sometimes you met them in the park."

Fairley nodded silently.

"So, no one but you had seen them before."

Fairley's nod was almost imperceptible. With sad eyes, he said, "I beg you to leave them out of this."

"I will, more or less," I promised, "except for a little something you said to me at the clambake. We were talking about dogs. About loving dogs. You said that it's in the genes. And that *they* were the same way. 'Dog nuts all.' That's exactly what you said."

Buck was running out of patience with me. "Let's move this."

211

"You're the one who taught me to fish," I told him. "We've hooked a big one. What you do with a big fish is play it."

Buck sighed mightily.

"It is in the genes," I told Fairley. "But the Rockefeller family has two branches. John D.'s branch. Benefactors of Acadia National Park. His brother William's branch. The mistake you made was not knowing which side of the family was the dog side. It's William's side, you see. On William's side, the Rockefeller family tree produces crop after crop of dog nuts."

"I was mistaken," Fairley conceded.

"If you knew these people the way you said you did, you wouldn't have made that mistake. You lured Norman Axelrod up here. I followed you. I was suspicious. I wanted to see for myself. And I did."

"Holly, what did you see?" Gabrielle asked.

"I tied the dogs," I told her, "so I could creep down this ledge and get a good look. I watched Norman Axelrod follow Malcolm Fairley to the top of the Ladder Trail. Malcolm said that was where the meeting was supposed to be. Only no one else was there. The fog had cleared temporarily. Then Malcolm headed up an abandoned section of the Ladder Trail. You can use it to get to the top of the cliff. Norman climbed up behind him. I saw no one else. I heard no one else. Then Norman's body fell from the top of the cliff. The sound was nauseating. I started to cut across and down these ledges, but you, Malcolm, came charging at me. You knocked me off the ledge, and I blacked out. I don't know why you left the job unfinished."

"This is outrageous!" Malcolm Fairley was furious.

"Norman was about to blow the whistle on your

212

Ponzi scheme," I continued, "until you lured him up here with the promise of meeting a benefactor. The foundation wasn't a Ponzi scheme after all! It was backed by the Rockefellers! And poor Norman could get to meet one! Then, since you couldn't actually produce one, you shoved Norman Axelrod off that cliff. What I saw yesterday were the *unseen things*. I saw that there are no benefactors. Anonymous is the least of what they are. They are the product of your imagination. Yes, I overheard you talking to one of them, and you obviously believe they're real. But they aren't. The foundation's benefactors *don't exist!*"

Thirty

"I HAD A BAD FALL MYSELF ONCE," MALCOLM FAIRLEY said somberly. "Head injury. The recovery is slow. Truth is, it was years before I was myself again."

I'd returned from the ledge to the trail, where I stood next to my father, facing Malcolm Fairley. Speaking of the man's face, let me note that I was struck by its honesty and familiarity. As I now knew, I'd met him only this week, but I *had* known men like him, or at least men who looked like him and who, in some invisible and intangible way, had the same air or feel about them. As malamutes recognize other malamutes, poodles other poodles, I'd identified Fairley as one of my own breed.

"Give yourself time," Fairley advised me. "Keep the stress to a minimum."

"If you actually knew the Rockefellers who've been Acadia's benefactors," I said slowly, "you'd never have

213

thought they were so-called dog nuts. I've been wondering about where you got that idea at all. At a guess, you read a book about the whole family dynasty. As homework, so to speak. Background research. And you read a paragraph or two about Geraldine R. Dodge, and you remembered her because she was *memorable*. Only, you didn't get her pedigree straight."

Malcolm Fairley told Buck, "Bangor's less than an hour's drive. There's a major medical center there."

"I know where Bangor is!" Buck roared. "So does everyone else here! What these people would like to know is where their money is."

"The foundation has consistently provided full reports," Fairley answered in the excessively rational tones that people reserve for lunatics. "Anita prepares the financial statements. She knows the workings of the foundation inside out." He guffawed. "She knows the details better than I do myself!"

If I'd been Anita, I'd have been unhappy to have the responsibility shifted to me. Steve, who had his arm around her shoulders, may have felt her muscles tighten or heard a change in her breathing. I saw no sign of a response.

"Isn't nonexistence very hard to prove?" Gabrielle asked the question abruptly, as if it had been lingering on her lips and suddenly spat itself out of its own volition. "I keep thinking about that. Like atheists and God! How would you ever *prove* that there aren't benefactors?"

"Gabbi," Quint said softly, "the point here isn't theological. And it isn't whether or not Holly saw anyone. It's whether or not the foundation has backing."

"What's needed," Wally said, "is an independent audit. Anita, when was the last one?"

214

"Recently," she said.

"Recently meaning yesterday?" Opal demanded. "Or recently meaning two years ago?"

"Don't you just love Gilbert and Sullivan?" Gabrielle exclaimed. "Not that this is the time or place. Why is it that serious worry always brings out the absurd in everyone?"

"It doesn't bring it out in everyone," Effie said. "It brings it out in *you*."

"Anita," her father said, "Wally has asked you the date of the last independent audit. That's a reasonable question from one of the foundation's investors, and it deserves a prompt, specific answer."

"I don't know the date off the top of my head," Anita said coolly. "The point is that these accusations don't deserve serious consideration. They're completely unfounded."

"What's *unfounded*," Buck charged, "is your foundation. Hah!" He's at his most obnoxious when he's pleased with himself. Unfortunately, when it comes to himself, he's easy to please.

As I'd done on about a million previous occasions, I sought solace in the company of dogs. As I climbed the slight slope to where the dogs were tied, my father was lecturing about Ponzi schemes. According to Buck, every characteristic of the Pine Tree Foundation was cause for suspicion, and taken together, the cluster of characteristics led to the conclusion that its proper name would've been the Ponzi Foundation. As I unhitched one dog, then the other, Buck pointed to the incredibly high rate of return, the payment of the initial investors, the old investors' reinvestment and their recruitment of new investors, and the reliance on the foundation itself as the only source of information about its dealings.

215

"Ponzi schemes collapse!" Anita Fairley countered. "They are houses of cards! What makes these charges so ludicrous is that the Pine Tree Foundation is thriving. Everyone connected with it is doing very nicely indeed, thank you very much. No one is absconding with anything!"

As I led Rowdy and Kimi back toward the group on the trail, we passed the big rock where Malcolm Fairley had spread his jacket to dry. Rowdy brought me to a sharp halt by stopping suddenly to sniff Fairley's jacket. The source of Rowdy's interest, I assumed, was either the scent of a dog that had marked the rock, or my own scent, which must have transferred itself to the jacket when my head had rested on its fabric. To Rowdy, the source wouldn't matter. In Rowdy's view, interestingly odiferous outdoor objects have no damned business emitting any scent except his. The nerve! The world is his fire hydrant. For the sake of civility, I speak euphemistically to Rowdy when informing him that people's belongings are not fire hydrants and are not to be treated as if they were. Instead of shouting, *Don't lift your leg on that!* I say sternly, *Not there!* Kimi sometimes requires the same command. She's not just a girl. She's a malamute.

So, as I was starting to say before my train of thought fell off its tracks and crashed in a brain lesion, I found Rowdy's interest in the jacket unwelcome. As I tell Rowdy and Kimi, if *I* don't want dog urine on my possessions, imagine how everyone else feels about it!

"Not there!" I told Rowdy.

To Rowdy's credit, he quit running his hydrant eye over the jacket. Perfect obedience to human commands is, however, contrary to the Alaskan Malamute Code. Instead of abandoning all curiosity about the jacket,

216

Rowdy switched to sniffing and nudging it. Unlike my father, Malcolm Fairley wasn't the sort of person who always carried dog treats, but he might have stashed trail mix, crackers, a sandwich, or some other snack in one of his pockets. Preoccupied with Rowdy, I took my eye off Kimi, who, obedient to the Malamute Code, Opportunism Provision, seized on my inattention to her to snatch the jacket off the rock so swiftly that by the time I saw what she'd done, she had it clamped between her teeth and was alternately shaking her prey to make sure it was dead and raising it proudly upward to give everyone the chance to admire her prize. When Kimi is in this victor-with-her-spoils mode, she shows no aggression; if you try to take her trophy, she won't growl, snarl, or snap. On the contrary, her attitude is maddeningly impersonal: She acts exactly as if the booty has mysteriously enmeshed itself in the gears of a machine that she has no idea how to operate. In theory, Kimi responds to the command *Trade,* which is an offer to exchange the filched object for a generous helping of roast beef, liver, cheese, or the equivalent. Indeed, she understands the command so perfectly that she ignores it until you open the refrigerator door. Acadia failed to provide even a rusted refrigerator. Except for worthless bits of fossilized cheddar, my pockets were empty.

While I was busy contemplating and rejecting the image of the cheesy debris as a tasteless symbol of the accusations still being tossed back and forth—valueless, unpersuasive—Rowdy's allegiance to the afore-mentioned Code drove him to make the most of my abstraction. Even if I'd been vigilant, he might have struck anyway. Kimi's braggadocio always provokes him. She really should learn never to lord anything over Rowdy.

Zoom! Rowdy shot forward and locked his jaws on what proved to be one of the capacious pockets of Malcolm Fairley's jacket. Sturdy though its fabric was, the jacket had been designed as outerwear for human beings, of course, and not, as the prolonged *r-r-r-i-i-i-p-p-p* of cloth proclaimed, a tug-of-war toy for Alaskan malamutes.

Alerted by the rough play of my big dogs and the sound of the pocket being torn off the jacket, everyone finally quit the bickering. Finding themselves the object of universal attention, the dogs showed off. Kimi, in possession of the ruined jacket, gave it another neck-breaking shake of joy. Looking beautiful and absurd, Rowdy stood absolutely still, the torn-off pocket dangling upside down from his mouth. A large white envelope protruded from the pocket.

Infuriated beyond all reason—I'd have paid for a new jacket, for heaven's sake—Malcolm Fairley stomped up to Rowdy and, in the incalculably stupid manner of a person who knows *nothing* about dogs, made a quick, doomed grab for the envelope. In case I haven't mentioned it lately, I must note that Rowdy is not only gorgeous, but friendly, winsome, and playful. Tactfully disregarding the clumsiness of Fairley's effort to initiate a game, Rowdy accepted his invitation by executing a charming front-end-down, hind-end-up play bow while simultaneously chomping down even harder than before on the pocket and its contents. What did Fairley expect! If someone tries to snatch something from you, what do you do? Tighten your grip!

Exhibiting a disgraceful lack of the lighthearted high spirits of even the average dog, not to mention Rowdy, Fairley veered toward me. "I want that *back*," he demanded childishly, "and I want it back right *now!* It's mine! Make him give it to me!"

I'd have complied. Even with no refrigerator in sight, Rowdy will usually trade.

But Fairley panicked. Turning back to Rowdy, he made another grab.

"Stop it!" I told Fairley. "You're making things worse! Stop it!"

Paying no attention to me, Fairley darted a hand at Rowdy. This time, he got a grip on the ragged remains of the pocket. The fat white envelope dropped to the ground. The upper lefthand corner was embossed with an airliner-and-suitcase logo and, in big letters, *Worldmaster Travel*.

"Going somewhere, Malcolm?" I asked.

Fairley lunged for the envelope, but Rowdy beat him to it. Instantly discarding the shredded pocket as second best, he went for the first prize and, within seconds, had it in his mouth.

I transferred both leashes to my left hand. With my right, I proudly reached out and said softly, "Rowdy, trade!"

As I may have mentioned in passing, this is one hell of a good dog.

The white envelope was moist and tooth-marked, but the plane ticket, the printout of Fairley's itinerary, and the colorful travel brochure were undamaged. Of course, I didn't actually read the ticket, the printout, or the brochure. I didn't really need to. And I didn't have time. As the word *Guatemala* was leaving my lips, Malcolm Fairley, correctly sizing me up as an easier mark than Rowdy, tried to wrest his travel documents from my hand.

Stupid, stupid! Rowdy is a friendly boy, but he does not like people to touch me without my permission. My greater fear, however, centered on Kimi. Rowdy might give a warning: a low growl or a menacing move. But Kimi? I was deathly afraid that she'd go directly for Malcolm Fairley's throat.

I underestimated Kimi's intelligence. As I'd feared, she shifted instantaneously from silent, vigilant immobility to snarling, violent action. Shooting upward, propelled by the drive of her sled-dog hindquarters, her muscles rippling, her eyes flashing, her ears flat against her head, a hideous growl roaring from between her exposed teeth, she flew at Malcolm Fairley, who didn't have time to evade her, but took her full projectile force on his left shoulder. He spun around as if he'd been hit by a bullet instead of a dog. Kimi's goal, I saw in retrospect, wasn't to knock Fairley off balance and off his feet. Her aim wasn't even his throat, his face, or the center of his chest. Rather, she delivered an off-center blow designed to knock him out of action and slam him away from me. Rowdy, her partner, backed her up with rumbling growls until Fairley lay doubled over on the ground. Then Rowdy moved in to loom over the moaning Fairley, who undoubtedly found the sight of those open jaws less cozy than I had. The entire episode, including the horrendous, terrifying noise of the dogs, lasted less than ten seconds.

At that point, my father startled everyone, especially Rowdy, by bending at the knees, wrapping his powerful arms under the eighty-five-pound dog, lifting him off his feet, and strolling off with him.

"Enough!" I told Kimi. "Leave it! This way!" Having done precisely what she'd intended, Kimi eyed me gently. As I led her from Fairley, I studied him for signs of blood and found none. Only later did I learn the remarkable fact of Fairley's condition: Far from drawing blood, Kimi hadn't used her teeth at all; she didn't leave so much as a mark.

Trembling, I halted, breathed deeply, reached for Kimi's neck, dug my fingers into her thick, infinitely comforting double coat, and briefly closed my eyes. When I opened them, Malcolm Fairley was seated on the ground. Looming over him in Rowdy's place was his daughter, Anita, slapping the air in front of her father's face with the travel itinerary, the plane ticket, and the brochure about Guatemala. I knew at once that I had never before seen a human being so fiercely and purely enraged.

"You son of a bitch!" she screeched. "So *this* is what you were up to! You sneaky son of a bitch!" Anita was not even slightly beautiful when she was angry. She was as bony as a witch and twice as ugly. "You son of a bitch! You were going to bolt and dump this entire frigging mess of yours on *me!* And leave *me* to explain your goddamned *imaginary* benefactors! You crazy bastard! Guatemala! Goddamn Guatemala!"

"Anna," Malcolm said, "I am already aware that you don't share my commitment to saving the rain forests, but—"

"The amazing thing about you—the irony! the damned irony!—is that you do care about the rain forests! You are absolutely sincere about saving the planet! What's incredible is that everyone believed in your anonymous benefactors because you believed in them yourself! You convinced yourself of their existence. You conned yourself, didn't you? But you didn't con *me*. Rockefellers! Hah! You want to know the difference between you and me, Daddy? You're sincere. But I'm honest. I'm a shyster, and I *know* I'm a shyster. But you're the murderer, not me, and you won't admit even to yourself that you deliberately shoved Axelrod off that cliff. *Before* you did it, you

221

convinced yourself that it was *going to be* an accident!"

Anita addressed the group. "I am no one's fall guy," she said with dignity. "My father did take your money. He set up a Ponzi scheme. A classic Ponzi scheme with a twist: the anonymous benefactors. You fell for it. Greed disguised as charity? You loved having it both ways. What you don't know is that my father is the only genuinely charitable person here. You asked where the money was? I'll tell you, in defense of my father's sincerity. He took your investments, he opened a brokerage account, he obtained a generous line of credit, and how did he use it? For personal gain? Not at all! He took your money and he drew on that line of credit, and he donated every cent he could get his hands on to every save-the-rain-forest group, every environmental lobby, every conservation organization, and every other bunch of mush-for-brains environmental do-gooders he could find. You want to know where your damn money is? My father gave it away. He donated all of it to *charity*."

Thirty-one

WHEN I MET HORACE LIVERMORE AT MY FATHER'S wedding, I recognized him immediately from dog shows. Horace is in his late fifties, I guess, a tall, burly, white-haired man who looks nothing whatever like the handsome, dark lone hiker the dogs and I had met at the top of the Ladder Trail. The hiker, Zeke, was a wedding guest, too, mainly because Gabrielle felt that Zeke had at least spotted something off about the Pine Tree Foundation, even if he hadn't been able to get anyone to listen to him. He worked for the brokerage house that handled Malcolm Fairley's account. The large amount of money that Fairley drew on his line of credit had aroused Zeke's suspicions. When his superiors dismissed his concerns, he decided to investigate on his own. In taking time off to go to Mount Desert Island and in volunteering for Fairley's trail crew, he sought an intimate look at the workings of the Pine Tree Foundation. In presenting himself as the prosperous young man he was and in demonstrating his hands-on determination to save the environment, he hoped to offer himself as a likely investor. After working with Fairley's trail crew, however, Zeke was impressed by the genuineness of the man's commitment. Indeed, he began to wonder whether Anita Fairley alone might be responsible for the Ponzi scheme, and Malcolm Fairley merely his daughter's dupe. The one who'd been almost ready to blow an effective whistle had been Norman Axelrod. Interestingly enough, Zeke had suspected that the anonymous benefactors were a fabrication, but poor Norman Axelrod hiked to his death in the hope of meeting a Rockefeller. If Axelrod had cared enough about his immediate environment to work on the reclamation of the Homans Path, he'd have met Zeke, of course. It's intriguing to realize that if the two had pooled their information, they'd have put a stop to the Ponzi scheme without giving Malcolm Fairley the chance to abscond. They'd have found another common interest. Zeke isn't a professional handler, but he does owner-handle his Belgian sheepdog bitch. Axelrod, however, would never have worked on the Homans Path. Once I remembered him, I knew that everyone had told the truth. He really did hate trees.

Axelrod was right and wrong about Horace

Livermore, by the way. Over a glass of wedding champagne, Horace shamelessly told me that he'd used small doses of arsenic to improve Isaac's coat. Horace maintained that he'd been hired to see that Axelrod's dog won, and since Isaac had been a consistent winner, Norm had had no cause for complaint. Axelrod's only mistake, in his handler's view, had been taking the dog away from him so abruptly. Look at Isaac now! His coat was in terrible condition. He wouldn't win so much as a booby prize at a pet fair looking like that. What a waste of a show dog! I didn't suppose, did I, that Gabrielle would be interested in sending Isaac back out with him again? No, I told Horace, I was sure she wouldn't. Somewhat to my surprise, Horace generously gave me the name of a vet who'd supply me with arsenic for my own dogs. Or was I already using it on Rowdy? Beautiful coat. Kimi's could stand a little help. Hormones would fix that. If I intended to do anything serious with her, I should get her on something. As far as my dogs' show careers went, I told him, my only intention was to have fun. Horace lost all respect for me. By then, however, I had little for him. He was not, however, an international smuggler. Norman Axelrod was correct in his suspicions that Horace was sneaking something into Canada, but wrong about what it was. To avoid being hassled by customs officials about crossing into Canada with a supply of aerosol cans, Horace always hid the aerosol spray-on cheese that his sister, Candace Livermore-Smith, used in training her Border collies.

Malcolm Fairley's escape was my father's fault. Buck should have known better than to carry a firearm in Acadia National Park. His shoddy excuse is that he was protecting a witness to murder. As if I needed human protection! But it was true that I'd overheard Axelrod and Fairley when I'd followed them up Dorr, and I'd seen Fairley push Axelrod off the cliff. True, Fairley hadn't used his hands. Rather, he'd used a booted foot to trip Axelrod. I guess that's what Anita meant when she'd talked about the murder. She understood that her father hadn't exactly *murdered* Axelrod. Rather, Fairley had told himself that Axelrod had had an accident. Fairley had used a boot on me, too. The second I saw and heard the fatal fall, I should have bolted up the slope in search of my big dogs. Instead, I hunkered down on the ridge. After all, I couldn't lead a murderer to Rowdy and Kimi! Fairley must have spotted me after Axelrod's plunge. Maybe he heard something. He appeared behind me in what seemed like seconds. He bumped into me almost as if by accident. My feet went out from under me. He couldn't, however, have finished me off without admitting to himself that he'd committed murder. I'm pretty sure of all this. I can't, of course, be certain.

My vet, Dr. Delaney, and his bride, Ms. Fairley-Delaney, were not at the wedding, which was held at Gabrielle's big house. In fact, if Gabrielle manages to hold on to the house despite her major financial losses—she'll be lucky to keep even the guest cottage— she should consider renting it out for large festivities. The house had room for many more guests than she and Buck invited. More people had attended the clambake for Malcolm Fairley than were present at the wedding. The ceremony was short and traditional, at least as defined in my family's tradition: The minister was also an AKC-licensed judge, and quite a few members of the bridal party were dogs. Mandy, Buck's golden, was hormonally fit to appear in public. She comported

225

herself with her typical air of perfection. Molly stood at Gabrielle's side. Isaac, Pacer, and a few other dogs were there, too. Against Buck's objections, Gabrielle invited Opal and Wally. Buck did not shoot them. After the ceremony, we ate lobster and drank champagne. Most of us did. Effie ate a tofu casserole that she'd made herself.

Malcolm Fairley wasn't there. The Pine Tree Foundation for Conservation Philanthropy was in bankruptcy, and Malcolm and Anita were charged with seventy-six counts of fraud and money laundering. Also, it's a long trip from Guatemala to Maine. We aren't sure exactly how Malcolm got to Guatemala. I certainly know how he evaded the law on Mount Desert Island. After the ruckus on Dorr, my father, still in his bold-alpha-leader role, convinced everyone to hike immediately back down to the Nature Center. In the case of Malcolm and Anita, he reinforced his alpha status by drawing his handgun. The tourists we encountered on our descent were alarmed at the sight of a firearm, but otherwise, all went as well as could be expected until our whole crew arrived at the Nature Center, where Buck intended to turn Anita and Malcolm over to the authorities. Instead of taking the culprits into custody, however, the two park rangers at the Nature Center politely asked Buck to surrender his weapon. Feeling the need to explain the situation, he refused. In the resulting melee, Malcolm Fairley slipped away.

The suspicion is that a friend with a private plane, probably a grateful investor in the Pine Tree Foundation, flew him to Toronto. From there, he took a flight to Miami, and then a flight to Guatemala City. He wrote to Gabrielle from an undisclosed location in Guatemala. She says she burned the letter, which, she maintains, was almost exclusively about the rain forest.

226

When pressed, she admits that Fairley briefly mentioned the benefactors. I asked what he said about them. "He sees them when he closes his eyes," Gabrielle told me. "He finds them a great comfort."

I haven't seen Dr. Delaney since the eventful day I discovered that he'd married Anita. My animals haven't been sick. Or needed any shots. I may switch vets. I'd like to forget him. I'm hoping for . . . amnesia.

Author's Notes

COULD SUCH A SCHEME FOOL ANYONE? IT DID. THE Foundation for New Era Philanthropy, of Radnor, Pennsylvania, lured investors with the promise of combining charity with high returns. According to New Era's founder, John G. Bennet, Jr., matching grants from anonymous benefactors made it possible to double investors' money in six months. The scheme collapsed. On September 22, 1998, Bennet was sentenced to twelve years in federal prison. New Era's victims included churches, charities, and universities, as well as such individuals as Laurance and Mary Rockefeller.

Acadia National Park's Homans Path remains officially abandoned. The reclamation project described in this book is, alas, imaginary.

For the appearance of Alaskan malamutes Sno Ridge's Gabrielle DeBoyd (Gabbi), Sno Shire's Trophy Edition (Bentley), and the late Ch. Nomarak's Malcolm DeBoyd, who is greatly missed, I am grateful to Bruce and Ann Ratcliff.

Dear Reader:

I hope you enjoyed reading this Large Print mystery. If you are interested in reading other Beeler Large Print Mystery titles or any other Beeler Large Print titles, ask your librarian or write to me at

> Thomas T. Beeler, *Publisher*
> Post Office Box 659
> Hampton Falls, New Hampshire 03844

You can also call me at 1-800-818-7574 and I will send you my latest catalogue.

Audrey Lesko chooses the titles I publish in Large Print. Our aim is to provide good books by outstanding authors—books we both enjoyed reading and liked well enough to want to share. We warmly welcome any suggestions for new titles and authors.

Sincerely,